UNCORRECTED
PROOF

NOT FOR
SALE

ALL THE WAY DOWN

OTHER TITLES BY ERIC BEETNER

McGraw Crime Series
Rumrunners
Leadfoot

Lars and Shane Series
The Devil Doesn't Want Me
The Devil Comes to Call
The Devil at Your Door

The Fightcard Series
Fightcard: Split Decision
Fightcard: A Mouth Full of Blood

The Lawyer Western Series
Six Guns at Sundown
Blood Moon
The Last Trail

As Editor
Unloaded vol 1
Unloaded vol 2

Stand Alones
The Year I Died Seven Times
Criminal Economics
Nine Toes in the Grave
Dig Two Graves
White Hot Pistol
Stripper Pole at the End of the World
A Bouquet of Bullets (stories)
All the Way Down

With Frank Zafiro
The Backlist
The Short List
The Getaway List

With JB Kohl
Over Their Heads
Borrowed Trouble
One Too Many Blows to the Head

ERIC BEETNER

ALL THE
WAY DOWN

Down & Out Books
3959 Van Dyke Rd, Ste. 265
Lutz, FL 33558
www.DownAndOutBooks.com

The characters and events in this book are fictitious. Any similarity to real persons, living or dead, is coincidental and not intended by the author.

Edited by Chris Rhatigan
Cover design by Eric Beetner

ISBN: 1-64396-010-5
ISBN-13: 978-1-64396-010-4

Dedication: a true story

Me on Twitter:
Why do I feel guilty if I don't add a dedication to a book?

My sister:
You can always dedicate one to your favorite sister who always buys and reads all your books.

Me:
Too obvious.

CHAPTER 1

As Dale rode up in the elevator he thought, *This is it, they know everything. I'm fired and then off to jail.*

He wiped damp palms down the front of his pants as the elevator doors dinged and opened. The pebbled glass door faced him, stenciled writing in an arch announcing this was the office of the chief of police. Dale went inside and spoke to the secretary.

"Dale Burnett to see the chief."

She gave him an expressionless look. "Yes, he's expecting you, Detective. Have a seat."

Dale moved to the row of four chrome and leather chairs, no magazines on the shin-busting low coffee table. Behind him the secretary pressed a button on the intercom. "Detective Burnett to see you."

Whatever answer she got Dale couldn't hear through the headset she wore, but he wasn't invited immediately in. He sat.

Fifteen years on the force. Seven since he left the beat to become a detective. All about to be thrown out the window because he'd been so goddamn stupid. A dirty cop. How the hell did that happen?

He'd seen it over the years. You can't be on the force and not catch a glimpse in the periphery, hiding in the shadows, creeping up the back stairs. But he'd resisted. At least he'd convinced himself he had. In truth, no one had made him an offer. And when they did...

Dale was still small time, as far as the greased palm set goes.

1

But his stock had risen in the past year when two other cops on the same payroll to the same kingpin had died, and died badly. Two bullets in the head for one of them, the other went missing for eight weeks until his body was found in the trunks of three different cars. Dale had gotten a promotion from the kingpin to the number one seat and it didn't sit well on him. He felt the pressure, saw how it ended for most dirty cops. He wanted out. On the days an envelope of cash didn't settle in his hand, anyway. But easier said than done. And with money flowing in, breaking free always got pushed off until next month.

And now this.

He looked up and caught the secretary watching him with upturned eyes, her neck tilted down to her computer screen pretending to type. Dale felt the bottom drop out. His stomach roiled. The descent started before he was ready. Shit. No time to cover up, obscure his tracks. Probably too many to do much about anyway.

Dale clutched his gut.

"Excuse me." He stood and sure as shit, whacked his leg on the table as he made for the door and the long sprint down the hall to the bathroom. Chief Schuster's private commode wouldn't do for this mess.

He kept it together long enough to kick open a stall, then dry heaved three times into the bowl. Nothing came up but long strings of spit and whatever dignity he had left.

Empty. Gutless. That was Dale. He spit a few more times, thought about jamming his finger down his throat to make it happen, hoping for the sweet relief he felt when he had the flu and finally vomited. But he knew the feeling would be fleeting. The disease remained.

He rinsed his mouth and returned through the pebbled door. The secretary gave her best sorority girl judgmental look.

"He'll see you now."

Dale wiped his palms again and did a quick exhale, then went into the chief's office to take his punishment like a man.

Chief Schuster wasn't alone. Three men flanked him, one in uniform and two in expensive suits. Schuster waved Dale forward. "Detective, join us."

Dale tried to pick out if one of the guys was his lawyer, maybe a fed. He figured they knew about some, but never all, of what he'd done. Maybe they knew more than he thought.

The only place to sit was a couch on the far side of the room from the chief's desk, so Dale stood in the center of the rug, ready for inspection by the intimidating group of men.

He kept his focus on the chief. "You wanted to see me, sir?"

He'd met the chief before, but he wouldn't call them friends. Dale generally steered clear of the higher-ups in recent years. Since he'd crossed the line from cop to criminal.

Schuster didn't seem especially angry. The other men all looked concerned, but their worry was not aimed at Dale. The chief set down a piece of paper he'd been reading. "Dale, you might think you know why you're here?"

"I'm not sure, sir." When in doubt, play dumb.

"It's a lot to unpack and it all stays in this room. Is that understood?" Schuster steepled his fingers waiting for Dale's response.

"Yes, sir."

"Good." Schuster turned in his chair to one of the suits. "You see, Dale, something's happened."

The younger of the two men in suits explained. "The mayor's daughter has been kidnapped."

Schuster waved a hand at the man in the suit, spoke of him like he was a son-in-law he hated. "Dale, this is Lewis Workman, chief of staff to the mayor."

Lewis nodded. Dale immediately forgot his name, mind still reeling. Wasn't this a bust? Didn't they know all about him?

"It's about who's got her." Schuster eyeballed him directly. "It's Tat."

And there it was. Busted. Tautolu Losopo, a.k.a. Tat, was a crime kingpin. The big man in town. Untouchable by the law, mainly because he had guys like Dale and a dozen others like

3

him on the payroll. Not to mention people in the mayor's office, the city council, the unions. He ran a sprawling conglomerate of criminal enterprise and operated with immunity.

And he paid really well. Three years now since Dale had become one of his go-to men on the force. Tat spoke, Dale acted. And the envelopes of cash kept coming in. Until now.

Dale wished he'd sat down and feared doing so right there on the rug. He locked his knees in place and stood firm to take his medicine.

The grey-haired man in uniform looked from the chief, back to Dale. His polished brass badge read Bardsley. "We need your help, Detective."

The statement almost didn't register. Dale had been daydreaming about his first day in prison already. Christ, he'd heard the stories of what they did to cops when they end up behind bars. His sphincter tightened just thinking about it. Then Bardsley's words sank in.

"My help?"

Lewis crossed his arms across his chest. "We didn't get to square one on negotiations to free Lauren. Tat won't budge." All three men looked at him like disappointed dads.

"We know about you. We know an awful lot about you." Chief Schuster waited for a response, but Dale remained silent. "We need your relationship with Mr. Losopo to help us gain access to him. So, we've got a little assignment for you."

"An assignment?" Dale couldn't hide his surprise. Where were the handcuffs? The leg irons? The Miranda rights?

Bardsley came around the desk and moved closer to Dale on the rug. Dale recognized him. A high-ranking cop who was trotted out for ceremonies and press conferences. Hadn't done any day-to-day police work in decades. Apparently still in the know, though.

"You're going in to get her. You can get access. You may be the only one. But make no mistake, Burnett, you still belong to us."

Dale swallowed the rock in his throat.

"We debated a major action like SWAT or some other tactical team, but it would put Mayor O'Brien's daughter in jeopardy. You know that building he's in. It's a goddamn fortress. Storming the castle just isn't an option on this one. We want you to go in and get him to release her."

"What makes you think I can do that?"

"We don't know if you can. If it fails, we break in with heavy firepower. But in this case, we're going with plan B first."

"If it fails, then I'm dead."

Chief Schuster was the only man to meet Dale's eye. "Son, as it is, you're looking at a few decades of prison time. That's if none of your fellow officers takes you down before that, once they find out your record." He held up a thick file on his desk, let it drop. "This is an opportunity to make a damn good impression on whatever judge you end up in front of."

Lewis piped in. "And to have an endorsement of good faith from the mayor himself for rescuing his only daughter."

Dale scanned the eyes of each man in the room. He hadn't expected a second chance. As second chances go, this one was somewhere between suicide mission and lost cause. Fortress was a good description of Tat's place. One guarded by a private army of very loyal soldiers.

But, as Dale saw it, "I don't have much choice here, do I?"

Schuster drew his hands into fists on his desk, awaiting Dale's answer. "No, you have a choice. We're not forcing you. But I know what I'd do."

"Not fuck up in the first place?" Dale smiled alone in the room. He let the grin slip off his face. "Okay. Let me give it a shot. But, um, can it wait an hour? I've got to go bury a dog."

CHAPTER 2

They gave him his hour and didn't ask questions. Dale didn't offer any explanation. How his marriage had dissolved and ended up with a dead dog as its mascot was too much to recount on his way out the door.

Dale got the basic information about the mayor's daughter. Name: Lauren. Age: twenty-four. Worked as a reporter for an online news site.

Schuster waved Dale onto the elevator before following him in. "I'll let her boss fill you in on the rest, but she went there of her own accord for a story on her dad's new drug task force and crackdown. I guess Tat didn't much care for the mayor's new policy."

"Yeah, I guess he wouldn't." The door closed, sealing them inside the cube, alone. "Seems like a dumb move to go there, even as a journal—"

Schuster grabbed Dale by the shirt and slammed his back against the wall of the elevator. He reached out a hand and punched the red emergency stop button.

"I want to make myself clear, you piece of shit. If you weren't useful to me right now, I'd have your ass in a sling and you'd be behind bars already. When IA brought me that file, I nearly went out and killed you myself."

Dale had no retreat. This level of anger was more what he expected when he went to see Schuster in the first place, but he hadn't expected it here.

"Assholes like you give the whole department a black eye. Greedy, childish punks who can't pass up a few bucks passed to you under the table. Who the fuck do you think you are?" Schuster pounded Dale's back against the wall again for emphasis on the rhetorical question.

"I never put anyone's life in jeopardy, I swear it."

"Shut up."

"The only people who got hurt were the dirtbags. The fuck-ups."

"*You're* the fuck-up, Burnett. When this is all over you will face the people you've wronged, including your brothers on the force. I'll see to it."

Schuster's face had gone heart attack red, strands of his silvery hair came undone and stuck to the perspiration on his forehead. Dale didn't try to defend himself, didn't try to make excuses. He knew this was the easy part of what was to come.

When Schuster seemed to realize there would be no fight coming from Dale, he pulled the red emergency knob back out and the elevator started moving again. Schuster straightened his tie, smoothed his hair, and ignored Dale for the rest of the ride down.

Dale tried to avoid slipping into the deep self-loathing he'd been capable of in recent weeks. Years of disappointing himself had taken their toll. He knew he deserved it—every insult the boys in the precinct were bound to hurl at him, every gob of spit coming his way.

His chance at a small redemption wasn't lost on him.

"Chief?"

Schuster continued to ignore him.

"I know I fucked up. I won't say I can make it right, but I'm ready for what you've got for me. I'm gonna do this job and try to do it right. Then I'll stand up and take what you've got. You're right. I deserve it."

Schuster didn't acknowledge him, but Dale saw his body loosen a little. He figured it was all he was going to get. He told himself to remember that little speech for his wife. That would take some explaining.

Dahlia Burnett hung up the phone after making the appointment. Their marriage had been rocky for a while and a child wasn't the solution. She refused to be one of those people who had a kid in hopes of bringing them closer together with a spouse they practically hated.

Hate was too strong. *Didn't know anymore* was more like it.

And now with something going on at work, something Dale only described as "complicated" before he left for the station this morning, a baby would make things exponentially worse.

Dahlia lay a hand over her belly. She tried not to get attached to the idea of a life growing in there, especially since she'd just made an appointment to terminate that life. But she couldn't ignore it. She had to allow herself to mourn—the thing she hadn't let herself do for her marriage.

She never expected things to go downhill once her husband made it off the beat, but that's when Dale started changing. Hardening. She used to love how he was the most un-cop-like cop she'd ever met. Now he was closed off, secretive, grumpy. Like living with a teenage version of herself.

Well, Dahlia could keep a secret, too. Like the baby Dale didn't know he had, and after today, never would.

Lewis returned to Mayor O'Brien's office with more bad news.

"There's another video."

The mayor let out an exasperated sigh. "Do I want to see it?"

"It's more of the same." Lewis pressed play on his laptop and a shaky cell phone video began playing. Tat was behind the camera, talking to Mayor O'Brien, but the image was of Lauren, his daughter.

She wasn't bound or gagged, wasn't bloodied. She didn't

look kidnapped at all, just annoyed. Her brief detention would make her news story all the more attention-worthy—and Pulitzer-worthy.

Lewis talked over Tat's ramblings. Nothing he and the mayor hadn't heard before since the first video the night prior. Direct messages to the mayor criticizing the new drug crack-down. Veiled threats of what would happen if he didn't back off.

"Chief Schuster has a man on it."

"A man? Singular?"

"They decided it was best to try inserting someone they think can get her out without a big gunfight."

"Jesus H."

"They still don't want to go to the press with this. I told them I'd give them four hours."

O'Brien pushed his chair back from his desk. "Why the hell would we want press in on this at all? Now or four hours from now?"

"Because it makes you look sympathetic, which we could really use right now. Do you need me to recite more poll numbers for you?"

"No. I know how shitty the polls are. I thought that's why we did this whole drug war thing."

"It is." Lewis walked the floor of the mayor's office like he owned it and Mayor O'Brien was only renting space. "That made you look tough on crime. This makes you look vulnerable. The worried father. You yourself a victim of these evil drug kingpins after your vow to take them down."

"I am a worried father. You know what Tat is capable of."

Lewis maintained his calm. "It's a show. He's made no ransom, just the idiotic call to repeal the new crackdown. Well, gimmie a fucking break. He's busting your balls and we might as well use this because this could be the only thing that might swing this election for you. We could get a ten-point bump from a missing daughter, come on."

"Jesus, Lewis. You're talking about my only child."

"I'm talking about your job. Lauren will be fine. Let's not squander the opportunity that just fell in our laps."

O'Brien rubbed the bridge of his nose. His all-American face had been carved through with lines during his first term. The golden boy mayor of last election was gone. He needed more makeup now when appearing on TV. He'd started to dye his hair. The entitled, silver-spoon-fed pretty boy was what people saw these days, sucking on the teat of special interests.

And they were right.

Mayor O'Brien stared at his subordinate. This brash kid from Yale who did everything by the manual for political ass-holes. But Lewis had steered him into the mayor's office and he was handling this latest downturn in public opinion. Lewis could be trusted. O'Brien studied the young man and hoped like hell it was true.

"Okay, what do you want? A press conference?"

"We'll work that out when we're closer. Let's see how this guy does first."

"And who is he again? Some kind of special forces or some-thing?"

Lewis turned to leave, exercising his control over the conver-sation. "Some crooked cop. They've got him by the balls so he has to do whatever they say."

"What the...? Is that really the best guy to go and get my daughter back?"

Lewis shrugged. "He's the guy they picked, so he's the guy we've got."

Lewis ducked out, leaving O'Brien alone thinking about hair dyes for when he stood in front of the press to announce his daughter had been saved. Or to tell them she was dead.

Dahlia watched the printer as it sucked up paper and laser jetted ink onto them. The steady noise filled the otherwise quiet house. For a few weeks they had the exuberant sounds of a puppy, but now even that was gone. Their last-ditch effort to have something to love in the house. If it couldn't be each other, maybe a third party would remind them what it felt like. When the puppy started panting and falling over, Dahlia thought for a moment the dog was being slowly asphyxiated by the toxic air in the house. The animosity and the simmering suspicion between the puppy's new owners.

Congenital heart defect was the real reason. A hole in his heart. Neither of them even cried. It all seemed so predestined. Last night, the puppy died quietly in his crate. Dale promised they would bury him in the backyard under a stone, but then he got that urgent call to come in to the station...

Dahlia leaned down and pulled the pages out of the printer. Directions to the clinic. She stared at the final destination, fifty-six miles away. The appointment time. Dale being late tonight would be a good thing. The papers were still warm from the printer but going cold. Like the life inside her. The one she didn't need. Didn't want. Not with Dale. Still...

The front door opened and Dahlia flipped the papers to the blank side and tried to hide the surprise on her face.

Dale looked somehow ashamed for being in his own home. "Hi."

"Hi."

"I only have a short time. So...do you want to...?"

"Yeah. I guess so."

Even for a funeral it was somber. The pup hadn't had time to get very big so Dale didn't need to dig a large hole. Five shovelfuls did the trick. Dahlia did finally cry when Dale set the black plastic trash bag in the ground. But she didn't feel like her tears were all for the dog.

Dale put his arm around her shoulder and warmth passed between them. A current of possibility, a spark that all was not lost. Neither one of them had any words for the dog or for their marriage. Finally, Dale cleared his throat.

"I gotta get going."

She moved away from his touch.

Dale started filling the hole. "When I get back, we should talk. Some things at work...things are different."

"Okay." *What did that mean?*

He set the shovel in the ground and leaned on it. "Hey, Dahl? I love you, okay?"

Yes, make it okay. Love him back and it will be okay. And she did love him. Somewhere in there. In memories. In photos. In his arm around her, same as it ever was. "I love you too, Dale. We'll talk when you get back."

"Yeah. When I get home."

She could tell there was a lot on his mind. A heavier weight than usual, which must have been crushing him. She let him go with a brushed kiss on the cheek. She had her own places to be that afternoon.

After he'd gone, she lifted her printed directions off the desk. The pages in Dahlia's hands had gone cold.

CHAPTER 3

Dale was overfed on information like a tick about to pop. He knew the job. Get in, get the girl, reason with Tat to let her go, and waltz out.

If he thought about it, he had to laugh. Who the hell was he kidding? Who were *they* kidding? Change the plan to: walk in and ask Tat for the girl, get shot between fifty and a hundred and fifty times, get stuffed in a drainpipe in more than one piece—then he'd have a much better chance of success.

The latest nervous Nelly chattering at him was Lauren's boss from the news website. Mike Arneson, late twenties and clearly nervous talking to the cops, spewed more details than anyone needed the way a murder confession goes when someone is trying desperately to unburden themselves.

"She's young, man. Twenty-four. I know she's got no practical experience, but her connections." He let that sit, waiting for some sort of acknowledgement or agreement from Dale. He got none. "I mean, with the mayor being her dad. I couldn't pass up that kind of inside scoop. We've been hurting for hits on the site. So she came in and pitched this story on what her dad's new initiative was going to do to the drug trade in the city. Well, shit, you can't say no to that."

"And you thought it was a good idea for her to go see Tat?"

"That was all her, man. She said she wanted the story from the horse's mouth or something like that. Tell you the truth, I didn't even know who the fuck she was talking about."

"Did you just move here or something?"

"About a year ago."

"Ah."

Dale turned at the sound of the door opening. A man came in with the telltale little suitcase of a wire.

"Uh-uh. No way. I'm not wearing a wire."

Behind the technician carrying the suitcase, another man entered. Dale's supervisor, the chief of detectives, Barney Nolan.

"Dale, you gotta."

"You trying to get me killed? This isn't a sting, it's a rescue mission. If Tat catches me with a wire—which he would about ten seconds in the door—I'd be target practice first and dog food next. You know that, Nolan."

Nolan put his head down, showing Dale the circle of pale scalp where his hair had vacated the premises. "You're right, you're right. I'm trying here, okay? I don't want to send you in naked."

"I might as well be."

Nolan looked Dale in the eye. Before he spoke, Dale realized, *he doesn't know yet.*

"I can't believe you volunteered for this crazy-ass assignment."

"I didn't have much say in it, Nolan."

"Still, man. Shit."

"Yeah. Shit."

Arneson shifted uncomfortably in his seat. "Do you need anything else from me?"

Dale shook his head. "I guess not. Let me ask you this, though. Was she trying for, like, an exposé piece? Was she trying to pin something on Tat?"

"No. She said he was one of those Al Capone types who operated illegally out in the open. She wanted his opinion on the new policies. That's all."

"And when did those policies get released to the press?"

Arneson feigned some heavy thinking about it. "This morning, I think."

"But she went to see Tat yesterday."

Arneson shrugged. "Like I said. Inside information. It was gonna be a great piece. Still is, but a slightly different one, am I right?" He attempted a smile but was shot down.

Dale pulled on his jacket. Slate grey, worn elbows. A working man's coat. "So she was the one who ended up telling him that his business was about to be shut down?" Dale turned to Nolan. "I can see how he'd be a little pissed."

Arneson began to whine again, sounding so much like a suspect, Dale wanted to read him his rights. "I told you it was her idea. I didn't make her go there."

"We know you didn't. Go home. Write about something else. This story stays here until you hear from me."

Arneson nodded; the press had been castrated and didn't fight back.

Dale stood. Nolan looked him over. "You're not even going to take your piece?"

"Would you walk into Tat's carrying a gun?"

Nolan nodded. Dale thought of one last thing.

"Can I make a phone call?"

Nolan smiled. "You're not under arrest, Dale. You get a call if you want."

Dale gave back a close-lipped grin. He mumbled to himself, "Yet."

Dale stopped a mile and a half down the road from Tat's complex to have a final face-to-face with Chief Schuster. After that, he was on his own.

"I don't need to remind you we're all counting on you, do I Dale?"

"I don't need to remind you this is a terrible idea, do I?"

Schuster sighed, frustrated and doubting his decision. "We want her alive and unharmed. I send SWAT in there and chances are good neither of those things happen."

"I'll do my best, Chief. This is a good-faith gesture. I know it won't save my ass, but I need all the karma I can get."

"We won't be able to communicate with you until you're out." Schuster pulled open the door to the police van. Cool fall air hit Dale like the lash of a whip. "Meet you back here."

"Let's hope so."

Dale stepped out of the van onto the four-lane road leading to the industrial park.

Four Pines Technology Park was supposed to bring jobs and new industry to the area. Four towers of office space, two warehouses, two manufacturing blocks. Shipping docks, an on-site gym, day care.

In the end, funding collapsed and the three-hundred-acre complex stood as a monument to the economic downturn. Only one tower had been fully built. Fifteen stories of glass and steel. A four-story skeleton sat rusting in the shadow of the completed building. The other two buildings hadn't even been started beyond concrete pads. Wide concrete squares and a massive pit intended for underground parking spread out over the clearing in the woods. Driveways that led nowhere, fountains with no water, signs with no lettering gave the complex a ghost town feeling.

Tat had purchased the acreage legally and turned it into his residence, his place of business, and a refuge for his employees for them to get off the streets and out of the gutter. Being private property, the cops couldn't search it without a warrant and somehow, those never seemed to get approved.

Ten miles out of town, Tat was out of sight and out of mind for the city's law enforcement. And with everyone he paid off in the police force and the city government, Tat's fortress was as safe as the White House.

Dale approached the fence surrounding the property. He'd been here before, several times, but always at night and always at Tat's request. Dale had kicked in the doors of suspects before without knowing what dangers waited for him on the other side. He'd been shot at, threatened, stabbed once with a carrot peeler. Experience taught him not to hesitate. You step up and do the job.

The single building was a thin rectangle. The idea of the park was to have several towers, four to start with room for four more, but every office would have window. That way the buildings would each only be two offices and a hallway wide. It also helped them keep heating costs down and a few other benefits that gave the design a Green Leaf certification.

The result was one tall knife blade cutting into the sky. A samurai sword shoved hilt-first into the ground. The perfect shape for a building of Tat's.

Dale pressed the buzzer on the gate and turned his face, smiling, to the security camera hanging overhead.

The gate buzzed and swung open, his familiarity gaining him entry. Dale sucked in a deep breath and went inside.

Lauren O'Brien had been told she looked like a mayor's daughter during the campaign. A Hollywood casting agent's idea of one, anyway. Blonde, pretty, slightly arrogant stare. She'd smiled her best politician's family smile at the left-handed compliment.

So far her abduction had been the Ritz-Carlton of kidnappings. The room where Tat had put her was plush, right off his office and comfortable for a week's vacation stay. Not at all like the cinder-block bunker she'd expected. Even her bodyguard was kind of cute, if you liked your men twice your size and mute.

When Tat entered, he didn't bother to knock. Muscular, buzz cut, and sparking with energy, he picked up in the middle of a conversation he'd started without her.

"Not a goddamn thing yet. You believe that shit?"

From her father? Yeah, she could believe it.

"I've been telling you this is a bad idea."

"No, you coming here was a bad idea. Breaking into my shit was a bad idea. Your daddy sending spies into my house was a bad idea."

"I'm not working for my father," she repeated for the tenth time since she'd been caught snooping around the lower floors.

"Not anymore." He bent at the waist and stared her down. "Your ass belongs to me now. And I gots to get paid to give you back."

Paid not in cash, but in influence. A loophole carved out of the new antidrug policy. An indefinite extension on the free pass Tat got from the cops. And maybe a little cash to smooth over the hurt.

"Have you told Tyler I'm here? Is he coming to see me?"

Her contact. Her inside man. Her boyfriend...sort of. The guy she'd been sleeping with for two months now.

"I told you, accountants don't get to come to the top floor. Around here, everyone knows their place. Maybe you oughta learn that, girl." Tat spun on his heel. "Time to give your daddy another call."

Lauren could only curse to herself and punch a velvet pillow. Her plan to dig up information for her story had not gone as expected. She got into the fortress like she wanted. Tyler had done his job, even if he hadn't know it was his job. Ever since then, things had gone to shit. But she knew her dad had a plan. He wouldn't leave her. He'd send the cops, the FBI negotiators. Someone, right?

15TH FLOOR

Much as he couldn't believe it, Dale's stomach felt less twisted riding in this elevator than when he rode up to see Chief Schuster that morning. Like a model home, this tower had been completed to show all aspects of the coming technology center and job creating engine. Right down to the piped-in smooth jazz music in the elevators. Tat decided he kind of liked the smooth sounds and kept the one tiny playlist of tunes that repeated every ten minutes.

Dale focused on the buttery sounds of Kenny G's saxophone. What was supposed to be inoffensive music while somehow managing to be about the most offensive sound Dale could think of. He actually felt relief getting off on the top floor.

Tat's office.

Dale was met at the elevator by a hulking meathead. He wore a tight-fitting jacket over a thin T-shirt threatening to pop every seam under his 'roided out muscle mass. He patted Dale down, found nothing.

The meathead waved Dale inside.

No one could accuse Tat of having good taste. He believed that success was measured by the amount of gold-plated surfaces one had. Politely, Tat's sprawling office could be called ornate. Realistically, the open space that took over half of the top floor looked like the palace of Versailles fucked a Miami hooker and fell backward into a vat of gold plating.

The wall paper crisscrossed with shiny gold hexagons. The carpet was a blood red. Mirrors hung so close to each other the room had a funhouse quality to it. It was enough to give you a complex, all those reflections of yourself all at once.

The couch was orange leather, the pillows animal prints, the art on the walls from the Motel 6 collection.

In the center of it all, behind his ornate, Hummer-sized desk, was Tautolu Losopo, crime kingpin. Tat had the good fortune to be named according to his Samoan upbringing with a name that also shortened to a nickname appropriate to the thick rows of tribal tattoos that snaked up both arms.

Tat's dark olive skin bulged with muscles. His buzz cut gave his head the look of a howitzer shell. His teeth shone white in his mouth except where gold caps covered both his canines.

His desk sat against the windows a good thirty feet from the door and Tat had to raise his voice to call Dale over. "Dale, get the fuck in here, man." White teeth and gold caps flashed at him like a werewolf snarling, but this was Tat's version of a welcome greeting.

Dale made the long walk across the room, taking inventory of the three bodyguards and four young women in the room. The men, also Samoans, all watched him closely while the girls ignored him vehemently, examining their nails, popping gum, texting on their phones in an effort to look utterly bored by his presence.

Tat's near boundless energy was hard to contain while sitting, but to stand would be to show respect to someone else in his place of business. Not going to happen. "To what do I owe the pleasure of your company?"

"Hey, Tat."

Dale caught his reflection in one of the many mirrors and he looked as nervous as he felt. He needed to relax. He'd turned down the wire, but he still came off looking like he wore a microphone under his shirt, hidden camera on his belt, and a backup team of officers stuffed up his ass.

"You heard about this fuckin' mayor?" Tat slapped a hand down on the black marble top of his desk. A thick gold ring clacked off the surface like a gunshot. "What's he tryin' to do to us, man?"

"Y'know, Tat, that's kinda why I'm here." Cut to the chase. Get the job done, get out, and get on with things. Even the idea of hurry up and go to jail seemed more appealing than standing in this office building any longer.

"You're here 'cause I let you be here, man. You work for me, remember?"

Dale felt properly put in his place. "Yes. True, but that's not all."

"The girl, right?" Tat's grin spread wide, exposing both golden canines again. "What the fuck, mayor can't take a joke?"

"Yeah, down at headquarters no one is laughing, Tat."

The gold teeth were covered as Tat's mouth slid shut, a pinched glare taking over. He snapped his fingers twice and two of the henchmen slipped out of the room on a mission. Dale didn't like the look of it.

"She came in here snooping around, man. Looking for shit. A reporter, you know? Writing some shit about me. Hey, unless it's some shit about how beautiful I am, you don't do that without my permission, you dig? I got to get the facts, man. Did her daddy send her here? This new law, man, this shit is bullshit. They're trying to shut me down."

Tat twisted his neck, trying to crack it. Nothing happened. Still pinned to his seat, his energy threatened to vibrate him right out onto his desk.

"So the mayor's is pissed I kept his little girl for a day or two? He ought to feel lucky I didn't put a bullet in her. Or maybe some of this." Tat reached down and grabbed a fistful of his crotch, pumped his hand a few times to emphasize its bulk, then laughed it off.

In his two years of dealing with Tat, Dale felt he was always one minor slipup away from a bullet to the brain. From a gold-plated gun, of course. Tat had no respect for the badge Dale carried, but Dale knew by agreeing to the first meeting and taking the first stack of hundred-dollar bills, Dale had disrespected the badge himself. The relationship got off on the wrong foot.

But Tat knew Dale as a man of action. A man who could get things done. One of Tat's rivals needed to go away, Dale could have him behind bars by the stroke of midnight, and if that was impossible, he'd have someone underneath the pavement of a new parking lot just as fast. Dale had scumbag blood on his hands at Tat's request. What Tat didn't know is that it all came out of a deep fear of Tat and a detailed look at the reports of the other two cops on the take before him—including autopsy photos of them after the fact. Dale didn't feel like being victim number three, and fear can make a man do some very stupid things.

Standing in front of Tat, unarmed, Dale was a newborn puppy still slick with afterbirth. No threat to anyone. Still, he needed to maintain an aura of a man who could come in to Tat's own building and make demands, or at least requests.

The two henchmen returned escorting Lauren O'Brien between them. Dirty blonde, pretty, and looking younger than her twenty-four years, she seemed more annoyed than scared. A pissy sorority girl.

"What the fuck is it now?" She acted like the two thugs had turned off her favorite TV show to bring her into the office. She looked up and noticed Dale. He thought he saw a hitch of hope in her eyes. She quickly covered it over with a thick layer of fake annoyance. "Who's this?"

Tat swiveled in his chair to face her. "His name is Luke Skywalker. He's here to rescue you."

Dale didn't feel like getting caught in any animosity they already had going against each other. "I'm just here to tell you, Tat, that things are starting to get ugly out there because of this little stunt. It would be smart of you to let me take her back to her father and you can sort this all out later."

"Is that what would be smart?"

Dale backpedaled. "I'm just saying, if you got a problem

with the mayor's new plan, this isn't exactly the way to get a debate going."

"He's listening to me, isn't he?"

"It's not a free ride anymore. For fuck's sake, I got busted. I'm going down."

Tat eyed Dale, tilted his head a little like a dog. "But you're my boy."

"Yeah. That's kinda it. They know everything." Dale hung his head low, mumbling to himself. "Christ, I hope not everything."

"So what are you doing here if you're busted? Why'd they let you come?"

"They're giving me a chance. You too. We make this right again and we both might have a shot."

Tat waved his ring-heavy hand, pushed out a puff of air like a steam valve. "I got them by the balls, bro. Ain't nobody can touch me. Alls I got to do is give 'em a twist."

Probably true, thought Dale. "Well, it might be my only chance."

Not the most likely strategy when dealing with Tat, appealing to his good nature, but it was all Dale had. He could feel Lauren's eyes on him, reaching for news of the outside world. Wanting to know her rescue was coming soon and hoping to God this wasn't it.

Tat rocked in his chair, thinking. The gum chewing from a girl on the couch behind Dale filled the silence.

"So you're gonna come in here," Tat started tapping the big gold ring on the middle finger of his right hand against the black marble, "and tell me to let my bargaining chip go? You're gonna tell me I made a mistake? You're gonna tell me to help you out because *you* got sloppy and got busted?"

Uh-oh. Dale didn't like the rising volume in Tat's voice or the pulsing vein bumping the tribal tattoo on his biceps.

"Tat, I just don't want to see it turn ugly."

Tat sat forward quickly, both palms down on his desk. "And how's it gonna get ugly? You know I'm the one who makes it ugly, right? Right?"

Dale saw the three bodyguards tense up. He heard shuffling of clothes and the sharp click of spike heels on the floor as two of the girls moved off the couch and beyond the rug.

"Sit the fuck down, you cunts." Tat kept his eyes on Dale. The heels clicked slower on the tile floor until they hit the carpet and then padded like bullets from a silencer as the girls obeyed orders to return to their seats.

"Look, all I know is, if I don't walk out of here with the girl, I can't guarantee what will happen next."

"If you walk out of here at all, you mean."

Dale felt his knees start to seize up. Trying so hard not to let them collapse ended up having the opposite effect. His legs were stiff and locked in place. He needed to pace, to move, but he didn't dare make any motion or Tat might attack like a well-trained pit bull. A lifetime of being beaten with a rubber hose, prodded with a taser, burned with cigarettes. Tat's hard upbringing left him without a single fuck to give to anyone in the world, least of all Dale or the mayor's daughter.

"Tat, you got no beef with me." Dale tried to shuffle his feet to loosen them a bit but make the motion invisible. "I've been good to you. I'm coming here as a courtesy because I don't want anything bad to happen."

"My hero."

"Tat, let me walk out of here with her. She's not doing you any good. You have people on the inside you can do this through. You don't need to piss off anybody else."

Tat thrust an angry finger toward Lauren. "You know what she told me? She said her fuckhead of a father promised that people like me would be gone from this city like ticks off a dog. Blood-sucking parasite, he called me."

"That's between you and him."

"Then you come in here and try to take something of mine. You try to take from me?"

"I'm trying to help you."

24

"On his fucking knees."

On the command, the same two bodyguards who led Lauren in crossed to Dale and each put a hand up under an armpit and kicked out the back of a knee. Dale went down to the rug, his kneecaps cracking hard as he fell. The third bodyguard slid over and put a hand on Lauren, so she didn't get any ideas.

Tat picked up the phone. "You wanna take from me?"

Dale did not like the sound of that but thought better of arguing anymore. More than anything else, he wanted to bring Schuster into the room and scream, "I told you so," at him.

Tat hit a single button and someone answered. Dale listened, fearing the conversation the way he'd fear a gun pressed to his temple. The chamber clicked on a full round. He heard his wife's name. His address.

"Pick her up. Bring her here."

Dale's gut stung like a fish hook gouged him. *Not Dahlia.*

"No. Tat. She's got nothing—"

Tat nodded and a fist hammered into Dale's skull. A knuckle-breaking blow on any normal human, but the bodyguard to his right seemed to take it without an ounce of pain. Dale's head swam in murky waters.

Lauren spoke, defying Tat to order the same kind of blow to her head. "Now what? More kidnappings?"

"He wants to take from me, I take from him. Maybe we swap."

Dale hung limp in the grip of the two men. "Please, not my wife."

"I made my point though, right?"

"Please."

Dale felt the uneasiness in his gut tighten, the dread turned ice cold and rock hard. He'd been facing down losing everything, but now he really was. And to bring Dahlia into it, he couldn't let that stand. He'd met men before who said their motivation for the awful things they did was that they had nothing to lose. He always scoffed at them, called bullshit on their excuses.

25

On his knees, in that gaudy palace paid for with drug money and spilled blood, Dale found himself with nothing left to lose and the realization freed him. The fear faded away. He didn't give a shit anymore what Schuster had planned. He didn't care what came out in a trial.

He looked up at the Samoan grinning gold teeth at him behind his desk and hated every inch of that motherfucker. Dale turned to his right, saw the butt of a gun jutting from the shoulder holster of the thick man holding him down. Promises of a broken nose from one end, a death sentence from the other.

"Y'know what, Tat?" Dale caught his breath again. Felt the rock in his gut. "I came here to do a job. You don't like it, that's your problem. Call them off my wife."

"I thought we had an agreement, Dale."

"Call them off."

Tat leaned forward, peering over the edge of his monolithic desk to see Dale better in his supplicate position on the floor. "I pay you and you follow orders. Isn't that how it works?"

"Call them off."

"Isn't that why I bought your badge?"

Dale spun and snatched the gun from under the jacket of the man on his right. Hands under the armpits? Fucking amateurs.

He swung the piece around and blew out the kneecap of the man to his left, felt hot blood tickle his lip. He brought the gun back and fired into the gut of the gun's owner. Two shots burrowed past the thick muscle. No amount of sit-ups can stop a slug from a .45.

The girls were up and screaming. Free to move, Dale dashed for the gaudy orange sofa when the bullets came. Tat's gold pistol dug chunks in the rug behind Dale as he retreated. A girl in a red bikini and a sheer sarong ran left, then doubled back right, crossing the path of Tat's wild shots. She caught one in each thigh and went down.

* * *

Lauren uncoiled like a spring. She spun in place and flattened her hand like a blade as she chopped at the neck of the man holding her. He grabbed at his throat and lurched backward.

Lauren pounced, seeing her only chance at escape. She straddled the man she'd karate chopped and reached under his coat for a gun. She wrapped two hands around it and gripped a little too tight. It went off in the holster. Startled, she let go of the gun, wondering if this guy had ever heard of a safety.

Dale crouched low behind the arm of the sofa and ripped off two shots at Tat's desk. Flecks of black marble spit into the air.

A thin fist hammered the side of Dale's head. A long red nail broke off and embedded in Dale's skin just above his right ear. He turned to see a girl in short shorts, a tank top, and six-inch heels pounding at him while screaming high-pitched nonsense.

Dale grabbed a wrist as it swung down at his head and yanked her, pulling her off balance. She tipped on her heels and fell onto the couch, bouncing on the plush cushions. Tat launched another volley of fire.

The girl with the broken nail absorbed a bullet in her ribs, her hip, her wrist, and finally her neck. She spasmed like a cell phone on vibrate for a second while the shots were pelting her body, then fell still, sinking deeper into the cushions.

Better her than me, thought Dale, but he immediately felt guilty about it. What had she done besides run with assholes and criminals? Dale *was* the asshole criminal.

"I tried to help you, Tat."

"Fuck you." More shots. Dale hadn't been counting, but Tat was letting them fly freely.

"Just let us go."

"Maybe I stuttered. I said fuck you." Five shots came from behind the black desk. Wild, undisciplined shots by a man used to having people do this shit for him.

* * *

Lauren reached into the jacket again of the man she shot. His chest was warm and sticky with blood as she lifted the gun out of the holster. He shrank into a ball, clutching at his side. She thought of shooting him in the head but knew she couldn't. He was unarmed, no longer a threat, and curled up like a little baby.

Behind her was the door she came through, an anteroom used to keep her prisoner but probably intended for Tat to bang any of the skinny, generic pieces of ass he kept around him like tchotchkes on the shelf. She could dive back through and shut herself in, but then what? Whoever this guy they sent in was, he sure had some balls on him. Probably going to get both of them killed, but she had to hand it to him for his tenacity.

She stood to the side of Tat's desk where she could see him crouching behind, slapping a new clip into his golden gun. He moved up to one knee and brought the barrel over the top of the desk aimed toward her rescuer. Without thinking, she raised the gun in her hand and fired.

The first shot ricocheted off the marble desktop. The second cracked through the computer screen on the desk. The third punctured Tat's shooting hand.

It was the loudest single profanity Dale had ever heard. Tat's up-from-the-depths scream made Dale look. He had to. He'd been curious to peek out from his hiding spot when he heard the other shots, but he was happy enough when none of them landed in him.

Dale saw Tat holding his own hand, a fresh flow of red coating both hands. The gun was gone, out of sight somewhere behind the desk. The mayor's daughter held her own gun now, aiming at Tat, not at Dale. A good enough time as any to move.

Dale charged forward, his gun in a two-handed, academy trained grip. He sidestepped to move behind Tat's desk, gave the golden gun a swift kick with the toe of his shoe, and aimed his pistol at Tat's head.

Tat greeted him with another high volume, "Fuck!"

"Call them off my wife." Tat ignored him. "Call them off, Tat." Dale looked at the desk, the phone Tat had used to call was in pieces. Plastic casing shattered by one of Lauren's wild shots.

As if she knew he was admiring her work, Lauren spoke up. "We gotta get out of here."

"Not until he cancels the guys going after my wife." Dale pointed the gun at Tat's head but was ignored.

"We're gonna have company soon." Lauren waved the gun in front of her to indicate the noise of the shootout to Dale. She also gave him a "duh" look.

Dale wasn't about to leave Tat behind, but he had no way to restrain him. One hand injury wouldn't keep a man like Tat docile for long. Dale remembered a technique he'd heard about some really fucked up Mexican cartels using. Figured it might be his only shot.

Dale stuffed the gun into his waistband. "Sorry, man. I gotta do this."

He stepped up and put a foot on Tat's ribcage, took up his non-injured arm in both hands. Dale pulled up and twisted, dislocating the shoulder with a pop and a gravelly crunch he thought didn't sound good at all.

Tat hollered a record-level swear word again. Dale reached down and took the wrist of Tat's blood-soaked arm in his two hands. He gripped tight to keep it from slipping out on the lube of thick red blood. The hole in his palm was open on both ends, shreds of flesh pushing out.

Dale tugged and twisted, Tat's shoulder popped and crunched. Two shoulders dislocated. The poor man's handcuffs.

Dale put a hand under Tat's armpit and lifted. "Let's go."

Lauren fell in behind them. "Is this it? Any backup?"

"This is it. They wanted to do it quietly. No gunfire and no casualties."

Lauren stepped over the splayed legs of one of the three dead girls in the room. She listened to the moaning of the man she'd shot get quieter as they moved across the wide room toward the elevators.

Mirrors reflected their long walk as Dale pushed Tat out in front, the big man hunched over and whimpering from his injuries, his arms slack at his side and his gunshot hand dripping blood freely over the thick pile rugs and then the tile floor.

At the doorway out to the former lobby, now entry into Tat's inner sanctum, Dale turned to Lauren.

"You'll tell your dad about this, right? Maybe with a little less blood."

"If we get out of here, he'll be giving you the key to the city, if that's what your worried about."

"What do you mean, if?"

"This is a huge building with a lot of people in it. I have a feeling getting out isn't going to be as easy as an elevator ride."

On cue, a high-heeled shoe blurred into Dale's periphery. A high-pitched karate yell came close behind it and Dale felt the sharp spike of the stiletto heel dig into his temple.

Dale let go of Tat as he tilted toward the floor, the impact of the kick ringing his ears. Another high yell sounded, but Dale was already on the ground. He rolled over to see a girl in her twenties he thought he had seen in the room when he first arrived. Her tight-fitting tube dress was hiked up her thighs exposing her red thong. When her foot came down from clipping Dale across the skull, the heel snapped off on the hard tile floor. She flailed for balance, her second attack thrown off by the sudden spin of the earth.

Her war cry never stopped. As the girl regained her footing and shifted her weight to attack with her good heel, Dale pawed at his belt, hunting for the gun he knew he'd stashed there only moments ago.

Above him, Tat spun in a confused circle trying to avoid the girl and maybe think about escape. His arms flung out from his sides like deadweight. Droplets of blood hit Dale in the cheek as Tat swung.

Dale couldn't find his gun, his brain temporarily fuzzed out from the kick to the head. As the girl reared back for another attack, he saw the quick flash of Lauren's hand and the gun turned butt-end first in her fist. The gun clubbed the young girl across the back of her skull and stunned her. She didn't go lights out, but she stopped yelling and it halted her attack.

Lauren whacked her again. Dale saw Tat start to make a run for it and thrust out his own feet to tangle in Tat's legs as he got moving. Tat fell, and with no arms to protect him, hit the floor hard on his chest and his face.

The girl followed him to the floor soon after.

Dale scrambled up. "Thanks."

Lauren spun the gun back around in her hand. "No problem." She turned her attention to the bank of elevators and the numbers in red digital readout climbing from below. "We gotta go."

Dale looked at the numbers ticking off Tat's backup team's inevitable arrival. "Yeah, but where?"

"Stairs. Here."

Lauren turned and ran. Dale had to scoop up Tat, his nose now dumping any blood not already lost to his hand. Dale felt his own streak of red sliding down the side of his face from the heel-shaped indent in his scalp.

Lauren made it to the stairwell using the building schematics she'd studied for a week before her meeting there. She'd been fascinated by how Tat came to possess the abandoned structure and how nobody could touch his criminal utopia inside. The building plans were public record and unless he'd altered them since moving in, she knew the layout of the fifteen stories as well as the architect.

Lauren pushed open the door and held it in place with her

body while Dale muscled Tat down the short hallway. "Come on, they're almost here."

"I need to get to a phone, have this asshole call his guys off."

"An elevator full of his guys are about to be here. We can find a phone one floor down. Now, go."

"Shit."

Dale pushed Tat through the door and into the concrete stairwell. A stenciled number fifteen was spray painted on the grey cement wall. Concrete dust from construction still gritted the floors and the scraping of their shoes echoed down the shaft.

Lauren stepped in and let the door slam behind her.

Tat blew out, spraying blood off his lips. "You're dead. Both of you. Dead." His voice came out stuffy and slightly muffled from the nose full of blood. Dale knew the feeling, the blood dripping down the back of your throat. He could almost taste the bitter blood in his mouth.

Dale pushed Tat forward and down the first steps. "Tat, I hate to say, I told you so." Dale had to grip his prisoner with both hands to keep him from falling face-first down the steps. "I tell you what though, we get to a phone and you're gonna call off your guys or you'll be the one who's dead."

CHAPTER 4

Dahlia looked at the clock, wondering how early was too early to get to the clinic. Sitting around the house made her fidgety, but the idea of arriving with too much time to spare and sitting in a waiting room for an hour or more with her eyes down, avoiding contact with the other women there made her queasy. She wondered if there would be music. Would she have to sit and read month-old *People* magazines about vapid starlets' lives being so goddamn difficult while she and her fellow moms-for-now crushed back tears and composed silent, internal eulogies for babies they'd never met?

Would she be trapped in a crowded room with a dozen other women all feeling the same gut-churning emotions inside, or worse, would there be one lonely teenage girl crying into an already wet tissue? She'd have to ignore her. Ignore anyone else in the place. Dahlia didn't have it in her to give her strength to someone else. She needed all of it for herself.

Times like these she needed a vice like smoking. Instead she checked over her directions again even though she had it memorized. The route was convenient. She could even stop for groceries on the way home.

Dahlia went to the kitchen to check if she needed eggs. The doorbell rang.

Grateful for the distraction, she went to the door ready to endure the practiced speech of a fringe political group or a crackpot religious sect. She found two tall men with dark, tanned skin and

33

tight black T-shirts on her stoop. They both had tightly cropped hair and one wore a neatly trimmed goatee. He took the lead.

"Mrs. Burnett, could you come with us, please?"

Dahlia pushed the door closed by a few inches. "Who are you?"

"We need you to come with us."

Being a cop's wife, Dahlia had been drilled in this situation before. Most of those instructions were as out of reach as the gun in the nightstand upstairs, but she remembered Dale being adamant—don't let them in the house. It's called a home invasion for a reason. Don't let them invade.

"What is this regarding?" Stall tactics. She looked beyond the two figures and tried to find someone in the street—a neighbor, the mailman. Empty.

"We really need you to come with us, ma'am."

They were polite, not getting all gangster thuggish with her. Still, they wouldn't say who they were. She couldn't see the bulges of guns, but they hadn't turned around. She knew she was being optimistic. This was a crime in progress of some sort. She had to know that.

"Do you have any ID or anything?"

The two men shared a look. Dahlia didn't like it. She slammed the door and spun the deadbolt, then ran into the house.

Behind her she heard two kicks, then the splintering of wood. She ran a circle around the sofa in the living room, no idea where to go or what to do. She saw the phone on the kitchen counter and bolted.

The two men moved fast. They split up, flanking Dahlia so she couldn't alter her path at all. In the kitchen, she was cornered. She scooped up the phone in her right hand and the man with the goatee reached her and slapped it away. The cordless bounced off the granite countertop and landed in the sink. A small series of what she could almost call sobs escaped Dahlia's throat. Panicked whimpers. Fear she knew no words for.

The clean-shaven man took hold of her right arm. The other

man put a finger to his lips and shushed her. "We're just supposed to take you in. No one's here to hurt you."

That's what they say right before they hurt you, Dahlia thought. She swung her left hand in a wide arc. The goateed man ducked away like a boxer and she brought her hand around, curling her fingers into claws before her hand met the clean-shaven man's face. She raked four red gashes across his cheek. He let go of her arm.

"Fuck. She cut me, T."

Keeping his boxer's form, T shuffled forward on fast moving feet and planted a right jab to Dahlia's face. She took the punch in stunned silence. The force of the hit spun her around and she hit her hip bone against the counter. She looked down and saw blood from her mouth splash on the granite.

"Lady, let's not do it like this."

Dahlia pulled open the drawer in front of her. She stabbed a hand inside and she spun, coming out with the first thing her hand wrapped around. She swung the thin-bladed boning knife out in front of her. T ducked away again, retreating toward a neutral corner.

His partner had been moving closer, looking to wrap her in a clinch from behind and subdue the wildcat. Seeing the knife arcing through the air, he lifted his hand as if he were blocking a punch. This punch had a six-inch steel blade on the end of it.

The knife punctured his palm and wedged itself between the bones. Dahlia held on as he jerked his hand at the sudden shock of pain. Her fist gripped tight to the hilt as he waved his hand left, then right. He stared at the tip of the blade peeking out from the skin on the back of his hand, his own blood pooling out around it.

"Fuck, dude." He grunted a pained caveman noise as they continued to move together with the knife stuck in his palm and she unwilling to let it go.

T waited for an opening. He made one quick move forward, but the tangled duo twisted and blocked him, putting his partner's back to him. T retreated to wait for another opportunity, not eager to get a knife through his hand or any other part of him.

The partner pulled again and Dahlia went with him this time, pushing forward with his momentum. His hand and the knife tip protruding from it went toward him. The blade dove into his neck. It caught his left side as he turned a second too late to avoid it. The blade bit skin but only for a moment. The puncture was only a half inch deep, but it severed something vital.

His arm went slack when the new pain started and Dahlia pulled the knife free, his bones releasing their grip on the blade. The man turned to face T, confusion on his face. T took a small step backward, away from the gore. He seemed frozen by the turn of events.

As he spun, the young man spewed blood. He covered the four bananas on the counter, the pile of unpaid bills, the empty mug and spent tea bag Dahlia hadn't cleaned up yet.

The dot of blood on her lip from the punch became insignificant. He turned again, trying to find T's eyes. They stood, the three of them, and watched him bleed. Dahlia against the counter, panting frightened sobs, T by the fridge, and the bleeding man beside the breakfast bar, neck rotating and spraying blood like a lawn sprinkler.

Dahlia tried to drop the knife, but her grip on it was subconscious now. Some deep part of her brain knew she might need it again. She looked at T and saw the horror on his face as his partner bled out while searching his eyes for help or answers.

His black T-shirt became blacker as it soaked through. The pumps of blood slowed. The cut looked so small, then it would open with another gush in time to the man's slowing heartbeat. She thought about her appointment again. *Would there be blood?*

The man started to slump. Dahlia broke out of her trance first. She ran.

The front door was imploded in on itself and hung open. She sprinted through the house holding the boning knife like a relay runner's baton and made a mini hurdle jump over the threshold and out of the house.

14TH FLOOR

They reached the landing for fourteen and Dale saw an elaborate keypad on the door. No simple push bar and they were in. This floor had a security system.

"The fuck is this?"

Tat slumped heavy in his arms, dazed by pain and unwilling to help his captor.

Lauren stepped around the prisoner. "It's a fingerprint scanner. This is Tat's personal residence. Only he can get in."

"If only he can get in, how do you know about it?"

"I've been researching this building for weeks."

"So how do we get in?"

Lauren gestured to the man in Dale's grasp. "Duh. It's his fingerprints."

Dale wasn't thinking straight. This whole thing had gone so off the rails, he was bound to make some stupid mistakes, but he looked like a rookie to the girl. He needed to shake it off, assume some authority over the rescue mission. Act like a goddamn hero and maybe the mayor would hear about it and say something nice to get his prison sentence reduced from a hundred to only fifty years. He was proud of himself up in Tat's office. He still had some moves. Tat was the worst part of his weakness, his time on the take. He was a damn good cop. He knew it. His record showed it. The top brass agreed. But it was what his record hadn't shown—until this morning—that would define him as a police officer.

"Which hand?"

"Right."

Dale went to reach for Tat's right hand and balked when he saw the bloody mess at the end of his arm. The ragged hole in his hand had gone a dark purple from the half-coagulated blood and the bruising. He had no choice. Dale lifted Tat's hand by the wrist. Tat let out a sudden yell, the combination of the pain in his hand and his dislocated shoulder tag-teamed to bring a shooting pain through his body.

Dale tried to be gentle as he wiped Tat's right thumb on Tat's own pants to clear away some of the blood and make a clean print. He set the thumb down on the tiny pad and gave it a gentle side to side rocking motion, perfect perp printing technique, just like they taught him at the academy all those years ago.

A tiny light went from red to green and the door clicked open. Dale felt the sudden urge to draw his gun.

The room inside was dark and quiet. Dale toed the door the rest of the way open and tried to look around the corners. Lauren waited outside, looking to Dale with a question mark, as if she wondered if she should be scared or not.

"Is it okay?"

Dale swept his eyes from left to right. "Looks like it."

He pushed Tat through the door and followed him inside.

If Tat's office was a gaudy attempt at impressing people with his wealth, his apartment was a tacky attempt at seducing the female of the species through sheer submission. The couch was a zebra print with a bear skin rug on the floor in front of it. Gold candlestick holders balanced on every surface next to pots of potpourri in strong floral scents. A heavy stone fireplace surround sat at one end of the living space and large canvasses of nude oil paintings hung under low-wattage gallery light as if they were actual art and not the horny fantasies of some middle-aged Picasso wannabe.

Dale lingered on a painting of two women with long Gene Simmons tongues in a sixty-nine position. He pulled his eyes away. "Nice place. Now where's a phone so you can call the guys who are after my wife?"

"Fuck off." Tat's voice was weak and slurry. Dale couldn't be sure how much blood they'd left behind in the stairwell, but he was glad it wasn't his.

"Lauren, you see a phone?"

"Hard to see anything in here." She ran a hand along the wall until she found a switch. She flicked it and a wide crystal chandelier lit up the room and threw diamond reflections off every surface like being inside Liberace's jockstrap.

"Who the fuck are you?"

The new voice made both Dale and Lauren jump. Dale turned to see a woman facing them, a .45 pistol heavy in her grip. She was pretty, Latina, busty, and slender enough to pose for the artwork on the walls.

She noticed Tat. "*Ai, papi.*" The tip of her gun drooped as she studied the blood stains and saw the slumped, defeated way he walked under Dale's guidance.

Dale raised his gun at her while she was distracted. "Question is, who the fuck are you?"

The woman snapped back to attention, brought her gun up to aim at Dale again. "What are you doing with him?"

"Looking for a phone."

"Let him go."

Dale shook his head. "He had that chance. Now he's got to do me a favor first."

Lauren saw some sort of opportunity and lifted her gun to the woman in a classic cop grip. "Put the weapon down."

The Latina kept her gun on Dale but turned her eyes to Lauren. "You're the reporter. The mayor's daughter."

"You must be Tat's number one." Lauren sidestepped to the right, away from Dale and Tat. "For this week, anyway."

"He said you had a smart mouth."

"What would you know about being smart?"

Dale kept up his eyeball search for a phone. "Ladies, can we get back to the phone here. Tat needs to make a call."

Lauren continued her sidestepping, drawing the woman's view farther away from Dale. "You know what being the mayor's daughter meant for me? It meant self-defense classes. Years of them. We don't get round-the-clock secret service like the president or anything. I was on my own, but my dad was paranoid. He wanted me to be ready for anything. So I took karate, taekwando, Krav Maga. You name it."

Dale was silently impressed.

"So you drop that weapon, or I'll take it from you."

Tat spat a gob of blood on the floor. "Carolina." The woman looked him in the eye. "Kill this bitch."

Lauren didn't wait for the girl to follow orders. She kicked out with a long right leg and connected with the wrist of Carolina's gun hand. Her pistol flew. The fight was on.

Dale pulled Tat back and pressed against the wall, his gun at the ready but afraid to take any shots while Lauren's limbs flung at their shared target.

Carolina had her own training, but it was school of the streets. Her fighting style was girl-fight vicious and punctuated by loud screams. She immediately went for a hair grab. She got a few strands between the loose fingers of her right hand, but Lauren spun away and mentally checked that box. *Watch out for the hair.*

She shot out a flat palm and hit Carolina in the center of her ribs. Carolina fell back, a deep wheezing sound coming from her empty lungs.

Lauren set her feet, her body turned sideways to make a smaller target and to get her feet in position for another kick. Carolina hit against a long credenza. She spun and picked up a clear bowl filled with blue pebbles of glass. A decoration that had no discernible use suddenly found one—as a weapon.

Carolina flung the bowl, and its shrapnel of glass beads, at

Lauren who blocked with both arms covering her face. The glass pellets clattered across the room pinging off every surface, the bowl shattered on the floor. Carolina lunged forward and tackled Lauren like they were in an alley fight.

As though emboldened by his girlfriend's animal viciousness, Tat found a surge of energy and tried slamming his head back and into Dale. He pistoned his neck three times quickly, looking to make contact with Dale's nose and break it. Dale shifted out of the way, tightened his grip on Tat's underarms, and when that didn't work, kicked at the back of Tat's knees and brought him to the floor with another guttural yell.

"Calm the fuck down, Tat. You're starting to piss me off."

Dale buried a knee in Tat's back to keep him in place. He didn't feel too bad since he kept Tat's face turned toward the two women brawling on the floor, a sight undoubtedly stirring sexual arousal in the sick bastard.

Lauren had reversed the clench on Carolina and now had the Latina in a choke hold. She looked at Dale. "You gonna help me?"

"What do you want me to do?" He indicated the man at the end of his knee.

"Shoot her or something."

"I'm a cop. We only shoot people when necessary."

"What the hell would you call this?"

Dale thought for a second and shrugged. He brought his gun around in front of him and squeezed off a round. It caught Carolina in the thigh. She screamed and Lauren leapt off of her.

"Y'know what, fuck this." Dale stood and grabbed the back of Tat's shirt, started dragging him across the smooth wood floor. He pulled him up to a door, opened it, and eye-measured the space inside the closet. He decided it was enough and pushed Tat inside. He slammed the door and took a lacquered black chair with antelope horns for arms from a small table and wedged it under the doorknob, sealing Tat inside.

"Check if she's got a phone."

Lauren reached down into the pants pockets of the writhing woman. Second pocket in she came out with a cell phone and tossed it to Dale. He caught it and dialed his wife. While he called, Lauren went to the closet and took down the chair.

It rang five times then Dahlia's voicemail picked up. Maybe she didn't answer the strange number, not knowing it was Dale. "Dahlia, it's me. I'm calling from a different number. I need to know you're all right. Pick up next time, okay?"

He dialed again. Voicemail. Third time. Same thing.

"Shit." Dale turned to see Lauren pawing over Tat's pockets, him off balance and leaning back into a pile of coats on hangers. She kept one hand on a gun pointed at his face and one hand rifled his clothes like a pickpocket on an off day.

Lauren kept her voice low in Tat's ear.

"You keep any records up here? Accounts, things like that?"

Tat ignored her, his eyes swimming and unfocused with pain.

"You help me out and I'll make sure he goes easy on you. Where can I find records of payments, things like that?" She gripped his chin in her hands and squeezed his face into a pucker. "And don't go telling me you don't keep records. Tyler told me you keep track of numbers better than the IRS."

Dale thumbed the phone off then hurled it against the wall, his emotions overrunning his good sense. With Dahlia at risk, he needed to get control of himself. He turned to see Lauren in close quarters with Tat.

"What the fuck are you doing?"

Lauren let go of Tat's face and dug into his pockets again. "Going through her pockets, I figured I should go through his. You never know."

"What are you looking for?"

"I don't know." She opened his wallet, passed over the money—all hundreds—and ignored his ID. She saw a thin card made of metal. Like a razor of steel cut into the same shape as a credit card. Some sort of pass key probably. She pocketed it and went on searching.

Dale kept vigil over Carolina. "Well, hurry it up."

Lauren finished with Tat, shut him back in the closet. "Your wife not there?"

"No. But she should be."

Lauren pointed her gun down at Carolina. "What about her?"

"Tie her up."

"With him?" Lauren nodded to the closet.

Dale looked around the room for options. "No. Keep them separate."

"Then what?"

"Then we get out of here. Fast."

They hog tied her using strips of her own shirt and left her in her bra on the bear skin rug. Dale tried to think if there was any good reason to keep Tat with them, but he thought moving fast was a higher priority. By now the building would have been alerted to the bloodbath upstairs and that Tat was missing. Dale and Lauren needed to move.

"You say you know this building well?"

"Yeah. By blueprints and stuff. I haven't been to the other floors in real life."

"You're one up on me. All I've ever seen is the top floor." Dale looked around him. "And now this."

Lauren straightened her clothes. She tucked away her gun. "You have a car downstairs or something? Some way to get away from here?"

"Yeah. There's people waiting for us. I need to get to my wife, though."

"Then we need to get out of here."

"Yep." Dale started for the stairwell again. "Let's go."

CHAPTER 5

Dahlia flat-palm slapped the back door like a misbehaving child. She'd made it as far as Mrs. Joosten's house next door. The elderly lady had been in a cold war over trash can placement and her thoughts on how early on trash day it was neighborly to set out the cans. They hadn't spoken in six months and Dahlia suspected Mrs. Joosten of stealing birdseed from their feeder.

At the moment she pounded the old lady's back door, she hoped to bury the hatchet. Or at least she hoped to find a hatchet and use it to defend herself against T, the goateed thug chasing her out of her house.

Dahlia still didn't know why the two men had come to her door, or where they wanted to take her so urgently that they would attack her to make her comply. She'd figure it out later.

She shot glances over her shoulder back toward her house. She'd sprinted out the front door, doubled back along the hedge and ducked through the gap where the shrub had turned brown and made it to Mrs. Joosten's back door thinking it would be less visible. It also blocked most of her own house from view so she couldn't see if T had followed her path or not.

Dahlia slapped the door again, three times—hard. She saw a shape move inside through the pane of glass that made up the top half of the back door, thin curtains with sections of fruit on them made the shape blurry. Mrs. Joosten opened the door. "What the fuck is so urgent you gotta pound on my door like a teenager at a whorehouse?"

Dale found Mrs. Joosten's mouth, with her mixture of sailor, trucker, and longshoremen dialect, incredibly charming. He even endured the cranky fits like the bullshit with the trash cans because he thought she was so damn funny when she yelled at him in the driveway. He used to say he'd arrested guys with arm-length rap sheets and a dozen years of hard time behind them who would blush at one conversation with Mrs. J.

"I need to call the police. Someone broke into my home and a man is dead."

Mrs. Joosten cocked her head. "Are you fucking with me?"

"No. We need to get inside. There's still one out there."

Dahlia heard the shrub move, a body slipping through the crispy brown branches of the dead spot where Mrs. Joosten's Corgi liked to pee.

"Go inside." Dahlia pushed the old woman forward and shut the door behind her. Mrs. Joosten noticed the bloody knife in Dahlia's hand.

"Oh, good God."

Dahlia followed her eyes and saw the knife, now a permanent attachment to her palm. "No, no. I had to defend myself. They attacked me."

Mrs. Joosten put up her hands and backed away from Dahlia. "What's going on?"

"I told you." Dahlia stopped herself from re-explaining. She knew raising her voice wouldn't help alleviate Mrs. Joosten's wariness of her, but it might motivate her into desperately needed action. "We have to call the police!"

Glass shattered. Dahlia turned. T's elbow was pulling back through the smashed glass window. Shards fell and crashed to the floor, splintering into tiny slivers. He reached through with his hand, tattoos down almost past his wrist, and turned the knob.

"Inside." Dahlia pushed Mrs. Joosten again and moved them into the living room. Mrs. Joosten screamed.

"Who the fuck just broke my door?"

45

Dahlia shoved her deeper into the room past a floral couch. "Where's the phone?"

"In there." Mrs. J pointed to the kitchen from where they'd come. Dahlia turned and watched T emerge into the living room. He slowed and looked around, confirming there were only the two women inside.

"Lady, you gotta get a grip."

Dahlia wielded the knife. "You tried to kidnap me."

"I asked you nicely."

Mrs. Joosten stepped to her right and picked up a fireplace poker from an iron set by her hearth. "You better get the fuck outta my house before I beat your ass like your daddy should have."

T blank-faced stared at the woman, a full foot shorter and fifty pounds lighter than him.

Dahlia held the boning knife out in front of her, the blood on the blade already dried. "We called the cops."

"You didn't call any cops. Didn't have time."

"She's got one of those lifeline things. Like she's fallen and can't get up. All she had to do was press the button and cops come running."

T shifted his eyes between the two women, trying to discern the truth. "Bullshit."

"Stick around and find out."

Mrs. Joosten lifted the poker over her head. "Stick around and get this up your dick hole."

T set his feet. Dahlia watched his body. Hours in the gym, military-grade muscle structure. She didn't see any weapons and somehow that scared her even more. She examined him down to his boots. She saw the bulge of a knife holster. When she looked again she noticed details in his all-black clothes. Another knife tucked into the waistband of his pants. At least she thought it was a knife. Too small to be a gun.

"Look." At his words she snapped her eyes back to his. "You come with me and we can all just walk out of here, okay?"

"Who wants to see me so bad?"

"A friend of your husband."

Dahlia almost dropped the knife. What the hell did that mean? Her husband dealt with cops, DAs, sometimes federal agents. Mostly though, he dealt with scumbags, criminals, drug dealers, killers. Lately she'd been wondering how closely he dealt with them. She felt a little more light shine on her answer. He'd said work lately had been "complicated." Is this what he meant?

"You're lying."

"I only know what I'm told over the phone."

Dahlia noticed T had been inching closer. Subtle, slow movements, but he'd made it almost even with the hard candy dish on the reading table.

She thrust the knife out farther in front of her, hoping to re-mind him of his dead friend back in her kitchen, no matter how incidental her role in that was. "Stay where you are."

"Just come with me."

Mrs. Joosten adjusted the fire poker into a two-handed base-ball grip. "Is this what you do, you sick fucko? You come around breaking in and raping old ladies?" Through the threat of death in the room, Dahlia still managed to be offended at being lumped in with Mrs. J as an old lady.

"This has got nothing to do with you, ma'am."

Dahlia wondered how long his polite gentleman criminal act would last.

"You're in my living room, punk. I'd say it has a lot to do with me."

"I'm only doing my job."

Mrs. Joosten took two steps forward. "And I'm only defend-ing my house like it says in the fucking constitution." She swung the fire poker at him, but she was still three steps too far away.

"Lady..."

She stepped forward and swung again. Too short.

"Cut it out."

She stepped and swung. Missed.

"Just go back in the kitchen and act like we were never here."

She swung again like she held a Louisville Slugger and his head was a fast ball. T leaned back, but the poker glanced off his collarbone as her swing sloped downward. As the momentum of her swing brought the iron poker around the far side of her body, T stepped up and reached for it.

He put a hand over the long metal bar and twisted it from Mrs. Joosten's hand. He turned so the small right-angle hook poked out. The little notch made for turning burning logs now looked like a metal claw to Dahlia as she watched him rear back and swing, one handed.

The short metal spike caught Mrs. Joosten above her right breast, which hung fairly low, so the bar wedged itself between two of her ribs in the middle of her chest. The old lady *whuffed* out air from her lungs.

Dahlia threatened with her knife again but didn't step into his radius of swinging. "Stop it!"

T pulled and the poker stayed stuck, the hook of metal notched around a rib. He pulled again, twisting the bar. It came free, unraveling the grey threads of her sweater as it came out. With a long string of wool dangling from the end of the poker, most of the fabric stained red with Mrs. Joosten's blood, he swung again.

Too stunned to defend herself, Mrs. Joosten stood by and took the hit in her upper arm. Again the spike pierced her, but without bone to catch onto, it came right out.

Dahlia watched in horror as the lid came off T's pressure cooker. His eyes went red with rage and he moved in closer to Mrs. Joosten. He brought the iron bar down again and again, sometimes only slapping the straight metal rod against her, sometimes driving the hooked spike into her body and tearing it out to leave behind an open gash of muscle and blood.

Dahlia started backing away, realizing she could do nothing

for Mrs. Joosten. She stepped backward toward the front door.

T grunted with the effort of beating the old woman to death. After she slumped to the floor, he continued to rain down blows. The slap of iron against skin was punctuated by the cracking of bones. The fire poker started to bend and the single string of wool had unraveled to wrap around the shaft of the poker until it became ineffective as a bludgeon since it was so well padded with yarn.

Dahlia slipped out the door unnoticed.

CHAPTER 6

Lewis entered the mayor's office without knocking. "No word yet."

Mayor O'Brien turned his head away from staring at nothing. "Seriously?"

"They said they'll update me when they know." Lewis held up a manila folder in his hand. "Meanwhile, we need to talk strategies for how to make the most of this."

O'Brien ignored his opportunistic chief of staff. "I gotta say, after it took eighteen years to get here, and six in office, this isn't how I saw it ending."

"It won't if we can spin this in our favor. And it already is in our favor. Your drug crackdown is paying benefits and for those who are still doubting it, or say it's just window dressing—what more proof of how serious you are than to have your only daughter fall victim to the very people you're trying to stop?"

O'Brien let out a cynical chuckle. "The very people."

"Look, Mr. Mayor, when you're done with this office, you'll be fine. Even if you never hold office again, you've got speaking engagements, probably a book to write, maybe a job at a cable news network. But when we go, we go on our terms. Not like this."

O'Brien sat back in his chair. "You mean not with everyone hating me."

"They don't hate you, sir."

"They think I'm corrupt."

Lewis stayed silent.

"They think I stopped caring about the city and the people. That I've gotten lazy and ineffective. You got a spin for that?"

Lewis held up the folder. "Yes, I do."

The mayor set both hands flat against his face, dragged them slowly down, and exhaled. He felt tired. So damn tired. He'd all but given up after the latest poll numbers. He'd been getting hammered in the press. The city was stagnating, and on his watch. Then the first rumblings of corruption allegations. They always start when there's an election. Put the candidate on the defensive. Even if he's totally innocent, make him say the words. Make him say, "I didn't take money. I didn't do favors. I didn't look the other way."

And if he had...

"What have you got, Lewis?"

Lewis moved forward, a grin on his face. He sat in the chair opposite the mayor's desk, a chair where most of the decisions were being made recently.

"I've asked the chief of police to move up the first round of sweeps through the known drug areas. This will pick up mostly low-level street dealers and users, but it looks good to the voters. Lots of hands in cuffs and usually on scary-looking dudes with neck tattoos and stuff."

"When do we tell people about Lauren?"

"That's up to you, sir. I still say, sooner is better. We want them rooting for her while she's still inside. If voters only hear about it after the fact, it has less impact."

"Don't you think it makes us look good that we got her out? Hostage rescues are always big deals." He had to look down at his hands. Jesus, had he just said hostage rescue? It was his freaking daughter who was the hostage. He hated when he started speaking Lewis' language, but he knew it was the language of winning elections.

"The good news is, when she gets out, she has a platform. She'll write about it and right in paragraph one is your war on drugs."

"If that's the angle she takes."

Lewis leaned forward. "What other angle is there?"

O'Brien again looked away. "Lauren and I haven't exactly been getting along lately. She's been crusading, typical rebellious kid stuff."

"How does it affect us?"

"I don't know." O'Brien spun in his chair. He stood and walked to the corner liquor cabinet, a fixture in the mayor's office since the end of prohibition. Keeping it stocked was only upholding a city tradition. "She's been hinting that she's looking into some of the allegations." He poured two fingers of scotch into a glass. No ice.

Lewis provided enough chill for the double and the rest of the bottle. "What does *looking into* mean?"

"I told you." O'Brien took a swig, making Lewis wait. "I don't know."

A condescending smile drew across Lewis' lips. "Right. I guess that's my job, to know. And when we don't know something, to find it out." He stood. "Guess I'll go do my job."

O'Brien watched him go, drained the rest of the drink. He stared at the bottle but didn't refill. He'd need to be sharp the rest of the day.

12TH FLOOR

"You handled yourself well back there." Dale walked two steps behind Lauren as they descended the staircase away from Tat's apartment.

"That story wasn't a lie. I really did take all kinds of self-defense classes. My dad made me."

"Daddy's little girl, huh?"

Lauren scoffed. "Yeah. Right."

They descended slowly, wary of predators. The stencil on the wall read 12th Floor. Dale noticed it as they passed. "What the hell?"

Lauren went on high alert. "What is it?"

"What happened to thirteen?"

She exhaled. "There is no thirteen."

Dale stopped walking. "What, because of, like, superstitions?"

"I guess so. The architect numbered the floors. A lot of buildings do that."

"Still? I thought they stopped with that crap. Everyone knows the deal. That means fourteen was really thirteen. Guess that explains all the bad luck up there."

"I hate to break it to you, every floor is bad luck in this building."

Feet hammered on the concrete steps. The echoes came from far below, but they were moving with purpose and the steady thrumming of impacts meant a lot of boots. Reinforcements.

Lauren turned back up the steps. "Move, move."

"Sounds like a lot."

"More than us. I guess we're going to twelve."

"Can't be worse than thirteen."

Dale drew his stolen gun and pushed on the bar to open the door to the twelfth floor. No keypad. Not Tat's private residence. Dale had no idea what to expect.

They found themselves in a long, dark hallway like a row of apartments.

"Where are we?" Dale asked.

"Dorms for Tat's men."

Dale pressed his back to the wall and dropped his voice to a whisper. "You mean the guys who want to kill us?"

"Yes. But from the sounds of that stairwell, they're on the job, so they're not gonna be in their rooms."

The doors were identical, the walls a dark green, the doors black. The space was utilitarian, almost military in its absence of personality. These were sleeping quarters only, not places to get comfortable and forget who you worked for.

Down the hall, a door opened. Lauren padded next to Dale and put her hand on the knob of the door closest to them. She turned it and motioned for Dale to go inside. The door opened silently as Dale watched a man exit a room ten doors up and on the right. He seemed to move with a purpose and didn't take time to scan around the hallway and notice them.

Dale slid into the open room and Lauren followed.

The room was dim and devoid of character. Dale swept the small square with his gun before turning to Lauren to whisper, "All clear."

"Thank God."

"How did you know it would be open?"

"None of the doors have locks. Tat's policy. A way to keep the men more honest."

Dale let his gun hand drop by his waist. He looked around the room for another way out, a way to help them escape. And a phone. He found nothing.

"So why were you doing so much research on Tat and this place?"

"For my article."

"I thought the article was about your dad's drug policy."

"It is, sort of." Lauren inhaled, then let it out slowly. "I'm going to expose the connection between my dad and Tat's operation."

Knotting his eyebrows, Dale looked at Lauren. "What connection?"

"I think my dad has been part of a citywide conspiracy to give Tat a free pass. Well, not free. There are kickbacks, of course. And this new policy is the biggest giveaway of all. It's set up to basically run everyone else out of town and leave Tat in place to run his trade unopposed."

Dale wondered if his name had come up in her research. He couldn't be too surprised by her revelation. He knew the mayor's office had a few on the take. He had no idea it went so high.

"Jesus. You're going to take down you own dad?"

"He's going to lose the election anyway."

"But, still."

"He's corrupt. He's taking money from a drug lord and telling his own police force to look the other way. If I can get the right documents to prove it, well, let's just say it'll be good for my career."

"Good luck finding those."

"If I find Tyler, I find what I need."

"Who's Tyler?"

"My boyfriend. Sort of."

"Sort of?"

"It's complicated."

Dale didn't have time for complicated. He went to the sole window on the back wall, pushed open the shade covering it. Nothing. Bricked over. No view. "Look, I'm not gonna defend your dad, but a lot of those cops and everyone else on up may have had reasons for first getting in on the take. I've been out on the streets and working this racket for a long damn time, since you were in grade school. It's not black and white."

"Yeah, well, it sells newspapers and wins Pulitzers." Lauren put her ear to the door and listened to the hallway. "I think it's clear."

"Okay." Dale drew his weapon again. "Let's get me to my wife and you to this Tyler so you can type this up and bring down your dad." He shook his head. "Fuck. Just don't make me look too bad in the article."

"Right now you're the hero of my story."

"Just don't do too much research on me when we get out of here."

The door swung open on silent hinges. Dale moved first, easing his way into the darkened hall. He turned to his left, a rudimentary check of his surroundings. Instinct. Training. Surely nothing would be there.

Only there was. Six men, guns drawn, confused looks on their faces.

Dale thought about reversing into the room again, but Lauren was right on his back. He used his forward momentum to propel himself across the hall and slam, back first, into the door opposite. The knob gave way, the lock broke and he fell inside as the first volley of shots hit the doorframe.

They'd been expecting to see Tat, Dale figured. No one knew where their captured leader was. They only knew Dale was a foreign body in their biology. An organism that had to be killed.

Dale found himself in an equally unadorned room. Same layout, same dorm room furniture. He'd tumbled to the ground when he went through the door and he scrambled for footing as more bullets hit the doorframe he'd just crashed through. Rough splinters caught the air as large caliber bullets pounded the wood. Dale knew the type behind the guns: Young. Inexperienced. Grew up on *Scarface* and *Goodfellas*. Haven't spent much time on a gun range. He might have a chance against them—they both might. When he thought of Lauren, he realized she hadn't followed him into the room.

The first figure appeared in the open doorway. Dale fired. Man down. The sight of the first of their team crumpling with a gut shot would certainly slow the rest down, maybe give Dale a second to think. A second ticked by, then another, but nothing came to mind. Five more out there, only one of him in a room with no exit except the doorway five gun barrels were focused on.

If he was lucky, a few of them would peel off and go after Lauren on the other side of the hall. Lucky for him, not for her.

Lauren brought out her fake cry she usually only used when asking for extensions on college papers or pretending to be upset about breaking up with a guy she thought was a real shit.

"He grabbed me, he shot Tat. Oh, thank God you're here. I thought he was gonna kill me."

The two men standing in the room with her were confused. They still held their guns at the ready, but finding only a crying girl wasn't even on the list of what to expect when they stormed into the room. They expected more of the team Dale must have brought with him, or maybe their captured leader waiting to give them a reward for his rescue.

But they got Lauren, the mayor's daughter. Everyone knew Tat had snatched her. And now here she was, hysterical and blathering about her ordeal.

"Calm down. Where's Tat?"

"You said he's shot?"

"Yeah. Yes. Upstairs. In his apartment." While holding her face in her hands to mask the fact no real tears were coming, Lauren had rubbed her fingers on her eyeballs to start them tearing up and turning red. By the time she met eyes with the two men, she looked like she'd watched the ending of *The Notebook* without a box of tissues handy.

She heard more shots across the hall. It was hard to hide her concern for Dale, but the two guns in front of her were a more pressing problem.

ALL THE WAY DOWN

***

Dale pushed the single dresser away from the wall and crouched behind it. He maintained a sliver of a view at the door from behind his barrier and saw when the second man tentatively stepped into the doorframe, an extended gun in both hands to lead the way. Tat's men were all black clad, all muscular and buzz cut. This one moved differently from the others, more professional and with a tactical precision Dale recognized from the SWAT team. Former member or current, moonlighting on the squad? Dale would have to go uninformed, but he was different from the young guns so eager to pop off shots like a movie star. No time to indulge this one or let him get a shot.

Dale took aim and blew out one of the man's knees. With a yelp, he pitched forward and dropped both guns. As soon as he hit the floor he scrambled to get his guns back, recognizing his momentary weakness. With someone shooting at you, the last thing you want to be is unarmed.

Dale knew it as well as the man on the ground, knew he held the upper hand. For a second, Dale was reluctant to shoot. What if this man was a member of the force? Even if he was doing work for Tat on the side as part of his death squad, it would come out that Dale had killed an officer, something he worked very hard to avoid in his years of service to Tat. Whatever good graces he could muster from this rescue mission, he would need.

His second of doubt passed quickly and he shot the man in the top of the skull as he reached a bloody hand for one of his fallen Glock 9s. This man wouldn't have hesitated to shoot Dale. He knew that.

Paramount right now: survival. Worry later about the rest of your life later, in jail. Time to pay up for your sins. If that guy had to pay a little sooner than Dale, then so be it. He didn't want Dahlia to pay for his own mistakes, or Lauren. So fight like hell, get out of here, and don't think twice about it.

* * *

The men were discussing whether to take Lauren in custody as a prisoner, or to treat her like a rescue and return her to the room Tat had made up for her. The posh guest suite on the top floor with the fifty-inch TV and Xbox system.

Lauren watched them, deciding when to make a move or if it would be better to let them take her back and sit tight until a real rescue team showed up. This one-man band wasn't quite cutting it so far. But they'd find Tat eventually. He'd tell them how she shot him in the hand. He'd get his pound of flesh. It's what Tat did and he did it well.

The shooting across the hall slowed and Lauren feared it meant Dale was dead. Some sort of action was needed. While they talked, facing each other, she reached around her back for the gun.

Dale saw the barrel of the shotgun before he saw the person attached. That part didn't matter much to him. The thin, Ikea barricade he'd made for himself was no match for a blaster like the one coming through the door.

He bolted for the only other door in the room—the bathroom. A booming shot exploded the wall next to him as he dove inside. He landed on his back and kicked the door shut behind him. He recalled a protocol but couldn't remember if he'd learned it in academy, or one-on-one from some cop mentor, or if he'd seen it in a movie once. He crawled for the bathtub.

The bathroom door exploded into splinters behind him as another shotgun blast chased him into his corner of no escape. Dale flipped himself up into the tub, possibly the only thing that could withstand a blast and not leave him full of holes.

Once inside he cursed himself or whatever son-of-a-bitch had suggested this as a hiding place. He'd stuffed himself in a coffin-sized ditch to await discovery with no escape plan and nowhere else to go. He started to wonder how thin the walls were. Obviously no one ever expected these office towers to house dorm rooms so chances were good these were thrown up quickly and shoddily. They certainly hadn't gone in for any decorating. If he could punch through to the room next door, maybe he could buy himself a few seconds to escape. But time for a remodel was short.

"Is he getting away?" Lauren pointed with her left hand out the open door.

Both men turned, guns aimed away from her and into the dorm hall.

She shot them both in the back of the head. When the bodies had fallen to the floor, a shudder ran through her. She'd taken aim and pulled the trigger fast so she wouldn't have time to think about it. Her only thought during her brief debate of whether they needed to be killed was, "They're going to kill me. Maybe not right now, but as soon as we get upstairs, I'm dead."

Her own survival instinct had kicked in and now two men were headless on the floor. She felt bad. But not too bad. She had, after all, nailed both shots on the first try. But taking a second to admire her marksmanship was a mistake. As she looked down at the men, her gut seized and she had to turn away. An unfamiliar smell consumed her. Fresh blood, brain matter. Death. She braced a hand against the window frame and held a hand over her stomach, anticipating the sickness.

Again the barrel of the shotgun led the way. Like a probe seeking heat or other signs of life, the gun showed through the hole in the door like it was testing the air. Dale fired three shots at the hole. Three shots and then *click*.

Out of ammo.

The shotgun pulled back and retreated into the outside room, but the question had been answered. He was still alive. For now. Dale knew he had only a few seconds before the blasting started again. He flung himself over the edge of the tub and onto the white tile floor of the bathroom. He shimmied his body across the shrapnel of wood chips and buckshot to the toilet and put one hand up high enough to lift off the tank lid. One hand wasn't enough to hold it for long and it fell and slapped him on the chest. He fought to not lose all his air and wondered if any ribs had cracked.

He didn't get long to wonder as another blast came through the door. He'd made a guess and come out right. Dale figured no one ever shoots at the ground. He stayed as low to the tile as he could as another shot filled the room with pellets and smoke. The mirror above the sink shattered and then shattered smaller when the long shards of glass hit the porcelain sink. Dale waited.

The barrel reappeared, tentative at first, then pushing deeper through the ruined door and above Dale as he lay flat on his back. When he saw the knuckles of the shooter's hand on the slide, he swung upward with the toilet lid in both hands and let it go. The heavy porcelain rectangle cracked against the metal of the barrel and thrust it upward. Dale rolled to his right and got up on his knees. Next to him the lid came crashing down on the tile and Dale was up to his feet. He put a hand on the barrel of the gun as it came down into firing position again, it sent a hot stab of pain up his arm as if he'd put his palm down on a hot stove. He shoved forward to get the hot metal out of his hand, driving the gun and the shooter back into the room and off balance.

After all three shots, the hole in the door was big enough for Dale to move through. His torso broke apart the rest of the door as he followed the falling shooter. The bottom of the door held and Dale's knees clipped the wood and tipped him forward. He fell on top of the man and pushed the barrel up so it was pointing away and lay against the man's head. He felt the air rush out of the shooter's lungs as they landed.

Dale slid his other hand on top of the shooter's hand and pulled the trigger. Another blast erupted and the barrel coughed smoke and buckshot while the long tube lay parallel to the man's head. It was painfully loud for Dale; he knew the other man had to be hurting. Plus, the barrel was hot, and the shot had exited about two inches above his head and left a black mark on the man's scalp that started bleeding immediately.

Dale pushed up to his elbows, straddling the man and watching the agony on his face as he jerked his head away from the gun sitting upside it. Dale drove a fist down into his nose and scanned the debris strewn floor for the two fallen Glocks his second victim had dropped.

A loud blast sounded above him, but not another shotgun shot. Dale lifted his eyes from the ground to see Lauren standing in the doorway and the sixth shooter falling through the air on his way to the floor.

The man's face was a mixture of surprise and exposed bone. The shot had torn through him from behind and entered at the base of his skull and left through his mouth. What was left of his jaw hung slack in a silent scream as he fell.

Dale scratched at the wood floor and kicked away from the shotgun shooter as he clawed forward to retrieve a Glock. He grabbed it, spun, and shot the last man twice in the chest. Not as dramatic as Lauren's shots, but dead is dead.

Dale flopped onto his back and tried to breathe deep. The room reeked of blood and the gun powder from blast caps. He looked up at Lauren in the doorway. "Thanks."

"Sure." She averted her eyes from the man she'd shot.

"Can we get the fuck out of here now?"

"I sure as hell hope so."

With a groan, Dale rolled himself onto his belly and pushed himself to standing. He bent over and picked up the second Glock, feeling the impact of the toilet lid on his ribs and soreness in nearly every other part of his body. His ears were still ringing from the shotgun. He did a proper scan of the hallway before going out, then put both Glocks in his belt and started for the stairwell door.

CHAPTER 7

Dahlia heard music. Muffled, like it was coming up through the sewer. The beats didn't match the chugging guitars. Every instrument sounded like it was being played by gorillas with rubber mallets.

She wandered into the middle of the street and followed the sound. Across and up two houses, she saw the windows shaking on a garage. Those kids and their band. She remembered now. They opened the garage at the last Fourth of July party and attempted to play for the gathered neighbors and kids. Their covers of nineties' heavy rock tunes didn't go over well, especially when they had to stop their version of "Smells Like Teen Spirit" three times to start over.

She sprinted over to the garage like a groupie with floor seats and pounded on the off-white vinyl. The cacophony inside stopped. At least it sounded like the singer's voice had finally dropped.

Once the noise ended, Dahlia pounded again. It was the frantic banging of a horror movie victim when the man with the chainsaw is only steps behind. She turned over her shoulder but didn't see T leaving Mrs. Joosten's house yet.

The garage door motor started turning. The grinding of the rusty chain drive didn't sound any worse than the band. Dahlia waited for the painfully slow ascent of the door as it folded in sections until it had rolled into the ceiling of the garage. She found four boys behind their instruments, all with sour faces that seemed to say, "Whatever, lady. We're not turning it down." There were two girls on a ratty found-on-the-curb sofa watching the band practice.

Dahlia forgot she still held the blood-caked knife in her hand.

"You gotta help me. Someone is trying to kidnap me."

The teenage indignation on their faces changed to bewildered skepticism. Were they being pranked? Was someone going to jump out of the bushes with their iPhone and pronounce their scared reactions were totally going on YouTube?

The singer stood with a guitar draped over his shoulders. Dahlia recognized him as the kid who lived in the house. A spray-painted bed sheet hung behind the drum kit announcing the name of the band as Ten Times Fast.

"What?"

"Someone is after me. He killed Mrs. Joosten."

The bass player flicked his neck to flip long hair out of his face which promptly fell back into place covering the left half of him. "You mean that dude?"

Dahlia turned and saw T half way across the street, approaching fast.

"Oh my God."

Dahlia backed into the garage. The band started moving and chattering. The second guitar player noticed the knife in her hand. "Dude, what the fuck?"

The two girls on the couch tucked their legs up under their short skirts as if keeping their feet off the ground would help keep them safe.

Dahlia immediately felt regret coming here. She'd put Mrs. Joosten in harm's way by entering her home, and now she'd endangered six teenagers.

The singer, Kipp she remembered was his name, stepped forward as owner of the garage. "Woah, woah, dude."

T still brandished the fireplace poker, now dripping with blood. His eyes focused fury on Dahlia. He acted like the band wasn't there. He moved quickly up the driveway and the girls on the couch let out small screams.

"Dude, back off, man."

T swung the iron rod of the poker and caught Kipp across the bridge of his nose. He fell back and landed on the bass drum, punctuating T's arrival with a slamming of cymbals as the neck of his guitar hit the ride and his arm hit the crash.

The other band members, in a show of solidarity, leapt into action. The bass player brought the strap up over his head, grabbed the neck of his Fender like a baseball bat and swung. The heavy four-string hit T's shoulder and sent him off course toward the couch.

The two girls screamed and sprang up clutching each other. They sprinted out the open garage door and ran down the street.

Dahlia watched as the second guitar player held his Gibson SG by the body and ran over to where T was trying to regain his balance on the arm of the couch and slapped the tail end of the guitar into him.

Kipp stood up with a fresh flow of blood running down from his nose. He'd never looked more rock 'n roll.

Dahlia stood back by the drum kit with her knife outstretched in front of her, wondering if the members of Ten Times Fast could really subdue T and save the day. The drummer had fallen off his stool when Kipp hit his kit. He struggled to right himself and as he stood, he gripped both his drum sticks in one fist, wielding them like a knife.

The bass player tossed a microphone stand at T and it caused a screaming feedback in their monitors. T hadn't expected the retaliation and he'd been caught off guard. He swung the fire poker out at the objects coming his way. The band members added a steady stream of profanity to their attack.

"C'mon, motherfucker. Fuckin' pussy. The fuck you think you are?"

With T a little bit on his heels, Dahlia was confronted with what the end game should be. To truly end the threat, she should kill him. But stab a man to death on the couch of a teenager's rehearsal space? Maybe the boys could pin him down long enough for the police to arrive. But with T mentioning a connection to Dale, would the cops even be a smart move for her?

She didn't get a chance to fully contemplate. T seemed to gather himself in an "enough-of-this-shit" determination. He pushed himself up to a full stand. He cracked the fire poker across the incoming bass as the kid tried for another hit. The fire poker shook from the impact and dropped from T's hand. He reached for his belt and came back with a black knife he flipped open with this thumb. A six-inch blade appeared in matte black with a keen edge in silver down the side.

The bass player hadn't seen it yet and went for another swing. T ducked to the side and shot his arm out with the knife. The blade bit skin and dragged along the bass player's forearm as his eyes went wide watching the slice happen. He dropped his instrument and it fell to the concrete floor of the garage and immediately launched more screeching feedback from his amp.

"Russ!" Kipp held a hand up to his bloody nose as he watched his band mate sink to the floor.

Dahlia reached out and grabbed the hi hat cymbal next to her. She took it and the stand and hurled it at T. It didn't fly far, but clipped him in the side with the hard brass edge of the twin cymbals. T wasn't expecting the attack from the side. He bent at an awkward angle as he clutched his ribs where the sharp edges dug in.

Kipp took his chance and threw his Stratocaster across the garage at T. The guitar hit him at the base of the skull and T fell to the couch.

The drummer finally broke free from behind his kit. "Let's go, man." He leapt over his fallen drum stool and hit the driveway running. The second guitar player held his guitar in one hand and followed.

Russ leaned back against the bass drum next to Kipp and couldn't take his eyes off his slashed arm.

Dahlia pushed herself out from the corner by the snare drum.

"Do you have a car?"

Kipp pointed to where a rusted Volvo station wagon sat by the curb.

"Let's go."

Dahlia reached out to help the boys motivate to the car. Unthinking, she grabbed Russ by his cut arm. He howled from such a primal place he may have unseated Kipp as singer of the band. Dahlia let go quickly, her hand painted red. "Sorry. Shit."

"Stop." T spun his head to watch them leaving the garage. In desperation, Dahlia heaved the boning knife at where he slumped on the couch. Her fist finally unfurled from holding the knife and it felt stiff. The knife wobbled through the air and fell harmlessly against the couch cushions.

She turned and ran for the car. Kipp and Russ followed close behind leaving a trail of blood in tiny drops. Dahlia knew both boys were injured severely. Russ looking at stitches in the thirty to forty range and Kipp undoubtedly with a broken nose. "I'll drive."

Kipp dug a set of keys from his front pocket and tossed them to her. Dahlia grabbed the keys out of the air and went for the driver's side door. She looked back at the garage. T was up and coming for them, knife in hand.

The car looked like hell and smelled worse. Old bong hits, after-gig sweat from all four members, and a moldy undercurrent to everything. She prayed the engine wasn't as filthy.

Dahlia cranked the engine as Kipp got in the passenger seat and Russ slid in the back seat. They both slammed doors. Kipp slapped a hand down on the golf-tee-sized door lock. "Lock it, lock it."

T reached the car. He punched at the window and Kipp slid away, almost landing in Dahlia's lap. She nudged him with her shoulder to clear enough space to move the gearshift into Drive and pushed her foot to the floor on the gas.

T got in one more punch to the window before the car peeled away from the curb.

CHAPTER 8

The lock pick snapped into place and the door eased open. Lewis pushed into the apartment past a uniformed cop. "Thanks, Mikey. Mayor's office owes you one."

The officer waved the offer away. "Aw, don't worry about it, Mr. Workman. I just hope she comes back a-okay, y'know?"

"I do know. This will help. Thanks." Lewis stood in the living room of Lauren's apartment, not moving and hoping that the cop would get the hint that he was free to go.

Mikey got it and put two fingers up to his hat. "Any time at all, Mr. Workman."

Lewis waited until the door closed before moving again. He stepped carefully around Lauren's place as if it were a crime scene. He kept his hands deep in the pockets of his long coat, his wingtips moved silently over the carpet.

Small kitchen, unremarkable living room with a couch, flat-screen TV, and a short wine rack with a half dozen bottles of red. Lewis couldn't understand why she didn't choose to still live in the mayor's mansion. Something about her rebellious streak hadn't ended with her teen years like most girls. Lewis had been watching her cause trouble for eight years now since she got her driver's license. During the first campaign, he'd thought she was a hot little piece of jailbait, but then Lewis himself was just out of college and thought anything with two tits and a crotch was good enough to at least take for a tryout.

It was a two-bedroom apartment. He went to her room first,

pulled open drawers he knew would be filled with only clothes. He ran his hands over her underwear drawer, paused on a thin black teddy, a set of garter belts. Lewis smiled. Lauren was all grown up now.

In the bedside table was an unopened box of condoms and a modest-sized pink vibrator. He had a good guess which got used more.

In the other bedroom she'd made herself an office space. This is what he wanted. Her laptop sat closed on the tiny desk, a cork board hung above with colored notecards outlining stories she was working on. She saw Tautolu's name, the address of the building. He saw a card with only the words: *new legislation?* in black sharpie.

Lewis opened her laptop and booted it up. The Macbook hummed to life and he pulled off his coat and sat down at her desk. He started in the obvious places—the desktop, the documents folder, a folder marked accounts. He scanned the first few lines of documents before moving on. He didn't know what he was looking for exactly, but he already feared she knew more than she should.

He clicked open a folder of photos and lingered a little too long on a set of shots from Key West the past spring. Lauren in a red bikini with two girlfriends. In almost every shot they held fruity, colorful drinks.

Lewis studied her cleavage, contemplated whether he liked her hair better down and flowing or up in a sporty pony tail. He zoomed in on one of her walking away, studying the roundness of her backside and judging it for the extra folds where her leg was taking a long stride. The kind of thing they would photoshop out of a magazine, or blow up to emphasize a celebrity's cottage cheese thighs, even though they were completely normal thighs he'd like to have wrapped around his torso.

He got back to looking and found a folder called Projects, and inside that was what he hadn't wanted to find. He clicked open pages of transcribed notes of hers, probably typed versions of some spiral notebook she kept somewhere.

She knew, and she appeared to know a lot, but nearly all her notes were followed by question marks. She'd made connections on payments but added notes like *Proof?* in the margin. She'd noted names and marked them with the question *payroll?* Worst of all, she seemed to have cracked the code on the way they were using the new drug law as a way to move out all competition for Tat.

If only the hot-headed and impatient Samoan hadn't flown off the goddamn handle when she showed up. And Lauren, if only she'd waited until the announcement twenty-four hours later, then Tat would have gotten the call explaining why he had nothing to worry about and was, in fact, about to double his business. For a fee, of course.

Some deep, narcissistic part of Lewis felt proud to see his project written out like this. The way it all dovetailed in so nicely to a fat payout for him and the others as well as a good chance of reelection and four more years of those fat payouts.

But these were notes on an article, an exposé. Between this and Tat's overreaction, Lewis' brilliant plan was being derailed before it ever worked up a head of steam.

Lewis, however, never made a plan A without a plan B. And Tat's little stunt could be the downfall of the whole scheme, or the best thing to happen to it. That greasy Samoan fucker could be replaced. Any of a half dozen would-be kingpins could be handed the keys to the city, and most would play along with less noise and maybe even a higher percentage.

Yes, this was bad news. But Lewis excelled at spinning bad news into good.

11TH FLOOR

Dale's father wasn't one to dispense advice, so when he did, it stuck. The one Dale remembered most was when his dad, while driving their VW wagon to a day at the lake, told his son: be the kind of man who wouldn't be ashamed to be alone in a room with his own shadow.

It took years to decipher the meaning behind his dad's statement, but he knew it now. Don't be the kind of asshole you wouldn't associate with.

Good thing Dale's father wasn't alive to see him now.

In the grey concrete stairwell, Dale thought back over the slow slide downward he'd taken. Little offenses easily justified, leading to larger indiscretions and more elaborate coverups. Past the tipping point from public servant to average game player to crooked cop.

This shot at redemption wasn't working out the way he'd envisioned. Better than some scenarios his mind concocted on the way over to the abandoned office park; like the one where Tat shot him full of holes the minute he stepped in the door.

His head was a tangle of motivations driving him down the steps. 1) Free the girl. 2) Save his wife. 3) Look good for the chief.

One and two were necessities. Three was a bonus. None of them looked likely.

At least he hadn't dragged Lauren into this. Not like Dahlia. Best-case scenario, she was sitting at home cursing his name and not taking his phone calls because he'd been such a shit lately and left her with the cryptic promise to talk things over later. The kind of thing you say when you're about to admit you're having an affair, but just need to stop off one more time and bonk the mistress in question. When Dale came clean with her, she'd probably wish it was something as simple as an affair. A mistress can't put you in prison.

Lauren, though, had invited herself to this party. Dale had to consider that by helping her escape, he was also opening himself up to becoming a subject of her research. He imagined the glee when she realized the man who'd gotten her out of Tat's fortress was also on the take and she had the exclusive one-on-one account of this two-faced criminal slash one-man SWAT team. He hoped she'd at least thank him in her Pulitzer acceptance speech.

Dale reached the landing and passed by the stencil on the wall reading 11th Floor when he realized Lauren wasn't behind him. He stopped and turned to see her standing still on the fifth step up from the landing, her head down and crying.

Lauren had been trying to hold it in, trying to keep her emotions in check until they left the building. The silence of the stairwell did her in.

She'd killed people. Bad people, yes, but dead was dead. The first man she shot upstairs would survive...most likely. At least she didn't have to watch him die. And Tat would live to see the inside of a courtroom and then a jail cell, the hole in his hand a reminder that he fucked with the wrong girl.

But her lucky shot was way more badass than she was. Squaring off against Tat's girlfriend was the first fight she'd ever been in outside a gym class with padded floors. She was grateful she could turn off her mind in the moment and do what needed to be done, otherwise she and Dale would both be dead for sure. But now that the adrenalin stopped pumping, she wept.

Dale came back up a few steps to be closer to her.

"What's wrong? You hurt?"

Lauren sniffed, worked hard to compose herself. "No. I'm fine."

"Clearly not."

She wiped the back of her hand across her nose, rubbed the heel of her hand into her eyes to dry them. "I'm okay. Really. Just needed a moment there."

Dale watched her. "The shooting, huh?" He understood. "My first, I threw up, so you're doing better than me."

"Don't give me any ideas."

"It's fucked up, I know. We had to, though. These aren't the kind of people you talk it out with."

"I know." She sniffed again, pushed the hair out of her face. "It's just hard."

"I get it. It's not your job."

She looked at Dale and thought he might look like he wanted to hug her, to help ease the pain. She wasn't entirely sure she didn't want him to, but he looked like it was a last resort move. If he absolutely *had* to do it, he would.

"I'll be fine."

He split the difference and put a hand on her knee, about eye level for him on the steps below her. "We're going to make it out of here. Only a few more floors to go. If all goes well, we won't even see another person."

"And if all doesn't go well?"

Dale hefted the gun in his hand. "We fight like hell until we make it out. We didn't start this."

Lauren scoffed. "Didn't I? Chasing a goddamn story. Wanting to bring my father down. Christ, what a spoiled fucking brat I am."

"No. You want to do the right thing, you just went about it the wrong way." He patted her knee, took his hand back. "Welcome to the club."

Behind Dale, the door to the eleventh floor opened. He spun to see a black nose at the end of a long snout lead the way out the door. The rest of the German shepherd nosed around the door and immediately started growling and snapping its jaws. The handler held a short leash and peered around the steel door following the dog's alert.

Lauren raised her gun, startled, and her feet slipped. She fell and hit the step with her butt and bounced. A shot exploded out of her gun. She bounced down a step and fired another shot. As she slid down two more steps, she involuntarily squeezed off two more rounds. By the time she hit the landing on her backside, the dog handler was dead, four holes in his chest and the dog stood snarling at the end of a slack leash.

Dale stood in a crouch, both arms out, but remaining still. He locked eyes with the dog who didn't flinch at the gunfire.

Lauren stifled a squeal as she sat eye to teeth with the trained attack dog. It remained in place, waiting for a command that would never come with his handler slumped against the wall behind him. Lauren scuttled back and quickly hit the bottom step with her back. She lifted her gun again, no idea if there were any shots left.

Dale's words were louder and almost scarier than the dog's bark. "Don't you dare shoot that fucking dog."

The gun trembled in Lauren's hand. She turned her eyes to Dale who remained locked on the shepherd, his own gun in his hand, but aiming at the wall.

"But...but..."

"Don't do it. I won't let you shoot the dog." The dog kept up a low growl as it shifted its weight from front paw to front paw, regarding Dale as an equal but not yet ready to submit to him as a master. "What's on this floor?"

"More dorms." Lauren tried to swallow but the back of her throat was dry.

"Inside."

"Me?"

"Inside. Go." Dale held the gaze of the dog by some primitive hypnosis. The shepherd let a thin line of drool slide out the side of its mouth. He continued to bare his canines at them, eager for the attack command, but disciplined enough to remain still until he heard it.

Lauren started to stand. Dale kept his voice calm now, his volume low. "Slowly." Lauren slowed her movements. She got to her feet and waited, like the dog in front of her, for more commands.

The sudden line in the sand startled Dale. Why draw the line here? Why draw it at all? After what he'd done, before today and including the last twenty minutes, a dead dog wouldn't go noticed by a police report, Lauren's article, the karma police or St. Peter. But something about seeing the dog brought into a fight that wasn't his put Dale in a forgiving mood. The damn dog couldn't help who it was. And Dale knew none of this was its fault. Right then, that was enough.

Dale reached out his gun hand and put two fingers on the open door. The dead man's foot had propped it open for them and Dale pulled it wide. He moved his feet incrementally forward, moving in front of Lauren and closer to the dog.

"Stay behind me until I say so."

He got no answer from Lauren except her slow movement. Keeping a hand on the door, Dale moved his body so his arm was extended and made a bridge over the dog. His midsection was close enough now he felt the hot breath of the angry dog through his shirt. The dog pivoted in place, tracking Dale's movements with his muzzle. For the first time the dog noticed his dead handler. For a brief moment, the dog stopped snarling and sniffed the air above the dead man.

Dale stepped over the corpse's leg and had a clear shot through the door. The hallway was empty, the man and his dog a lone patrol.

75

"Okay, come around me. Go on in."

Lauren moved like she held an open jug of nitroglycerin. She gladly kept Dale's body between her and the dog. With one big step over the dead man's hips, she was inside the hallway. Dale eased his body around and the dog went with him. He'd maneuvered himself so the shepherd was facing the door now, all four paws on the outside of the threshold, and Dale was clear to make it inside, but the door wouldn't close with a dead guy in the way.

Dale stepped over him and set both feet on the interior side of the door, the dog's growling ratcheting up in pitch as if he knew what came next.

He whispered his instructions to Lauren. "You get his legs and I'll get the top half."

They each put a foot gently on the man, ready to push. "One. Two. Three."

Dale kicked at the man's hips, pitching his body forward onto the landing. Lauren kicked at his knee, pushing his legs out of the way of the door. Dale pulled the steel door shut as the dog barked loudly and leapt. He felt the impact on the door as the dog crashed into it, locked in the stairwell.

Dale exhaled. "Okay, now what?"

Lauren looked down the darkened hallway, doors on either side. "I guess we go to the north stairwell now."

"I guess we do."

CHAPTER 9

For a change Lewis' hand rested a moment on the doorknob to Mayor O'Brien's office. Normally he would walk right in, tell the mayor how it was going to be—what to say, who to say it to—and know with full confidence O'Brien would comply like a well-trained dog. This time, though, Lewis was about to engage on a much tougher sell, but with a much higher reward.

He pushed into the room. "She knows."

"Knows what?"

"A lot."

O'Brien sank into his chair. He acted like his daughter had just walked in on him screwing the maid. She knew his backroom dealings, his payouts and bribes. She knew the worst thing she could—the truth.

"How?"

Lewis paced the floor. "I don't know." He played it for anger. A betrayal by the only offspring of a powerful man. He faked thinking through every option, shaking his head as if throwing out ideas too heartless or too impossible.

"Jesus, Lewis, she's gonna sink me. My own daughter."

They'd discussed it many times—O'Brien hadn't harbored high hopes for his reelection, but he didn't plan on jail time or a public shaming. The way the polls had been going lately, when this came to light—the realization of all the fears and accusations, even the most paranoid sounding indictments of his opponents—he'd be run out of town on a rail. Maybe they'd bring back tarring and feathering. It had been a hundred and fifty years since a good old-fashioned lynching in this town. That used to be wholesome family entertainment in the town square.

Lewis began his pitch. "The article's not written yet."

"But she knows, you said. Everything?"

"Everything. Or near enough." He had to make her research sound more definitive than it was. She still had a lot to prove, but Lewis didn't want to give her the chance.

"My God, and she's with Tat right now. What's he gonna do to her when he finds out?"

Perfect. The blubbering of an emotionally stunted man-child. Exactly the Mayor O'Brien he counted on to come to this party.

"It could end badly for her, sir. We talked about that possibility."

O'Brien composed himself before he spilled any tears. It went unspoken between them that the tears were for his imploded career, not the potential threat to his daughter, the backstabbing bitch.

"I know, I know." O'Brien wiped at his eyes to erase all evidence of a near-miss cry.

"But maybe..." Lewis stopped his pacing, squared up to his boss. "The possibility is our strongest asset right now."

O'Brien waited in silence. Waited for instructions. Lewis would know. He'd know how to fix it, to make it all better.

"What if..." Lewis brought a finger to his lips as if he were figuring it all out right then, not an hour ago in Lauren's apartment while jacking off to her bikini pictures. "If this hostage situation ended badly for her." Careful not to say her name. Downplay the human element. "You have to admit, it would be the best possible outcome for us."

Lewis waited for his words to penetrate the thick, dyed-hair skull of the mayor. Wait for it, wait for it.

"What the hell does that mean?" Anger in his tone, bristling at the suggestion.

"I'm just saying," *Downplay, we're just spitballin' here.* "If she is a victim of the vicious men you're trying to stop, it puts a personal spin on your commitment to justice that we cannot buy."

"A victim? What's that mean, victim?"

"Mr. Mayor." *Say it. Pull off the band-aid.* "If Lauren dies in this, we get a ten-point bump in the polls. Maybe fifteen. No one can compete with the sympathy vote, and your rock-solid commitment to the cause is clear."

O'Brien stood, slowly. He walked in a daze over to the liquor cabinet and poured a short scotch. He gave Lewis another slack-jawed glance, listening to the words echo in his head. He downed the drink in one, then turned and fast-balled the tumbler at Lewis.

Lewis curled up like a school girl at a rubber spider. The glass sailed past him and exploded against the baseboard next to the sofa.

"That's my goddamn daughter."

Lewis heard the strong words but listened to the weak voice saying them. Daylight. "Tell me I'm wrong, sir."

With a hard face, O'Brien let the tears overflow his eyelids. Lewis countered with a stern look of his own. "Tell me I'm wrong."

The reality of it, that Lewis was exactly right, depressed Mayor O'Brien more than the thought of his little girl dying. The idea that this plan made so much damn sense drove hot spikes through his head. And the razor-bladed truth that tore at his heart, is that he wasn't saying no.

CHAPTER 11

Decisions, decisions. Dahlia swung the car over three lanes as she changed her mind. The boy beside her with the broken nose moaned while the boy in the back seat with a nine-inch gash in his arm squeaked a high-pitched note of pain.

Kipp's voice came out a cotton-filled mumble. "Where are you taking us?"

Dahlia had been driving toward the hospital. Russ in the back had leaked a lot of blood and some intern was going to get serious practice on their sutures, and Kipp needed his nose set so he could breathe properly again. She wondered if the same parents who bought him all that guitar gear and microphones would pony up for a nose job in a year when the sharp left turn his new nose took wouldn't be presentable to college admissions officers.

"We're going to the police station." Dahlia decided the precinct would get all three of them the help they wanted. She could find someone who knew Dale, get some answers, and maybe get him on the phone. Only a few blocks away from the carnage on her street and she slowed the car. The threat was over for now.

The piece of shit Volvo was easy to follow. The rust blotches and badly patched dents gave the finish a skin cancer patina and every time they started up from a stop light, the car belched a puff of black smoke as if it wanted to be followed.

He hung back almost two full blocks and still tracked the car without trouble. He'd put in the call to Tat to ask for advice since this thing was getting out of hand. Nobody answered.

T tried not to read too much into it. Probably busy with that dude who came by uninvited and stirred shit up so this errand was needed in the first place. With no instructions from the head office, T was on his own. He didn't want to hurt the kids. He'd been in a band when he was sixteen. A hip-hop thing, no guitars. And they never played any gigs, but they had fun at a few house parties rapping over other people's beats.

The old lady was regrettable too, but necessary. With both kids already injured, he could overpower them and grab her with little problem. He ought to break their fucking knees or something for the abuse they gave him with a bass guitar to the head and all that, but the injuries they'd already sustained were good enough. T wasn't a sadist or anything. Just a man with a job to do.

Right at the moment, he decided to pull them over and get the job done.

Damn her, she pulled into a fucking police station.

Dahlia parked and escorted the boys to the front door. They got a crooked look from a guy leaving the building, probably thinking she was a cop bringing in a new collar that she'd worked over damn well.

Inside, she dropped the boys off and explained the very basics to the officer at the desk. A crazy man had attacked her in her home. She ran and he followed and attacked the whole garage full of teens. She left out any whys about it because she didn't know.

She made sure to drop Dale's name and she was escorted into a waiting room. Dahlia stopped off to say goodbye to the boys. "Thanks for trying to defend me. You may have saved my life."

Kipp smiled, his nose swollen and clogged with dried blood. "No problem, Mrs. Burnett." When he showed his teeth, they were stained red.

"Thanks for getting us out of there." Russ' face was pinched in a permanent wince as even the slightest whiff of air sent jolts of pain through all the exposed nerves in his arm.

It was a good bet that one or both of them were trying to sleep with one or both of the girls from the couch. As they walked away, Dahlia couldn't feel too bad about their ordeal because she knew damn well those boys were going to trade their story and their scars for some serious action in the coming weeks.

Dahlia sat and the officer stopped before closing the door after him as he left. "Can I get you a drink?"

"Some water would be great." She hadn't realized how thirsty she was until he mentioned it, then she felt like a gallon wouldn't be enough and she knew she was in for one flimsy paper cup. Better than nothing.

He nodded and stepped out, closing her in the room. She sat in the silence for a moment before realizing she was in an interrogation room. *God*, she thought, *what terrible things have happened in here?*

T hung up the phone, his plan now in place. He sat parked across the street from the station, watching. As long as he had his cell phone out, he might as well try Tat again.

He dialed and it rang, but voicemail picked it up, Tat's message nothing but a huge bass drop from a song T didn't recognize.

Weird to get no answer on Tat's direct line, but nothing he could do about it. Tat had other guys to deal with whatever went down at the building. His job was out here, and it should be moving along nicely right now.

He dropped the car in gear and drove around to the back of the station.

* * *

There was a light knock at the door and Dahlia realized she'd drifted into a daydream.

"Come in."

A different man entered than had dropped her off. He didn't have any water.

"Mrs. Burnett?"

"Yes."

"Come with me, please."

She didn't like how his words echoed the man at her door this morning, but this was a cop. His badge hung on his chest right in front of her. And she was in a police station. Nothing could happen to her here.

10TH FLOOR

Dale put out a hand to stop Lauren. He held a finger to his lips. *Shhhhh.* They were three steps from the tenth-floor landing and he smelled smoke.

He pointed down and Lauren followed where his finger aimed. They both leaned gently over the railing and saw the top of the man's head. He was down on eight, it looked like. Still, they couldn't go any farther without him hearing them.

The man brought the cigarette to his mouth and soon after a cloud enveloped his head as he exhaled, and the smoke drifted up the stairwell. The barrel of an AR-15 slung over his shoulder pointed straight up.

Dale leaned in close to Lauren's ear. "What's on this floor?"

"Tat built an apartment for his mom."

Dale pulled back, gave her a raised eyebrow. She shrugged. He looked at the door, the heavy push bar entry. Heavy and loud. They needed to distract the man downstairs. Lauren watched as Dale searched the barren surroundings for some tool to create a distraction. Bare concrete steps, cinder-block walls, grey metal handrails. Nothing of use.

Dale patted his pockets, then fished in the tiny front pocket on the right side of his jeans nobody ever seemed to use except him. He brought out a quarter from the tiny change pocket. He leaned over, took aim, and let it fall.

The quarter sailed past the smoking man on eight and kept falling until the sixth floor when it veered off and chimed against a railing. For a tiny coin, it made quite a racket once it started hitting the long metal tubes of the railings and hard concrete steps.

The man ditched his cigarette, unshouldered his gun, and began clomping down the steps.

Dale pulled open the door to ten and found the back of a chest of drawers. He spun a look over his shoulder to Lauren, but she gave no explanation. Guess Mom didn't use the back stairs much. Might as well put furniture right in front of it. Not like the fire marshal is coming out for inspections anytime soon.

Dale put a shoulder against the chest and pushed. The front legs caught on a rug. He turned and waved Lauren over and together the two of them shoved the chest into the room enough for them to enter. Once the stairwell door was closed, Dale exhaled.

"Who the hell are you?"

The voice startled Dale, even though it was old and frail sounding. He turned to see a woman in her sixties, small with dark olive skin like Tat's, and brown kinky hair. He didn't need to check with Lauren. He knew they'd found Tat's mother. He also remained still because of the black eye of the gun barrel staring at him from her hand.

She sat on a small settee, her body sunken into it as if she were a throw pillow. The gun was steady in her hand but looked too big for her. She'd have been better off with a Derringer like the kind women used to stash in their garters, but instead she held a massive revolver and waited for an answer to her question.

Dale kept calm and completely still. "We're just passing through, ma'am. Sorry for the intrusion."

"You don't work for Tautolu. I know all the boys in his employ. So I ask you again," she drew back the hammer on her gun, "who the hell are you?"

Lauren tried on a sweet smile. "You know me. The reporter? The one your son is..." She searched for the right word to describe her kidnapping and imprisonment but came up blank.

"Y'all look like intruders to me."

"No, ma'am." Dale hated the thought of making it through the gauntlet of paid thugs only to be taken out by a decrepit old lady. He saw a cane on the cushion beside her, a trio of pill bottles on the side table. "We're keeping an eye on things. Like I said, just passing through." He turned to Lauren. "Shall we?"

Dale took a few steps. The gun erupted in her hand and punched a sizable hole in the wall, almost dead center in a wallpaper rose.

"I didn't say you could move."

Dale saw the gun shaking now, the recoil a jolt to her frail arms and the weight of the pistol too much to hold aloft for so long. "We're not here to hurt you." Dale wondered if it came to it, would he be able to?

"I think maybe I oughta call someone." She fumbled for a cell phone out of her pocket. It was too much for her to hold both the phone and the gun at the same time and she did a half-assed job of both. Dale stepped over the divide between them and wrapped his hand around her gun. With a quick twist it jumped from her hand. He thought for a second about flipping the butt around and giving her a crack across the cheek in exchange for her warning shot across his bow, but he remembered the shepherd in the hallway and decided to give her at least as much respect as a dog.

"You sonofabitch." She reached for her cane.

Dale turned to Lauren. "You wanna help me out here?"

"Help you beat up an old lady?"

Dale turned back to the couch in time to see the grip of the cane slide free from the staff and a glinting knife escape its hiding place. He leaned back as she bent forward at the waist and slashed at his face. The knife was a good six inches long and her wide, arcing slice caught the tip of his ear. Dale yelped.

Lauren sprang into action. She dodged around the coffee table, clipping a silver dish of hard caramel candies as she went. She reached the old woman and put both hands around the wrist holding the knife. Immediately she felt as if she was applying too much pressure. The bones under thin skin felt like they were bending under her grip. The woman cried out, then dropped the knife where it stuck in a couch cushion.

Dale slapped a hand over his ear. "Jesus Christ, what next?"

Tat's mom sat up straight. "Don't you blaspheme in here."

Lauren wrestled lightly with her. She easily held the upper hand, but the woman kept fighting.

Dale looked at the blood on his hand, then put it back to keep up pressure. He scanned the room for a mirror to assess the damage. He saw a phone on a desk along the far wall.

"I'm going to try to call Dahlia again." He pointed from Lauren to the old lady. "You watch her."

"Watch her do what?"

"I don't know. Make sure she doesn't have a hand grenade stuffed up her skirt."

Dale crossed the room and lifted the phone, accidentally putting it to his cut ear. He winced in pain and switched sides, a smear of blood on the receiver already. He dialed and waited.

Tat's mom stopped struggling. Lauren let her wrists go. "You'll be good?"

She nodded.

"Okay. We're not out to hurt anyone."

"What'd he do to you?"

"Dale? Nothing."

"No. My boy." She looked at Lauren with watery eyes, red veins permanently etched into the whites. Lauren saw the look as someone who expected the worst possible news.

Lauren tried to look as nonthreatening as possible. "What's your name?"

"Esmerelda."

"Well, Esmerelda, he didn't do anything. He was actually quite nice and accommodating."

"You don't have to lie to me, girl. I know my boy. I know

who he is."

"I'm serious. He kept me here, but he didn't...take advantage or anything. The food's been great. It's...yeah. It's fine." Lauren had a thought. "For my article, I've been looking for some records of the business here. Do you have any of that stuff around here?" Worth the risk, she decided. Maybe Esmerelda was sitting on something she didn't know the value of.

The old lady seemed to sink deeper into the couch. "What are you writing about in your newspaper there?"

"My dad, mostly. The new antidrug law. How it affects your son."

"And how's that?"

"To put him out of business is the idea."

Dale joined them again, his hand still to his ear. "Still no answer. I'm worried."

Lauren knew she could offer little reassurance. "We'll be out of here soon."

Esmerelda looked up at Dale, seemed impressed at her handiwork with the knife. "Did you kill him?"

Dale looked to Lauren, then back to the old woman. "No. We didn't."

She nodded. Turned her eyes away. "Someone will. Someday."

Dale let that hang in the room for a while. He looked at Lauren. "Back to the other stairwell?"

"Let's take the elevator."

"Great idea. I can't get out of here fast enough."

"What about her?"

Dale looked to the tiny woman practically a part of the couch. "I don't know."

"Just take me to my room. I won't be any bother."

Dale exchanged a look with Lauren; they silently agreed it would be okay. Lauren put a hand under her arm and Dale stepped closer to do the same from the other side. They got her to her feet and started to lead her away like an invalid.

They got a few feet away from the couch and Esmerelda

spun and brought her heel down on top of Dale's foot with a crunch. He yelped again and, while distracted, she brought a flat hand up and boxed his bad ear. This time Dale yowled and let go of the old woman, hopping away on one foot to nurse his wounds and yell some more.

Esmerelda swung an elbow into Lauren's gut. Lauren doubled over from the unexpected blow and Esmerelda took off at as close to a run as she could manage. Lauren saw her going and sucked in a deep breath before following. It only took a few steps to catch up and Lauren tackled the old woman from behind and brought them both to the floor.

Dale saw all this from ten feet away and couldn't believe it. Keeping pressure on his bleeding ear again, he crossed over to where the two ladies grappled on the floor.

"Careful with her."

Lauren rolled off and stood up. She looked down and evaluated her victim thinking maybe she had cracked a few ribs or even a hip. But the feisty old broad started sitting up on her own. Lauren, guilt ridden, bent down to pick her up again. As soon as her face got near, the old woman grabbed a fistful of hair and pulled.

Hearing Lauren cry out, Dale had enough. He tried not to think about it, crossing the distance between them quickly. He balled up a fist and punched Esmerelda across the jaw as hard as he could. She went out like a past-their-prime prizefighter. A tight fist of guilt squeezed Dale's stomach.

The woman went limp in Lauren's arms and the grip on her hair went slack. Lauren eased her down to the floor, then stood up straight. "Thanks."

"I did not want to do that."

"I know. It's okay."

"Can we get the hell out of here? This is getting ridiculous."

Dale pressed the button on the elevator and watched the old

woman's chest rise and fall as she slept off the punch, flat on her back. He rolled his eyes, "Okay, shit. Let's get her someplace more comfortable."

Lauren gave him a crooked look, but she went along with him.

Four minutes later, Esmerelda was in her own bed, a posh four-poster with gold and deep crimson bedding. She was also tied up, one hand to each of the posts above her head. Her legs were free. No sense torturing the old lady. Dale had even kept her hands a little loose. He didn't want to cut off circulation or accidentally snap one of her brittle bones. He worried for a moment about leaving her too much room to escape, but then he looked down at the passed-out sexagenarian and felt silly. Last thing he wanted on his conscience in his new attempt at a life of good was an old lady any worse off than she already was after he punched her in the face.

Even thinking it brought a shiver. Punched a grandmother in the face. Good lord. Every bit of graft he'd taken over the years was a pinched gumball compared to that.

Dale turned his back on Esmerelda and walked out. Out of sight, out of mind.

In the dark confines of the closet, Tat grew tired of waiting. The initial shock of his wounds, large and small, had worn off partly due to the quiet comfort of the closet.

None of his men had been by to let him out. Points off for them. But then again, he didn't know how many those two psychos had killed.

Tat turned his shoulder to the door. His arms hung limp at his sides, the dislocated sockets unable to create any movement. He sprang himself the half body length across the closet and hit the door. Pain rocketed down his arm from his shoulder to the hole in his hand. He bit his lip to hold in a scream. Bad idea. The worst. It took a good minute in frozen silence before he was sure he wasn't going to pass out.

Tat leaned back against the coats and pressed into the back wall of the closet. He lifted a foot and tried kicking at the door, but there was barely enough room to get his leg half straightened. The lock held tight.

This was not good. Suckered by a fucking cop. A cop on his payroll, even. And that reporter. If this ever got out...

Tat needed one of his men to come get him. This was his house, his castle. He'd built it to avoid shit like this. Impenetrable. Now he had two parasites inside. Bugs that needed to be squashed.

CHAPTER 12

The officer waved his arm out straight, turning his palm up like a maître d' ushering Dahlia to her table. "Ma'am. After you."

Dahlia took the chance to look at his watch. There were no clocks in the interrogation room she'd been sitting in, and though she'd only been there a minute or two, she hadn't checked the time since she ran out of her own house. Less than an hour had passed. There was still time to make her appointment if she got out of the station house soon.

It was a cruel reminder, but she smiled at the fact that she could let herself think about things other than her own survival now that the ordeal was over. Now if she could only talk to her husband. The threat of death made her want to see him, maybe even forgive him and work things out. Maybe.

"Did they have any luck tracking down Detective Burnett? Dale Burnett?"

"I'm not sure, ma'am. This way." He guided her away from the main lobby, which was fine by Dahlia. The fewer criminals she rubbed shoulders with the rest of the day, the better. She'd had enough to last her a year.

"Did the boys get to see a doctor? Is someone on the way?"

"I'm not sure, ma'am. Right through here."

This guy didn't know much. He looked young. Probably second or third year. Maybe just moved over from the night shift. He aimed her toward a door leading out the back of the station. Dahlia went where he pointed.

92

She pushed through the door and found herself facing the alley in back of the station. She stopped and turned. The friendly officer's body filled the doorway blocking her reentry into the police station. He smiled. Reilly, his name tag said.

"Am I being released?"

"Please step out, Mrs. Burnett."

"Who's going to take my statement? Do I get to sit with a sketch artist? Where's my husband?"

"Please, ma'am."

The uneasy feeling from her own front door crept over her. She didn't like being told what she was going to do and where she was going to go. What was with the men today bossing her around and telling her how it was going to be?

Car tires crunched on debris in the alley. Dahlia turned around and saw the familiar car of her attacker easing down the alley between a brick wall and a dumpster.

She spun her head back around to Officer Reilly. He stared at her with a hard look, his body unmoving from his roadblock position. She only had one way to go and it was toward the man trying to kidnap her. Kidnap or kill. At this point, she'd lost track.

"What's going on?"

Reilly stayed silent. He crossed his hands in front of him down around his waist. He looked to her like a soldier at ease.

Dahlia swung her head from Reilly to the car and back again. She added up the situation in her head. She'd been sold out. No way she'd make her appointment now.

Dahlia broke into a sprint. She ran straight for the car. T had opened the door but hadn't yet stepped out. He watched the wall of the alley closely to be sure his door didn't hit the brick and mar his paint job.

There was barely enough room for her to make it between the car and the building wall on one side and the dumpster on the other. But Dahlia didn't plan on either route. She ran for the hood of the car. T froze, not sure if he should get all the way

93

out, or duck inside and be ready to give chase.

While he dithered indecisively, Dahlia vaulted herself onto the hood, left two small divots as she ran across it and then set one foot on the windshield, one foot on the roof, then was down onto the trunk and took a leap off the back and landed two-footed on the alley floor. She ran expecting a bullet in her back.

The car engine growled to life. The high whine of reverse gear being pushed to its limit filled the alley. T drove as fast as he reasonably could while maintaining a straight line and not crashing into the narrow walls of the alleyway. It wasn't as fast as Dahlia could run.

It was the only gym workout she enjoyed. Running on a treadmill gave her time to listen to podcasts, audiobooks, play music. All those classes—zumba, spinning, pilates—they all had an overly perky instructor chanting or barking instructions and Hallmark-level encouragement at you. Dahlia wanted to be in her own world when she worked out.

She reached the end of the alley and turned left. T would reach the street soon, then he'd gain his advantage. She decided alleys were the way to go. Half way up the block, she ducked into a new alley across the street as T backed out of the alley behind her.

She dropped to a more sustainable running pace. Her breath was already coming heavy and fast. She'd started in a sprint and had to get the balance back or she'd be out of steam in another half block. Dahlia pumped her arms and took long strides. She'd made it halfway down the block by the time T's car turned into the alley behind her.

This was an unfamiliar part of town. The type of area she'd never go to. Four- and five-story apartment buildings, nice in their day but rundown now. Fire escapes rusted on building sides. Graffiti marred the walls. The windows on street level all hid behind bars.

Only two blocks from the police station and she felt like she was in an unsafe neighborhood, and it had nothing to do with the car bearing down on her or the man behind the wheel who had already announced his plans to abduct her and whom she'd seen murder her elderly neighbor and slash a kid's arm.

Dahlia reached the alley's end and dodged a fast right. T blasted out onto the street a few seconds behind her. His car squealed tires as he turned to pursue her. She ran for another alley, her only hope of outrunning a car.

She darted in between two buildings, her lungs burning with the effort and the tangy odor of piss and old food rotting in the garbage cans behind businesses backing the alley.

T tried to take the corner too fast. He skidded and ran his rear panel into the corner of a building at the mouth of the alley. Dahlia turned at the sound of the impact and saw him slapping the steering wheel and mouthing, "Fuck, fuck, fuck." Ahead, Dahlia knew her time was short. She slowed her pace and reached for the nearest door. Locked. She scurried up to the next, an overflowing trash can to the left of the door told her it was a Chinese restaurant. Also locked.

T's engine sprang to life again. He started motoring down the alley, more reckless this time. The car was already damaged and now he drove pissed off. Dahlia was nowhere in sight ahead of him. The narrow passageway was clogged with garbage cans and the walls of the buildings were pockmarked with alcoves hiding doorways and awnings meant to keep rain out of back doors.

Dahlia tried a third door and found it locked as well. On her fourth try, the door sprang open and she ducked inside.

CHAPTER 14

The intercom buzzed. "Your wife, sir."

Mayor O'Brien looked up to see the door to his office swing open before his secretary's sentence was even done crackling over the speaker.

"Lori, what a surprise."

Mrs. O'Brien moved quickly across the room. Her face was pinched with concern, undoing thousands of dollars of cosmetic surgery meant to erase lines like the ones she was forcing onto her face. Still beautiful—statuesque was a word used often in the press—Lori O'Brien was a consummate first lady of the city. She maintained a busy schedule of civic center openings, symphony fundraisers, art museum receptions, and charity luncheons. She knew nothing of her husband's dirty dealings, and he wanted to keep it that way.

"Is there any word about Lauren?"

"None yet, I'm afraid." O'Brien held his true thoughts inside like no secret he'd ever held from her, and he'd been holding on to some whoppers in recent years. His job right then, much like his job with the rest of the citizens of the city, was to reassure her. The last thing he was going to tell her was that Lewis was waiting down the hall for him to make up his mind whether he wanted to have his own daughter killed to keep his secrets safe. "It's going to be fine though, Lori. They have their best man on the job."

"What do you mean, like a negotiator or something?"

"Something like that. Now you know there's nothing more we can do, so don't go obsessing over it and driving yourself crazy."

"Then what else am I supposed to do? I can't go around acting like everything is normal."

O'Brien got up from his desk and went to the bar. He poured his wife two fingers of gin, threw in a splash of tonic and dropped in a wedge of lime. He brought it to her and kissed her cheek before handing off her favorite drink. He loved how old fashioned she was about her alcohol.

"I know it's maddening, dear." He motioned for her to sit and then perched himself on the edge of his desk. "We're going to get her back. Don't worry about it. These things take time."

It took every ounce of his best political mask to keep from breaking into a run for the bar again and drinking gulps of scotch straight from the decanter. His lies by omission to his wife and his constituents had become a way of life, but to so boldly lie to her face about the life and possible death of their only child was testing his façade like never before. He finally understood how guys like Bill Clinton and John Edwards felt when they stood in front of TV cameras with their wives an arm's length away and lied through their teeth about the women they were seeing, or at least getting blown by.

But would Bill ever contemplate ordering Chelsea to be taken out?

Lori took a long gulp of her drink, draining half of it in one. "I never thought this would happen to our family, Mike. I mean, it's terrorism. It's the same thing."

"Let's not fly off the handle here. It's terrible and it's scary, but the men involved are petty criminals, not international terrorists. I know it feels that way to us here and now, but this will be over soon and we can get back to normal."

"Back to the election?" There was vinegar in her voice. Bitter, blaming of her husband.

"Among other things, yes."

97

"Just don't use this to score points, okay Mike?"

O'Brien swallowed hard. "Okay."

"You promise?"

"How would I anyway? This isn't the sort of thing you set up a photo op for."

Lewis entered again without knocking. He stopped short on the rug when he saw Lori. "Oh, sorry. Mr. Mayor, we need to go prep for the press conference. We've only got twenty minutes."

Lori gave her husband a chilly look. In a city of disappointed voters, she was number one on the list. She finished her drink in one more gulp and set it down.

"Give me a minute, Lewis."

Lewis backed out of the office like a good servant.

O'Brien took his wife's hand, cold from the ice in her drink. He placed his other hand on top of hers, feeling the protruding diamond ring setting on her engagement ring, the one he'd had redone with a diamond twice the size of what he originally gave her twenty-six years ago.

"There are political realities and there are political opportunities. This is only a reality. I want to be the one to announce her abduction, not some news anchor getting a scoop. This isn't about the election. All I care about it getting Lauren home."

"I get it." Lori swigged the rest of her drink and stood. "That's when the photo op happens. Mayor and daughter tearfully reunited." She crossed to the door. "Hope you have some onions in your pockets so you can make some convincing tears."

CHAPTER 15

"What's the time?" Chief Schuster sat in the back of the tactical truck feeling pangs of a long dormant claustrophobia.

"Forty-two minutes, chief."

"Too soon for me to worry?"

The officer in charge nodded. Schuster resumed watching the tiny video screens displaying nothing. Shots of trees surrounding the old office park. They'd parked so far away to avoid detection by Tat's goon squad that they'd rendered themselves useless. He could be back in his office for all the damn good he was doing here. He could be in a bar somewhere drinking a single malt or getting a massage from a teenage Thai girl. He could think of lots of ways to better spend his time, and he had plenty of wasted time to think.

Sending Dale in after the girl had been a punt. Nobody could come up with a better plan. The final consensus was to try this and when it failed, send in some real firepower. But if they went in heavy first, they'd be crucified in the media. So sending Dale, a crooked goddamn cop, wasn't exactly sending in Seal Team 6.

Schuster had to admit a little bit of a payback element in his decision to go along with Dale as the inside man. He wouldn't cry any tears if Dale ended up with a bullet in his back. Or his front. Dirty cops made the whole department look bad. And the buck stopped with the chief, so the inevitable fallout questions wouldn't go to Dale, they'd go to Schuster. And then the mayor's office would need to act tough and properly outraged, so they'd hang him out to dry.

He was in what you'd call a no-win situation. Unless Dale could do it. Unless that weaselly little crap factory could make good on his promise from the elevator to do his damnedest to pull off the near impossible. He had the motivation—to keep his ass out of jail. But they all knew he was going up no matter what. But for how long hung in the balance.

Schuster hated the idea of Tat and his empire, and how helpless he felt to do anything about it. Handcuffed by the mayor's office into inaction, for whatever hidden bureaucratic decision lay behind that call. And now sending in a crooked cop to do a hero's work.

Crap. Maybe he should get drummed out of office. This was the dumbest damn decision of his career.

"I need some goddamn air. This place is like a coffin."

He stood up, hunched over in the back of the van. The officer in charge opened his mouth to protest but saw Schuster's determination and a glisten of sweat on his forehead and decided to let him go.

9TH FLOOR

This is all my fault, thought Lauren. Until that moment she could easily lay the blame at her father's feet, at Tat's, at this weird bulldozer of a rescuer. But no, she had to admit, none of this would be happening if she hadn't tried to get all Geraldo on this story and go into the lion's den or snake pit or whatever you would call this fifteen-story death trap. Okay, fourteen with that phantom thirteenth floor.

Men had been killed. Bad men, but still. And now an elderly lady had been cold cocked because of Lauren. All in pursuit of a story, which she also had to admit was a thinly veiled attempt at poking her dad with a stick. When she started she had no idea she'd turn up so much on him. She knew nothing of the extent to his corruption. She thought of the political ads that were currently skewering him and making accusations. She had to laugh. If they only knew.

She felt bad. Guilty. Like a spoiled child. She was still going to write the article though. First in a series. The corruption, the abduction, and the escape. She might leave out the KO'd septuagenarian, but she still had her eyes on the prize. She needed evidence. Facts. Paperwork, something. If she could only get to Tyler...and if Tyler hadn't already heard about their escape. Sure, he worked in accounting, but he was still a good soldier, loyal to Tat. If he found out he was being used...

* * *

Dale pressed the first-floor button in the elevator and cast a last glance at the gaudy and lavish living quarters of Tat's mom. The tacky furniture, bad art, and faux opulence made him wonder who the hell had come out to this abandoned office park and done contractor work to turn a floor of a glass-walled office building into a condo for Scarface's mother.

As the elevator doors closed, smooth jazz filled the steel box. Grateful to be on his way out, he let loose a long exhale. The ticking clock in his head finally started slowing, too. He had to have burned close to an hour of his allotted time, but now freedom was only a short right straight down. His mind could drift away from the simple here-and-now thoughts of brute survival.

He'd tried to be good. Tried to do the right thing. Really, he could have told Schuster to fuck off. Taken his turn at bat in front of a judge and dealt with whatever sentence was handed down. He didn't have to make this good faith extraction behind enemy lines. But that's where he was.

Tat was the enemy. Him and all of his kind. When Dale walked in, he'd been one of them, worthy of any of the bullets the men had gotten today. All of them could have been etched with Dale's name. But now, with a girl to save and a wife to rescue, he knew he stood on the right side again. He also knew it would be too late. But at least he knew.

"Gonna be good to get the hell out of here."

The elevator moved and he felt his stomach drop a bit as it began the descent.

Lauren nodded but looked at her feet. "Yeah. Sure will." She looked up at him. "Hey, would you mind if we make a quick stop on the fourth floor? You see my contact, Tyler—"

Before she could finish the bell dinged and the elevator slowed to a stop. The digital readout said 9. One floor down. Someone had pressed the button.

Dale moved his body in front of Lauren as he turned to face the opening doors. He'd been given no time to reach around and draw his gun.

The man on the landing to the ninth floor was more shocked than they were when the doors opened. His eyes went wide and he took a single step back as he quick-drew his pistol from a hip holster.

His ear hadn't even stopped bleeding and Dale found himself in another fight for his life.

Dale had no choice but to lunge forward and put a hand under the barrel of the 9mm, giving the shooter a level stare. He shoved the gun upward and the man fired a round that pierced the ceiling of the elevator. Dale's hand flared hot from the shot. He let go and made a fist with his good hand. He cracked the man across the jaw and the shooter went soft in the knees.

Lauren screamed as bits of the plastic light cover fell on her head. She cowered in the tiny elevator, no place to run.

Dale brushed aside the pain in his hand and reached up to wrench the gun from the strange man's grip. Still reeling from the punch, the gun came loose easily. Dale grabbed the man by the T-shirt and went to shove him forward, but the man snapped to attention. He countered Dale's shove and pushed forward himself, a bigger and stronger man than Dale.

Dale's feet scrambled to stay beneath him as he backpedaled. Dale pulled, using the man's own momentum against him and spun, whirling them both into the open elevator.

Lauren screamed again.

Dale pushed the man to the floor, his legs flopping over the tops of Lauren's shoes.

"Out." Dale barked the order as he let go of the T-shirt and aimed the gun. Lauren yanked her feet free and hopped over the body in front of her, tangling her legs in his. She bumped Dale as she leaned for the elevator door which was trying to close again and again but kept bumping against the man's sprawled legs. Lauren got free of the tangle and stumbled into the dark entryway. The floor was polished concrete, the walls dark grey.

Kicking at the man's legs, Dale held the gun on him while trying to stuff the man into the elevator. The man pulled his left leg inside, away from Dale's kicks. He put a hand down around his ankle and came back with a small pistol.

Dale leaned and started backing away. The man got off two shots before the door closed on him. Both went over Dale's head.

He turned to see Lauren standing in front of a thick metal door leading into the rest of the floor. "Go. Just go."

Lauren turned and stepped into a long dark hallway. Dale followed then turned on the door, slammed it shut like a set of prison bars and turned a heavy crank to lock the door solidly from the inside. When the man made the return trip to the ninth floor on the elevator, no way could he get inside. It gave Dale an uneasy feeling to think of what might be waiting for them on the ninth floor that required such a heavy and impenetrable set of doors, but his more immediate survival took priority.

Dale stared down the hall. As tacky and opulent as the floor above was, this was spare and cold. The hall was merely polished subfloor, shiny concrete in a dark grey. So were the walls. On either side of the hall were rows of doors much like the dorm floors, but there were all heavy steel with thick rivets like a ship's hull. They each had a thin opening about eye level with a thick plexiglass window.

"What is this?"

Lauren peered into the window of the first door. "I read about this but wasn't sure it was real. These are torture rooms."

Dale nearly shivered. He was reluctant to look through any of the windows.

"They're like cells." Lauren seemed genuinely fascinated. Seeing the rooms in person appeared to make her forget all about their assailant.

Dale hadn't forgotten. "Torture rooms?" He gave in to curiosity and peeked through a window. Inside was a nearly empty room, except for a single chair in the center under a cone of overhead light. The chair had arm and leg restraints and looked to Dale like a decommissioned electric chair. "Jesus..."

"Yeah. Kinda crazy, huh?"

They started walking door to door, looking in as they passed. Empty room after empty room, some with more equipment than others. Dale saw a wall rack. One set up with a tub for water to simulate drowning. One had what looked like a workbench with tools. None of them had any people in them, and Dale was grateful.

He continued to grip the gun in his burned hand.

Lauren let out a gasp. Dale stepped over to the window she'd looked through. There was a man inside, strapped to a chair like Dale had seen before. He was naked and his face pummeled bloody. Thick black cables ran from heavy clips on his pectorals to a bank of car batteries. It looked like they lifted the entire chassis from a Prius and brought it into the room.

Clamps pinched his nipples, his ears, one on each hand and finally his scrotum. Dale winced. The pressure of the heavy clips alone would be agony, let alone getting electric shocks.

Dale looked again, but there was no one inside with him.

Lauren turned the knob and the door opened.

Dale reached for the knob to snatch it back, but the door had swung too far inside. "What the hell are you doing?"

"Don't you want to help him?"

"I don't even know him. Maybe he's the bad guy."

"You really think that?"

Dale didn't. He stepped into the room. Once in, he noticed the man's feet sitting in a bucket of water. The areas on his body where the cables made their connection were bright red and turning to dark purple. Raised blisters dotted the areas of contact and a sour, cooked meat smell hung in the air. Dale couldn't help thinking this could be him if Tat ever caught up with them. If he hadn't fought his way out of the office upstairs, he might already be down here with cables clamped to his junk.

Dale peered closer at him. "You alive?"

The man jolted like he'd been shocked again. He pried his swollen eyes open and recoiled at the sight of a new face. He turned to see Lauren and shrank in the chair. She made a point of not looking down at his naked crotch and the jumper cables clamped there.

"It's okay. We're gonna get you out of there."

Dale stowed the new gun and started unclamping the naked man. He started with the ears and worked his way down to the genitals where he did not like what he saw when he removed the clamps. Each clamp had taken almost all of Dale's grip strength to remove. Putting one of those on your body would hurt like a bitch, and he knew it.

The testicles under the clamp were dark purple. Blood under the surface. Swollen too, like hard boiled eggs.

Dale put a hand under the man's armpit. The naked man tried to help in the effort to get him standing, but he was so weak, he couldn't keep a grip on Dale's arm.

The man slid forward, his skin slick with sweat and oil. Dale couldn't hold him. Lauren clamped a hand over her mouth as she watched the tortured man slump to the floor.

Dale reached down to try to get him back up, but he felt different somehow. Dale felt the need to check his pulse. He poked at his neck for a minute before realizing it wasn't his finger placement. The man was dead.

There was a rustling behind them. Dale and Lauren both turned to see a man in the doorway. Hanging from his hands was a fresh set of jumper cables. He wore a black rubber apron, knee-high rubber boots and thick rubber gloves, like he was going gardening in the mud or else performing an autopsy. Either way, the job he was dressed for was going to be messy.

He gave the same slack-jawed expression the man outside the elevator had given them.

Dale drew his gun. The rubber man flicked his wrist and the jumper cables shot out like a bullwhip and the heavy brass clamps cracked against the gun metal and sent it flying from Dale's weakened, powder-burned hand.

The rubber man yelled as he spun and flattened a palm against a large button on the wall. Round and flat like an emergency power switch. Behind Dale the bank of batteries sparked to life.

Dale hadn't been watching where he tossed the cables on the floor as he released the tortured man, and now that the power returned, he discovered several of the cables touching each other and making cross connections. The exposed brass clamps started sparking where they touched, shooting a light show across the floor and jumping like snakes, separating from one closed circuit and bouncing across the floor to touch another cable for a split second and send a miniature bolt of lightning flying.

The rubber man ran around the outside of the room and came up to the bank of batteries from behind. Dale and Lauren were too stunned by the sparking chaos in front of them to react. The rubber man lifted a set of cables and came at Dale.

Dale ducked and shifted to the side. The clamps swung past his head and connected in the air, spat sparks that burned little bee stings into the flesh on the back of his neck. Dale went for the gun. Rubber man tackled him from behind.

They fell to the hard subfloor. Dale was an arm length away from the gun. Rubber man squeezed on a clamp and shoved it down at Dale. He pinched the flesh on his upper arm behind the triceps. Dale felt the bite. Dale reached out futilely for the gun as rubber man came at him with the jaws of the second clamp open and toothy. If the connection was made the current would blast through Dale's body from one side to the other, crossing through his heart. Add to that the overturned tub the tortured man had been steeping in. Dale now lay in a thin layer of water.

A burst of light flashed in Dale's eyes and the smell of burning flesh became stronger. Rubber man rolled off Dale and slumped to the floor. Lauren stood over him with a cable in each hand, light smoke curling from the brass tips.

"Hit him again." Dale crawled for the gun. Lauren bent down and zapped the rubber man again on the thin strip of exposed arm flesh right above where his long gloves ended.

Dale snatched the gun from the floor and stood. "That's *it*."

He'd tried to be good. Tried his hand at redemption, but he'd had it. Lauren needed protecting, Dahlia needed saving. He knew how to do this part. He could do it and still be a cop. He didn't need the other half anymore. It might not be strictly by the book, but he never met a cop who played by absolutely all the rules.

He stood over the rubber man and shot him three times in the heart.

"Anybody else gets in my way, they're getting the same thing. I'm fucking done with this place."

Lauren didn't know what to say. She was a little bit scared, a little bit grateful that he was acting like a real anything-goes protector now. Hopefully they wouldn't need it. My God, how much worse could it get?

CHAPTER 16

The door cracked against the wall making a cannon blast sound of metal on cinder block. Dahlia had pushed the door open with such force she stumbled forward into the room, losing her balance and ending up on all fours looking up at a table with four men. Three of them had guns drawn on her.

She froze, the slow creak of rusty door hinges behind her. The space used to be a restaurant of some kind, but that was a long time ago. Now it stored boxes, housed a desk in one corner and a round poker table in the middle, but the men sitting there weren't playing cards.

One stood, a man with a shaved head and a white tank top. Tattoos circled his neck and decorated his biceps. The Virgin Mary and heavy gothic script of names and dates underneath. Fallen comrades.

"The fuck, Gil?"

The fourth man at the table, a fat man and the only without a shaved head and tattoos, put his hands up in a surrender gesture. "She's not with me. I swear it, Pooch. I don't know who the fuck she is."

Dahlia noticed two stacks on the table—one of money and one of bricks of something obscured by layers of plastic wrapping and tape. They could only be one thing.

Out of the frying pan...

"Someone is trying to kill me." Dahlia stayed on all fours, looking up at the men through wisps of hair that had fallen in her face.

The standing man, Pooch, kept his gun on her. "This is some bullshit, Gil."

Gil pushed back from the table a bit, his sizable gut kept him from getting close in the first place, but now he seemed to be planning a retreat. "I swear, Pooch. She's not with me. Tell him, honey. Tell him you don't know me."

"I don't know him." Dahlia grit her teeth against the frustration. She'd broken into a garage full of kids who couldn't defend her, though they tried, and now she'd broken into a room of men who could obviously take care of T, but they might prove to be more dangerous than him.

"Who's trying to kill you?" Pooch eyed her suspiciously. "I don't see nobody."

"He's following me. I ran away."

Pooch traded looks with his two partners. Nobody seemed eager to roll out the welcome mat for Dahlia. "I think maybe you came to the wrong door." Pooch turned to the shaved head man to his right. "A door that shoulda been locked."

Dahlia started to straighten out. Pooch's head spun around to her. She stopped her motions. "I'll go. I'll leave. But can I go out the front? He's right behind me and if I go out in that alley again..."

Gil eased back in his chair again, angling for the door. Pooch tightened the grip on his gun. "Something don't smell right."

"I swear to God—"

All eyes went to the open doorway. T slid his body into the space, filling it with his gun drawn. Pooch and his boys regarded him, then Pooch made his decision. "Aw, hell no, man."

Pooch shot first. T dove into the room firing as he went. A bullet punched the poker table and a puff of white powder went up from one of the plastic-wrapped bricks.

Dahlia flattened onto her belly and crawled for the corner as gunfire traded overhead. Pooch and his two boys launched their attack while trying to take cover. As if to avenge his betrayal,

Pooch shot Gil twice in the chest. He never had time to get out of his chair.

T ducked into a dark corner behind a tall shelf stacked high with boxes and rolls of paper towels. He managed to get one of the shaved head men with a shot across the forehead. The man slumped out of his chair and Pooch turned his attention to the new intruder again.

Dahlia crawled forward, hoping to reach the front of the storefront and slip out during the gun battle. Ahead of her, Gil slid off his chair and fell into a heap blocking her path. She had to adjust course and crawl around him.

The bullets slowed. Pooch huddled next to the wall, stealing glances at the back of the room where T hid. The other man sat at the poker table and reloaded his gun. T took the chance and leaned out to fire a single shot that caught the man above his heart. He slapped a hand over his chest as if someone had suddenly started playing the national anthem. The wide-eyed, stunned expression on his face stayed as he gasped for air. One lung had already gone flat.

Pooch watched his last partner and he caught Dahlia moving on the floor. Instead of waiting to get shot, he wanted out. Gil was already dead, and the men Gil worked for would get theirs later and Pooch could get repaid for any money he left behind. He couldn't do any of it if he was dead, though.

He pulled away from the wall and ducked behind the poker table, the empty air-sucking sounds moving past his ear as he slipped behind his dying partner. Thinking he was taking a hostage, he dipped down and grabbed Dahlia's arm, yanking her to her feet and spinning her to act as a human shield as he moved toward the door.

"See you in hell, motherfucker." Pooch squeezed off five rapid rounds at the dark corner where T hid and then pushed Dahlia outside.

"Thank you." Dahlia struggled to keep up as Pooch made for his car.

"Who the fuck are you?"

"I'm nothing to do with that. I'm just a woman. He was trying to kill me."

"Clearly. You don't work for Gil?"

"I don't know who that is."

Pooch stopped, spun her toward him by the fist wrapped around her arm. He put the gun between her eyes. Down the block, a shop owner ducked inside. Across the street someone gasped. Pooch ignored them. "Say that again."

Dahlia couldn't catch her breath to speak. She stammered, the hot circle of the gun barrel burning a ring into her skin. "I...I don't know any of you. I swear. I was trying to get away from that man."

Pooch looked her in the eye. He did most of his business on handshakes and trust. A few hundred grand a year in street drugs and a few girls on the side he pimped out. Everyone had a few girls. He worked in a game of trusting untrustworthy people. He felt like he got pretty good at sorting out who would screw him over, and who he could do business with. Something about this girl's eyes. And the fact he'd never seen her before. He didn't want to, but damn it, he believed her.

"Why's he trying to kill you?"

"I'm not sure. Something about my husband, I think."

Wasn't it always? Pooch pushed her forward toward his car. "We can't stay here."

"I can't go to the police."

"Who said anything about that?"

"I'm just saying. They set me up."

"Lady, I wouldn't take you to the police no matter what."

They reached a wide Pontiac. Pooch yanked open the passenger door. "Get in."

CHAPTER 17

Roy was a fixer. As far as Mayor O'Brien knew, Roy didn't have a last name, and as for the job description of what a fixer did, he was equally as vague.

Roy's expression was unmoving and emotionless. "I fix things. Solve problems. Make uncomfortable situations go away."

All for a fee, thought O'Brien. A well-earned fee as it had turned out in the past. Twice before Lewis had brought Roy onto the payroll, but this was the first O'Brien ever met him. Better to keep them separate in most instances, but this required the face to face. Special circumstances.

Lewis acted the mediator. "So, that's the outline." He paused, waiting for Roy to ask follow-up questions. Waiting for the mayor to give an answer.

The plan Lewis outlined, and one he emphasized would need prompt attention, was to have Roy go down to the building and be there when they came out. *If* they came out. In case Lauren exited the building standing, Roy was to take the shot, then the machine would kick into gear to place blame on Tat and his bloodthirsty men. Not a hard sell.

Lewis had placed phone calls to chief Schuster to get a progress report and had been told no news is good news. He didn't know what the meant, but she and the rescue team—rescue man—weren't out yet. No communication at all, in fact.

"Time is ticking, though." Lewis folded his fingers together, put his two index fingers to his lips. Serious, anxious. "We need an answer, Mr. Mayor."

O'Brien shifted uncomfortably in his seat. It unnerved him even more how unflappable Roy was. The man had barely budged an inch since sitting down. An eerie calm oozed off the man like an odor. Somewhere underneath that, though, O'Brien knew he was a tensed coil waiting to strike. The man could kill you with a knife hidden on his body, a pen off his own desk or even a magazine from his coffee table. Roy was a killer. It's how a lot of his problems got "fixed."

"I really don't think I can authorize this." O'Brien put a hand to his temple, a stress headache pounding behind the bone.

Roy finally spoke, a quiet, raspy growl. "It'll go quick. Painless."

O'Brien took little comfort. "I don't think you understand—this is my daughter."

"Everyone is somebody's kid." Roy's blunt assessment of the value of human life reassured the mayor of his capabilities in the job, but offered no reassurance to his own heart-rending decision.

Lewis leaned in again. "I know it's not easy, but we've got to think of the consequences if the story gets out."

O'Brien met Lewis' eye. "You mean if *she* gets out." He held the vicious stare and Lewis stayed firm.

"You didn't want me to talk about the benefits to the election. This is the other side of that coin. This is life when we don't win. This is jail time. Loss of all your assets. Every penny you've saved they will trace back to one of Mr. Losopo's accounts. We've been careful, very careful, but there is always a trail."

"I'll be ruined."

Lewis nodded. "Unless you do this."

O'Brien admired Lewis' coldness. His calculating style that never said the words out loud what "this" meant. He never said kill, never said Lauren's name, never said shot or shoot. It was always, "the target" or "eliminate" or "the threat." Not the first time O'Brien thought it was Lewis who should be in the mayor's chair and not him. Maybe then the decision would be easy for him. Not that he had kids. His life was the office, the campaign, the back-room deals to be struck. They were his children. Would he shoot one of them in the head?

"Well, would you?"

Lewis furrowed his brow at the mayor. "Would I what?"

O'Brien realized, *shit, I said that out loud.* "I just wonder, would you do it if you were in my shoes."

Lewis maintained his steel gaze locked with the mayor. "You know I would."

Exactly the answer he expected. But what the hell did the kid know? It's different when it's your own child.

His thoughts swirled like he was being forced to make this decision while drunk. Christ, he wished he was drunk. The rationalizations took hold. He didn't start this fight. It was her. She initiated the investigation. She wanted to bring him down. She went and talked to Tat behind his back, and what did that get her? Kidnapped.

There was a long list of political opponents in his wake who learned up close and personal that if you bring a fight to the mayor, chances are you will lose. Did he want to add Lauren to that list of political backstabbers and opportunists?

What O'Brien wanted right then was for Roy to move. To fidget, ask for a glass of water, blink, for God's sake. But Roy sat patiently and waited for an answer.

CHAPTER 18

Dreams of murder filled the darkness. Tat's eyes had adjusted as much as they were going to and the thin strip of light coming from the gap between the bottom of the closet door and the floor didn't offer him any view of his surroundings. So his mind wandered.

Could have been the isolation and sensory deprivation, could have been the blood loss, but the visions were vivid and detailed.

He'd skin the cop alive. Dale. That guy. He'd seemed like such a loyal soldier. Tat recognized the pangs of guilt that kept the best ones in line. The ones who didn't feel bad at all about betraying the badge were the ones who got cocky, asked for too much. Changed terms of the deal, or God forbid, asked favors.

How many had come to Tat looking for girls, piles of blow for weekend parties, hookups in Vegas or other places they assumed he knew a guy who knew a guy? That one bastard, Rector, he had to balls to ask Tat for a dozen girls for a week-end party. Tat gave in the one time and sent the girls out to the address he gave them. Forty-eight hours of prime tail for free, and when they came back, they said it wasn't exactly a party. Just Rector alone in a rented beach house and all dozen girls serving at his pleasure and feeding him Viagra.

Soon after, Rector was taken off the payroll. He turned up in a drainpipe with exactly one dozen stab wounds.

Dale had been a good boy. Gave his information, lost the occasional file. Did it all for peanuts, relatively, and never rocked the boat. Until today. Now a dozen stab wounds would be too good for him. This stunt was triple-digit territory.

Tat had almost fallen asleep while standing, leaning against the bed of coats. Or was it passed out. His arms had quieted to a dull thrum of pain like a bad tooth you get used to living with. His hand only hurt when a whiff of wind passed through the open hole, but that was almost swollen shut and the skin around the edges was surely dead. He listened intently for every noise outside the door, wondering where the hell his rescue squad was. They sent one for the damn girl, why can't his own guys get off their asses and find him?

He'd scared everyone away from coming into his floor is what it is. He made that point deathly clear. You don't come to his home or his mother's floor. All business takes place up top, or on the floor you've been assigned. The place was diverse enough he shouldn't ever have to invite work into his residence. You keep that shit separate.

Now he felt the consequences of his choice. Alone in the dark, fantasizing about ways to kill a greasy cop and a bitch girl who first violated the sanctity of his building.

He'd built the nearly perfect fortress to keep them out. All of them. Everyone. Tat didn't want to go full recluse, but he liked knowing who came and who went, where all the locks on the doors were.

Then he had to go and get careless and let a fly in through the screen. And now there was nothing to do but sit and think of ways to swat it.

8TH FLOOR

Slow day on the torture floor. The only occupied room they found now had two corpses in it and Dale and Lauren were on the move.

At the end of the long, dark hall the floor opened up. The rooms ended and the hall widened to a building-wide open area ahead of a railing and balcony looking down onto the eighth floor. Really, how many torture rooms do you need? So Tat, in his wisdom or by some recommendation from whatever sick puppy designed this fortress of criminality, chose to link this industrial, no frills floor to the floor below, an equally unfinished space. Also drab, dark, and unadorned by paint, carpet, lighting fixtures or anything you'd hope to find in an office.

The balcony overlooked an empty space below, a wide metal grating staircase connected the two floors. Movement between the two spaces was easy, obviously linking the floors in their usefulness and their staffs. Dale was a little frightened of another floor sharing a staff with the guys who worked the torture rooms, he admitted.

But down meant out and down was the only direction Dale and Lauren were interested in. So they headed down the metal steps.

Once down on eight they were confronted with a series of metal cages. They could see almost from one end of the floor to the other through the metal, chain-link walls of the cages, one after another. Inside each cage were cots, four to a cell, and on nearly every cot was a girl.

Dale stopped at the bottom of the stairs and looked at the three dozen pairs of eyes staring back at him. He felt Lauren come up next to him. "What the hell is this?"

"Oh, shit." Lauren had been so distracted, her knowledge of the building layout had escaped her for a moment. "These are the girls."

"I can see that."

Lauren's eyes skipped across the faces staring back at them. "More like concubines."

"These are all Tat's girls?"

"You know as much as I do. I only know this is where he houses all his working girls."

"Holy..." Dale let the thought hang. The girls all stared at the two new faces, mute and nervous like abused dogs in a shelter, untrusting of anyone.

Lauren moved her gaze from one girl to the next. All young, all brown skinned and scared. She doubted many of them could speak any English, doubted any of them knew they'd end up here when they agreed to work for Tat, if they agreed at all. Slavery, that's what she was looking at. Modern slavery in the service of sex with strangers. Almost immediately she thought the sickening worry that her dad had visited, or been visited by, one or more of these girls.

The day her relationship with her father changed was when she found out about his affair. It never got out to the public, but it nearly tore the family apart. She was a media consultant on his first campaign. Lauren remembered meeting the woman at the Christmas party, but Lauren was only fifteen and she didn't recognize their obvious flirting.

She overheard a vicious fight between her mom and dad about the media consultant. He swore he'd never do it again, mom countered with, "That's what you said last time."

The hurt in her mom's voice was something she'd never

heard. Lauren realized then that she had been living with the public wife of the candidate for a long time. Rising through city council ranks and now to the protracted mayor's race that seemed to go on for a year. Her mom had been in permanent photo-op mode and keeping a varnished and graceful veneer for all to see, even her daughter. But now it had cracked.

She never trusted her father again. And it was the secret, the fact it never came out in public, that shaped Lauren's career choice more than she realized. This was her chance for revenge. For her and by proxy, her mother.

So the idea of her dad being visited by a teenage prostitute wasn't inconceivable. One more item to add to her research list, though there had been a number of things so far in her investigation she hadn't wanted an answer to. Or at least she went in to the first few expecting to find nothing, and then dealing with near nausea when she learned the truth. This one, she might not want to know, ever.

But any man who partook in the abuse of these girls ought to be outed, exposed. Her dad? He deserved to be exposed, shamed, humiliated. His balls crushed in a vice.

Lauren itched to get out of the building so she could sit at her computer and get it all down, to not lose any detail so people could see what she saw. The pale green of that girl's loose-fitting top and how it matched her eyes. The fear in the younger girls' eyes and the deadness behind the older girls' blank stares. The way the metal wires of the walls crisscrossed in patterns that made it difficult to see to the end of the row without them blending together to form a nearly solid wall.

The oddly frightening specter of the empty cells, filled only with questions about where the former occupants went.

Where windows should have lined each wall behind the cages, only flat metal panels stood in place. The entire floor was cut off from sunlight or any vision of the outside world.

Dale's voice broke her tunnel-vision trance. "We can't leave them."

Lauren looked at him, saw the same revulsion she felt reflected in his eyes. "We can't take them with us either."

"We can let them go at least. Let them make it out too, just like us. Maybe there's power in numbers."

Lauren did a quick head count. "There's got to be thirty of them."

"I know."

"How do we get them out?"

"That I don't know."

Dale stepped forward to the nearest cage. The four girls inside retreated to the far side of the cage without a word. He noticed none of them wore shoes, their faces were dirty, and their bones showed through the loose clothes they wore. Runway-model-skinny girls for your sexual pleasure. Exotic foreign lasses who won't talk back, because they don't speak your language.

He watched the girls eye him up and down. The blood drying on his neck from the knife wound to his ear, his dirty clothes and bloodstained shirt—some his, some from others. He certainly didn't look like salvation.

He pulled at the door. Locked tight. The mechanism reminded him of prison cells. He followed the metal workings up to the ceiling. He was right. All the cells were linked together by thick metal hinges and bars right out of a max security cell block. At least Tat had a sense of humor about his headquarters.

He tried to meet the eyes of the girls inside, but they all looked away. "Wait here."

Dale walked down the row of cells, the girls moving in a mass away from him wherever he went, backing away from the chain link when he arrived, stepping back up to it after he'd passed to watch what he was doing.

Lauren followed too, not asking questions, just trying to memorize the faces of each girl to tell it later.

At the far end of the hall Dale found a corner station for a guard, it seemed. A small desk, a bank of video monitors with feeds of cameras mounted above each cage. He hadn't noticed them before, but he scanned the ceiling now and matched the small black camera box to the view on each monitor screen.

There was no dinner plate-sized ring of keys hanging on the wall. No row of buttons with a number for each cage on it. He found nothing to help him open the locked cells.

Lauren approached the small desk. "What are you looking for?"

"I'm not sure. Some way to open the doors."

"Don't you think somebody has the keys on them?"

"Probably. I don't know. Where are they, then?"

"These girls don't look like a real priority. Not exactly the kind of place that needs a twenty-four-hour guard on staff, is it? I bet Tat thinks his men have better use of their time."

Dale searched the walls around the small guard station. Beyond him was the landing to the elevator behind a thick metal door inset with a square of plexiglass. They could leave. He and Lauren could continue their mission to get out of the building and they could send help later. Somehow it didn't seem like enough.

Dale felt helpless to save Dahlia. He was helpless to save himself. He stood now in front of thirty girls he could save, he could help.

"What about that?"

Dale looked up to see Lauren pointing behind him. On the wall was a large button on a box like a light switch. It was painted grey like the walls and blended in. He'd seen it but glossed over it thinking it too easy. Might as well have had a Press Here sign mounted over it.

"That's nothing." He pushed it to prove his point and a great metallic rattle echoed throughout the floor. The gears turned, hinges swung, and at once every door opened like meal time on the cell block.

Dale and Lauren stared at the wide open doors. The girls

didn't move.

Dale stood and went to the first open cage. "Come with us. You're free now. You can go." The three girls inside stayed put.

Dale looked to Lauren for help, maybe a female telling them it was okay would hold more weight. "Really, you can leave. Come on. Everyone, come on."

They both waved their hands, beckoning, like new owners with untrained puppies. The girls traded silent looks with each other, bare feet rooted to the spot.

Dale felt exasperated and confused. "Why won't they come out?"

"They're scared shitless."

"They don't have to be anymore." He went to the next cage. Two girls inside. "Come out now. It's safe. Safe." Dale adopted the rising volume and overly pantomimed body language of a man speaking to people outside his native tongue.

"Safe now. Okay. You go. Can leave. Tat is gone. Not going to hurt you anymore."

Dale noticed a glimmer of recognition when he mentioned Tat's name.

"Yes. Tat won't hurt you anymore." He decided to tell a small lie to make them feel safer. It might as well have been true. "Tat is dead. Dead and gone." He dragged a finger across his neck, then tilted his head and hung his tongue out the side of his mouth to indicate the state of deadness.

Finally a murmur ran through the crowd of girls. They traded whispers between cages. An excited energy moved through them as if they were one organism.

Dale increased his volume, encouraging them to take advantage of their new freedom. "Yes. Tat dead. He's dead. Shot." He pantomimed a finger gun. "Shot dead."

Most of the girls had moved to the open doors of their cages now, though none had stepped out. A girl in a tan tank top and short blue skirt stepped forward. Her long black hair was greasy and the nipples on her tiny, almost adolescent breasts showed through the thin cotton shirt.

"Dead?" Her accent was undefinable to Dale. He smiled and nodded his head eagerly.

"Yes. Dead."

The girl turned to her cell mates and they spoke hurriedly in their own dialect. The message passed quickly between cages from small group of girls to small group. The energy built until the girls finally crossed the barrier of the doorways and flooded the hall.

Dale and Lauren shared a look of accomplishment, of pride that something good could come of this clusterfuck of a day.

The girls moved as one, a mob of bone-thin teenagers in too-small clothes. Dale's excitement turned to confusion as they seemed to gain a burst of hidden energy. When they screamed they did so as a group. The fear and timidity in their eyes changed to anger as the gang charged their would-be liberators.

Dale started backing toward the exit door. "What the fuck are they doing?"

Lauren put a hand on Dale's arm. "They're going to fucking kill us."

The girls attacked. A flurry of tiny fists pounded on Dale like a sudden hail storm. Lauren skidded backward, trying to stay upright and swinging her own fists at the approaching girls. Fifteen girls surrounded Dale and punched, kicked and scraped at him. At once his ear wound opened up again and blood flowed freely.

He didn't know what to do. It was like being attacked by an all-girls school. There was no force behind their punches, but working together he felt like he was being pummeled by a pillow case full of oranges. Dull thuds bruising his body all over.

Dale curled into a ball while he thought of what to do.

Lauren had cornered herself. She reached out and flipped the guard desk over to act as a barrier between her and the group of girls attacking. The desk was no more a deterrent on its side than it had been upright, but the action and the loud sound drove the girls into retreat for a moment, long enough for her to set her stance and act like she was prepared for the next wave.

She still had a gun in her belt, but she didn't want to bring it out. How could she convince them she was trying to save them?

Bony fingers grabbed Dale's hair. He screamed as he was pulled along the floor, more feet kicking at him and hands swatting him. He ran the same scenarios about his gun. He couldn't shoot them. He needed to make them understand. He needed to explain his lie, maybe that would do it. But first, he needed them off of him.

He spun his body, kicking out his legs in a way he hadn't done since he tried to learn breakdancing in high school. His legs swept six girls in a semicircle around him. Their brittle, branch-like legs bent and they fell to the ground. The fingers released his hair.

Dale swiveled to his knees, his fists balled up and ready to go, but when he saw the face of the girl nearest him, saw how young she was and how fragile, he couldn't swing. Punching an old woman in the face put him over his limit for the day.

The girl had no such reservations. She clenched a tiny fist and socked Dale in the mouth.

They went straight for Lauren's hair. It was a cat fight, and a very lopsided one. At least ten girls crowded around Lauren, reaching in for locks of her hair. Lauren swung at them blindly, her head tilted down from all the pulling. She felt her fists connect with ribcages that hurt her knuckles, elbows that stung like hitting wood. This was going nowhere. She felt her skin bruising, softening up. She couldn't see Dale but doubted he was faring any better.

They weren't going to get the hint that they were being rescued.

Lauren felt a tug at her scalp and swore she felt some hair pull loose. That did it. She reached around behind her and found her gun with a fumbling hand. Blindly she pulled it free from her waistband and raised it over her head, fighting through a tangle of skinny arms.

Dale had taken to pushing girls, shoving them back into whoever stood behind them and sending two at a time to the floor. They didn't stay down long and they came back angrier. They all shouted nonsense at him. Words he didn't understand said with emotion he couldn't misinterpret.

He kept the throng marginally at bay while fists and feet still hit him from all angles. It was like falling down an endless flight of stairs.

A gunshot rang out, rattling the cages. As one, the girls screamed and scrambled.

Oh, no. Oh, no, Dale thought. She didn't.

Feet thundered past his head as the girls all retreated to their cages, like a fire drill had been called in reverse. They all scurried back inside in a well-rehearsed group.

Lauren pulled the trigger again, but the gun was empty. Luckily, the one shot seemed to have done the trick. The girls flowed like water back into their containers. Once she could see the last girl slip inside, she turned and kicked the grey button on the wall and the doors closed again, en masse.

Lauren ran to Dale crumpled on the ground.

He turned to lay flat on his back, nose bleeding, ear bleeding, lip swelling and cracked.

"You didn't kill one, did you?"

Lauren tried to catch her breath which had been beaten out of her. "Warning shot."

Dale nodded and they both stayed in place, trying to recover.

CHAPTER 18

The car was some seventies vintage thing. Dahlia didn't know much about cars, and classic cars even less. It was one of those cars that was an eyesore in its day, but now young men like the drug dealer in the driver's seat bought them and fixed them up. New paint, new leather for the seats. Made the cars look presentable again, even though they were still gas-guzzling, non-airbag death traps of steel and chrome.

"So tell me about the guy who just shot up my place."

Dahlia knew she wasn't getting a charity ride. This guy was a criminal. He thought he could get answers from her and that's probably the only reason he took her along. "Thanks for saving my life."

"Enough of that. Who is the guy? If you think this is over, you're fucking wrong."

"I don't know who he is."

"Bullshit." Pooch sped the car deeper into a part of town she didn't know.

"I really don't. He came to my door, tried to abduct me, and I ran."

Pooch chewed his lip, thinking about how to get this guy back. "Well, does he want you dead or does he want you alive?"

"Alive, I think. I may have pissed him off though."

"I'd say you did."

"If you can just get me to..." Dahlia had no idea where she would be safe. Home was out, the police proved unreliable, she didn't know where Dale was. She almost chuckled thinking the safest place she could be was at her appointment, which she could still make.

Pooch's mind kept on spinning. "So why'd he want you? Like a kidnapping or something?"

"I guess."

"Are you, like, rich or something?"

Dahlia scoffed. "No." Not on Dale's cop salary, she thought. The only way they'd get rich was if he started getting kickbacks or bribes on the job. If he went "on the take" as they said. But not a wuss like Dale. Never gonna happen.

Pooch sped along, the big V-8 engine making a rumbling growl as they bounced on soft shocks over uneven pavement. "He must have thought you were worth something if he's coming to grab you."

"I guess so. I really don't know what he thought I could give him."

Pooch reached into his belt and drew his gun. He set it in his lap, aimed at Dahlia. "Why don't we find out, huh?"

CHAPTER 19

Chief Schuster ran both hands through his nearly grey hair. He slapped his palms, slick with grease from his scalp, onto both knees. "We gotta do something."

The officer in charge, Greely, looked at his boss from the command center inside the cramped mobile SWAT truck. "Like what?"

"I don't know." Schuster stood but kept his shoulders hunched. The confined space made him anxious. Even though he could have stood up straight, he felt the roof bending down on him. "It's been an hour."

A military-sounding uniformed man with perfect posture didn't look up from his console as he called out the time. "Fifty-four minutes."

Greely let his hand hover over his walkie button. "Chief, we're ready to go when you say the word. I can have two more trucks down here in ten."

Schuster turned away. "No, no. Hold on. Let me think." He opened the back door and let it swing open. He stayed in the back of the truck, staring out at the tree line separating them from the acreage of the office park. "How do you think he's doing in there?"

"Honestly, sir?"

Schuster turned to Greely. "Yes, honestly."

"It's been a while. They could be talking, working out terms. But it seems like a long time."

Schuster had been telling himself it was a good thing if Dale ended up dead. Saves him a trial and the embarrassment. His secrets could die with him. But the girl...

"Do you think he'd kill the girl? Tat, I mean."

"There's no way of knowing, sir."

"It's not her fault."

"No, sir."

Lord, the shit that would rain down from the mayor's office if his daughter died during the rescue attempt. Loading up three vans worth of tactical teams seemed like a sure bet for either a crossfire killing or just pissing off Tat enough so that he put a bullet in her brain only to make a point.

Schuster had a gun in his back and a knife at his throat. No way to turn that it wouldn't end poorly. He stared out over the trees. "God damn you, Dale. You owe me this. You better come through."

The machine hum of the truck's nervous system bounced around the metal box. One of the men shifted in his seat, another cleared his throat.

Schuster turned back to Greely. "Stand down. We'll give him his time. My word means something around here."

7TH FLOOR

Any way Dale rolled on the hard floor, his body protested in agony. A hundred tiny fists left their mark, tenderizing his flesh until there was nowhere left to find comfort.

The girls all chattered in their own languages, several different ones floating overhead. Dale closed his eyes, knew he had to get up, but stayed down, needed a few minutes more.

Lauren leaned on one knee. Her scalp hurt, her ribs were bruised from the kicks. "We need to keep moving."

"I know." Dale stayed on the floor, his eyes remained shut. "I feel like I've been run through a clothes dryer."

"We didn't see that coming, did we?"

"I shouldn't have lied."

"Hey, you got them out of the cages."

Dale tried to smile but his lip ached. His right ear was muffled, clotted blood blocking the sound. "Thanks for rounding them up again."

"I'm just glad it worked the first time." Lauren pushed up to standing. "That was my last bullet."

Dale thought about giving up. Pressing the button again and letting the girls go wild. Not a bad way to go, death by thirty prostitutes. Alone, Lauren might stand a better chance of walking out the door unnoticed. Or she could go back with Tat, wait out the little stunt he was pulling, maybe make a deal with the mayor, and she'd be out of here without any of this abortion of a rescue attempt.

He could send her out with a message for Dahlia. That he was sorry. That he died trying to do something good. She wouldn't have to bother with a divorce. She'd get his life insurance and what she was entitled to from his pension. Not fully vested, but it would be something. He could send Lauren out with the numbers on the safe deposit boxes, but they were all under his name only. Dahlia wouldn't be able to get at them. Maybe once she showed them a death certificate. Maybe.

The thought of leaving all that money to wither away hurt as much as his bruised legs. And the idea that one of Tat's men was out there right now looking for her. No, bringing her in. No way it would take one of Tat's guys this long to find her. What the hell would she be walking in to now?

Dale wondered if Tat had been found in the closet yet. He wondered who else in the building knew anything about what was going on.

Too many unanswered questions to lay down and die. And a bunch of weak girl-fight slaps from a few dozen twigs in short skirts wasn't going to kill him. He'd done worse to himself doing yard work.

He rolled onto his front and got on all fours. He held in a groan. Had to make Lauren feel safe, not like her savior was an old man who can't take a punch or fifty. Dale pushed up and stood. The girls' chattering quieted as they all watched him stand.

Dale looked at Lauren, wondering how bad he must look. Based on the expression on her face, pretty bad. "So what now?"

Her hair was in a tangle on the crown of her head. She dabbed at her lip with a finger, checking for blood. "Elevator again, I guess."

A metal clank startled them. They both thought the cell doors would open again, but they didn't move, and the sound came from down the row of cells. Over by the steps they used to come down from the torture rooms, a section of the floor lifted up. A trap door cut into the floor. Two men appeared from below.

"The fuck are you? What's all the racket up here?"

Dale drew his gun, making his ribs ache anew. The two men threw their hands up. Dale noticed air filtration masks hanging loose around their necks, white smocks over their clothing as they poked halfway out of the trap door.

Lauren drew her gun as well, knowing it was empty but also knowing an empty gun is an effective motivator when the person you're pointing it at doesn't know.

Dale marched forward. "Hands up." The two men looked at each other, recognizing they were already holding their hands up. Dale tried to clear his head as he walked, to stay straight and steady so the two men wouldn't see the pain he was in. As he walked by the cages, the girls all chattered like birds.

Dale spoke over his shoulder at Lauren. "What's down there?"

"Let's see...we're on eight..." She remembered. "The lab."

They reached the open trap door. "Down." The two men turned and walked down the steps. They came down into a sprawling laboratory. The seventh floor finally looked like something the architects of this complex imagined it would be used for. Though Dale doubted this was a lab for any sort of medical research or high-tech computer components.

A half dozen workers hunched over tables in air filtration masks and white paper booties on their shoes.

Lauren stared in wonder at another floor she'd only read about.

The taller of the two men with their hands up looked at Dale. "You're the guy."

Dale pushed his gun in the man's face. "What do you mean?"

"We heard there was shooting up on the top floor. Some trouble, and they were looking for someone."

Shit. Word was out.

The lab worker was nervous. He was paunchy around the middle, not the military-grade muscle men in Tat's army. "We're just lab workers." He spun around to acknowledge the rest of the team. The others, still with their masks on, looked if they were wondering whether to put their hands up or to keep working. "I'm Elton. We're not gonna...I mean we wouldn't—"

"Shut up." Dale scanned the room.

Elton woke up that morning thinking this was the day he should quit. And now this. Of course, he thought that every morning. He wasn't using his chemistry degree exactly the way he expected when he secured his first scholarship. Running a lab for Tat had been lucrative, but he felt like a fool wearing his breathing mask every day when the real threat was anywhere but on this floor of the complex.

Dale looked at the tables and bubbling chemical works, a question playing across his face like he was wondering if they should ask for masks of their own. "Meth?"

Lauren squinted at the vials and vessels on the long tables. "I don't think so. It's set up for meth, for cutting coke and heroin. This looks different." A light inhale of recognition made Lauren give off a gasping sigh. "It is, isn't it?"

Dale crinkled his brow. "Is what?"

Her reporter instincts were overriding her fear. And the experiences of the last sixty minutes were threatening to kill her fear altogether. "You're branching out, aren't you?"

Elton looked down at his bootie-covered shoes.

"Krokodil. Am I right?"

Elton avoided her eye, looking around the lab at the listening workers, wary of saying anything out loud that could get him in trouble around so many witnesses.

Lauren grinned, adding another mental note to her story, or perhaps the follow-up story all about the drug problem in town. "I am right. Jesus Christ. You're going to let that loose on the streets?"

"It's an experiment." Elton blushed as soon as he said it.

Dale watched the man's reaction and asked Lauren, "What's Krokodil?"

"A new drug. It came from Eastern Europe. More addictive than crack, more dangerous than heroin. Eats you alive from the inside, for anyone stupid enough to take it."

Elton let a shameful half smile worm across his face. "There's always someone stupid enough."

Dale saw the resigned sadness in his face. "You can put your hands down."

Elton and his shorter partner did. The room seemed to relax a little.

"So this is where Tat makes all his product?"

"Some of it. Some still comes from South America, Mexico, Canada."

Dale shook his head and whispered to himself. "Right under our noses." Manufacturing hadn't been on Tat's list of offenses, as far as the police knew. Dale was paid to look the other way on a lot of things regarding Tat and his operation; this one blind-sided even him.

On a table near the back wall, beside a tall window that had been blacked out, a beaker of acrid-smelling liquid bubbled over because the worker at the station had been eavesdropping on the conversation.

A cloud of white mist rose from where the liquid boiled over and he scrambled to lift the glass off the flame and quickly mop up the mess.

Elton looked worried. "Hey, watch it. Pay attention, all right?"

Lauren knew why. Any of these bottles or beakers could turn deadly, either by releasing gasses or heating too high and bursting into flames. Most of what they were cooking with was combustible and the rest was the type of ingredients that needed the heavy filter masks everyone wore.

Everyone except Lauren and Dale.

Her eyes studied the lab, the workers with their blanked out faces. "We should keep moving."

"Yeah." Dale kept his gun gripped tight as he pointed to the far side of the room. "Elevators this way?"

Elton nodded. "You're leaving?"

"We've been trying to leave. Maybe this time it'll take."

"Can I go with you?"

Dale stared at him, saw the fear in his eyes. He looked at Lauren, who shrugged.

"Why do you want to do that?"

"Look at us." Elton waved a hand around the room. "We're making vile drugs for unsuspecting people. I'm supposed to be working on cancer research."

The shorter man spoke with an accent. "I was working on bioengineering in Brazil."

"You want to come too?"

The shorter man nodded. Dale looked around him. "All of you?"

Heads nodded behind masks. He turned to Lauren again. She didn't seem to have any answers. "It's not that different from the girls, is it?" Didn't make quite as good a story for her article, but it would do.

"I guess not." Dale chewed his lip. The smell grew throughout the room. Ammonia mixed with an auto body shop with a little bit of low tide thrown in. "God dammit."

Elton turned to his coworkers and gave commands to get out of their white suits. They started removing masks and peeling off the white coveralls. All but one, Dale noticed. A worker in back at some sort of packaging station. There were no beakers or burners at his table, only piles of small glycine bags filled with tiny amounts of powders and crystals like rock candy.

As the group began to gather around to be led out, Dale focused on the unmoving man. Above the rim of his mask, Dale could see terrified eyes. He noticed he could not see the man's hands, hidden under the table. Dale took a step forward.

It was like he set off a trip wire. The man stood up, a .45 in his hand. He shouted something in Spanish and moved the gun side to side, targeting, then changing his mind and getting his sights on someone else. The crowd buzzed and cowered together.

Elton called out to the man. "Mario, what the hell are you doing?"

Dale put out a hand to calm the nervous crowd behind him. It had been a long while since he'd been in a standoff with a perp, but he'd been here before. He was still at least thirty feet from the man who had moved away from his table and backed against one of the blacked-out windows. Too far to be sure about taking a shot, and this Mario was aiming at a much larger mass. Anywhere he put a bullet, someone was going to catch it.

Dale called over his shoulder to Elton. "I thought you were only lab workers. You weren't going to cause me any trouble."

"They make sure we are armed."

Lauren, standing next to Elton, looked at him incredulously. "All of you?" Elton and his shorter assistant nodded.

Dale shook his head twice. "Anything else I should know?"

Elton and the assistant traded a look. Lauren nudged him with her gun. "Tell him."

"Every station has a panic button."

Dale tensed. "Like a self-destruct?"

"No, not like that. It warns them if we get breeched."

Dale turned away from Mario. "Warns who?"

A shot rang out in the open space. Mario had fired once, a wild bullet that punched the wall only a foot down from the ceiling. They may have had guns, but it didn't mean they could shoot. The crowd of workers screamed and tried to get closer to each other, a mass of tangled bodies trying to make themselves small.

Dale turned back to Mario. "Put it down." He could hear the heavy breathing going on under the mask. The .45 twitched and shook. "Put it down and come with us."

A high-pitched bell sounded and the floating sounds of Al Jarreau led the way as the elevator opened and five men poured out onto the lab floor. Tat's militia, armed to the teeth. The panic button had been pressed.

AR-15s, Glock 9s, bulletproof vests. Dale was watching the reason Chief Schuster and the mayor didn't want to storm the castle in the first place. And they were all coming for him.

Bullets flew. In an instant the air was alive with buzzing hornets of metal, the sound bouncing off the walls and ceiling in the big, open space. Dale dove for cover, rolling and turning to see blossoms of red open up across the chests of several workers.

Lauren hit the floor and barrel rolled under a table. All around her hissing liquids began to fall in an avalanche of broken glass. The automatic weapons unleashed a brutal wave of destruction as the men marched forward into the room.

After the first few seconds, stage two of the fight began, much to Dale's surprise. The sound of a dozen handguns firing filled the silence after the initial burst of machine gun fire. Every lab worker had drawn their guns and was shooting back.

The five militia men split ranks and dove for cover. A bullet clipped one in the head. He fell and the pistol in his hand slid across the floor and ended up a few inches from Dale. He reached out and took it, knowing he was almost out of bullets.

Tables of lab equipment disintegrated, liquids mixed together into a toxic stew. Flames erupted.

Lauren stayed under her table, pinned against the wall with a growing puddle of vile liquid building on the floor in front of her, making a chemical lake of any escape route. She watched a lab worker get shot and fall, making a barrier between her and the shooting. She saw the pistol on his belt, undrawn and unused. She reached around and took it, unlocked the clip, and saw it was fully loaded.

Three militia men remained. Another frantic burst of gunfire from an AR-15 tore through the room. A lab worker had made a dash for the elevator, which still hung open and still leaked smooth jazz, though it was covered up by the cacophony of the gunfire. The worker ran low in a crouch and the gunman raked his line of fire across the wall too high at first, then lowered his aim in a line Dale could track by the bursts of bullet hits on the concrete wall. The bullets tore into the elevator's call button. Sparks flew and the elevator dropped suddenly.

The worker sprawled out face first, shot through the chest a half dozen times. The open elevator doors hung there, but the elevator car dipped out of sight.

From low on the ground, Dale saw the white clad feet of Mario, still in his coveralls, running forward. Dale rolled on his back, aimed over his head, the world upside down for a moment, and fired two shots up at Mario as he came closer. Bursts of red sprang from his chest and he fell. Dale clicked his trigger again, but his gun was empty. He dropped it and took up the spare.

The gunfire slowed. Lauren peered over the body blocking her from view, and saw ten more bodies strewn across the lab floor, as well as the orange glow of flame. She turned behind her and saw Elton leaning over his shorter counterpart and shaking him by the shoulders, but the man had gone limp.

Acrid smoke filled the room. Dale knew he shouldn't be breathing it by the way it burned his nostrils. He looked out and saw no movement. He turned to the far wall and saw Elton letting a man go and crawling away. Dale moved toward him.

Lauren pushed her human shield forward and slid him around to make an opening for her to get out from under the table. She followed Elton as he moved forward.

The three of them met near the cracked leg of a table dripping a blue liquid down the side. Elton looked at them, rather desperate. "We have to get out of here. Find a mask if you can."

Each person scrambled to a find a fallen air filtration mask. The first one Dale picked up was soaked through with the very chemicals he was trying to avoid. Lauren found one back near her hiding table and Elton got one from around his partner's neck.

A loud pop sounded and a new burst of flames erupted on the far side of the room. The last remaining militia man stood and launched a volley of automatic weapon fire at the sound, but he hit only a growing inferno. The small explosion had spit flaming liquid ten feet in all directions.

Elton spoke muffled through his mask. "We gotta go."

Dale wondered if he was the only one who saw there was still a man with a machine gun in there with them. But it was either death by fire, death by inhalation of God knows what, or death by firing squad. And the whole damn point was to get the hell out of here. Dale stood first.

They ran in a serpentine motion for a few feet, then Elton broke off.

Gunfire followed them, smashing table legs and what glass wasn't broken yet. The gunman traced Elton's escape route, leaving Dale and Lauren to reach the doorway first.

Elton reached his destination, a wall switch not unlike the door locking mechanism upstairs. He punched a button on the wall and initiated a lockdown sequence. Heavy steel roll doors fell down over the blacked-out windows. A thick metal door moved on gears from the ceiling to block where the regular double doors were.

Elton made a sprint for the exit and caught a bullet in his leg. He faltered, then fell. The metal fire door nearly closed.

Dale tucked his gun in his belt. "Shit." He reached forward as another burst of gunfire sounded. Dale could feel the heat from the flames inside the room as the metal door started to cut them off in the cooler, outer area. Elton grabbed his hand.

The shooting stopped. Out of ammo. Might not matter to Elton anyway. Dale pulled, but Elton was large. The door was three feet from closing. Dale slid forward on his butt, put a foot on the lowering door and used the leverage to pull Elton as hard as he could.

The big man slid forward and banged a hip on the door as he went through. He tucked his legs tight to his chest as the door came down the last twelve inches. Lauren reached in and took his hand, pulling him farther into the room.

Dale started to breathe a sigh of relief, but his foot slipped off the metal door and shot forward as the thick barrier locked into place. His toes were trapped underneath.

The screams were louder than the bullets.

Dale was on his belly, his right foot sole up and angled under the door. He remembered the time he got his fingers shut in the car door as they were loading up to go to Great Adventure. They had to cancel the trip and two of his fingers were in a cast for three weeks. Nothing compared to this. Nothing. He pounded the floor in agony.

Lauren came to him. "Holy crap. Are you stuck?"

He grunted out an affirmative. She moved closer to look. His shoe was bent under the weight of the door. The mechanism was locked tight.

"How do you raise this door?" Lauren looked at Elton.

"You don't. Only the fire department can override it."

She knew arguing with him would be pointless. She looked at Dale's shoe again. Blood was seeping through. She bent low to him. "It looks like it's only the big toe. Maybe the one next to it."

"Fuck, it hurts."

She put a hand on his shoulder. She couldn't think of anything else to do. Pull him until it came loose? Or came off?

Elton, blood smeared on his cheek, scooted over on his backside. He clutched at his leg where a bullet had torn into his calf. "What can we do?"

"I don't know." Lauren tried to will her brain to think.

"We can shoot it off." Elton drew his gun.

Lauren drew her new, fully loaded gun and held it on him. "Like hell you will. Drop it."

Elton threw his hands up again. "Hey, come on. I'm with you guys."

Lauren had developed a deep distrust of Elton and all his lab buddies in the past three minutes. So far no one in this building proved trustworthy, so she was done trusting.

"I said drop it."

Elton let go of his pistol. Lauren turned to Dale, his eyes clenched in pain. "I hate to say it, Dale. But he's got a good idea. It's the only one we've got for now." Dale shook his head. "And we don't know how many more of those men are coming."

Dale set his head against the floor, forehead down. He breathed deep. "Do it."

Lauren took her new gun and pointed it at Dale's foot. She set the barrel against the shoe, touching the metal of the door to get the minimum toe that she needed to break him free. She wondered if she should count to three or see if he needed to bite down on something. She decided he didn't need to know when it was coming and before she lost her nerve, Lauren fired a single shot into Dale's shoe.

CHAPTER 20

She thought of the baby. Clutching low across her stomach where the seat belt burned a red welt into her skin, Dahlia figured there was no way it could have survived the crash. She felt like she barely did.

Better than him, though.

She pulled the bloodied body of Pooch off the steering wheel and finally silenced the horn. The hard plastic wheel of the old Pontiac had bent across the top where Pooch's forehead hit it. As his body slumped into the seat back, his front and bottom rows of teeth drooled out his mouth on a slime of blood and saliva.

Dahlia had sat with the horn blaring for what felt like a long time but could have only been a minute before she felt strong enough to move. No airbags in a vintage car, only solid steel.

She turned, slowly. Looking again at Pooch, she saw how his chest now had a divot in the center where his ribcage collapsed. Somehow her arms had held and saved her from doing a header into the dashboard. She'd braced herself just in time, though her elbows hurt like hell from the impact.

After Pooch drew his gun on her, a gold-plated beast she thought at first looked like a toy, Dahlia first decided to go for sympathy.

"I'm pregnant, y'know."

"Is that why that boy wanted to snatch you?" Pooch was single-minded on the money he could possibly get for her.

"I told you I don't know why. I think it has something to do with my husband, but that won't help you at all."

"He, like, a banker or something? Stock broker? Lawyer?"

"Cop." That shut him up for a moment. "Detective."

Pooch thought about it, then pushed forward. "Is that who I send the ransom note to?"

Dahlia was more annoyed than scared, for some reason. The escalating traumas of the day had dulled her senses. She felt manipulated by Pooch. At least with the boys in the band she didn't get double crossed.

"There's no ransom, no reward. You've got the wrong idea. That guy wanted to take me somewhere, to see someone."

"I thought you said kidnapping?"

"That is a kidnapping."

Pooch screwed up his face in deep concentration, his eyes aimed out the windshield of the car, his one hand on the wheel leaving the other for the golden gun. Dahlia decided he was an idiot. A dangerous idiot, but not someone she was going to succumb to after outwitting T and his man, then some crooked cop. Dale always told her, in the event anyone tries to make you get in their car (too late) don't wait to get to the destination. If you've made it that far, they have the advantage and chances drop by half that you will ever make it back alive.

She'd screwed up Dale's advice on the home invasion, she didn't want to screw this up too.

His mind was otherwise occupied with plans to get the phantom money he thought was out there waiting for Dahlia's return. Between that and driving with one hand, Pooch was distracted. Enough for Dahlia to form her own plan. Not a great one, but she zeroed in on hers first and that made all the difference.

Pooch had driven them out of the city and toward the river. The buildings changed from retail and apartments to warehouses and shuttered factories. There had been a time when one of the nation's largest vinyl record manufacturers was headquartered here. And a company that made flagpoles employed more than two hundred people.

Now the area was ghostly. The businesses that still hung on like barnacles under a ship did so behind high, razor-wire fences. The empty buildings looked overrun by the homeless.

Dahlia didn't want to get any deeper into the wastes.

With Pooch concentrating to the point of a headache, she leaned over and in one motion unclipped his seatbelt with a thumb and wrapped her hand around the steering wheel and gave it a violent twist to the left.

The car dipped low on ancient shocks and veered for the sidewalk. Pooch fought her on the wheel, dropping his gun to get two hands on. She pushed with all she had, using her right arm to brace herself against the dash. They aimed for a telephone pole. He veered the car back a little bit right, but not enough.

At the last second, Dahlia put her other hand on the dash, locked her elbows in place and shut her eyes. The left headlight hit the pole and the car came to a sudden stop. Glass from the windshield exploded into the car and Dahlia heard Pooch's body thump against the wheel. She missed the second thud of his head whipping viciously to the side and hitting the crown of his skull on the post between the windshield and door.

The back tires lifted off the pavement, then slammed down announcing the arrival of the car. The front end was creased nearly to the engine block by the pole, which leaned away as if it were trying to avoid to oncoming car. Steam hissed from the crushed engine.

The sound of glass tinkling down to the floorboards slowed, then ceased. Bits of the windshield stuck in Pooch's hair and clung to where blood flowed from his nose as his body slumped forward on the cracked steering wheel. The horn started blowing the alarm.

Dahlia lifted the gun from under a layer of broken glass. Time to figure out where she was.

CHAPTER 21

"I need an answer, sir." Lewis stayed in his seat watching O'Brien's back as his boss hovered at the liquor cabinet. He watched the mayor shoot a glass of scotch, hang his head, and set the glass down.

"You're saying it will be fast?"

Lewis looked at Roy. He knew the mayor's question was for the fixer, not him. Lewis nodded to the man for him to answer.

Roy, devoid of emotion, calmly assuaged the mayor's fears. "Fast, silent, painless." O'Brien nodded. "Tell you the truth, it'll be nice for a change."

Lewis gave Roy a chastising look. He tried to calm the boss with his own logic. "Fact is, sir, we probably won't even need Roy at all. If we haven't heard by now…"

O'Brien turned. "What? If we haven't heard, then what?"

Lewis accepted the challenge in O'Brien's voice. He swallowed. "Then she's probably already dead."

The thought had occurred to O'Brien. In a strange way it was the best-case scenario. It's one reason why he didn't fight the crazy notion of sending in a one-man rescue squad. He couldn't be sure which was more likely to backfire—one man or a small army.

"It's hard, Lewis. You've got to understand." O'Brien looked up, got nothing from Roy's eyes. No sympathy, no sadness, no fear. He turned to Lewis again. "I'm losing my daughter. You see that, right?"

"Sir..." Lewis shifted in his seat. Time to seal the deal. "Didn't you lose her a long time ago?"

The little punk was right. Lewis knew O'Brien's family better than he did most times. Lauren began pulling away years ago, during the first campaign. She felt none of the thrill of victory when they won, didn't give a damn when they moved into the mayor's mansion, didn't care about city functions, didn't do squat for the first reelection campaign.

Much of that could be chalked up to Lauren being a teenager. Moody, temperamental, and robbed of her normal teenage years by the spotlight forced on her by her dad and his choice to seek office. But what was it now that she was a woman in her early twenties? Residual teenage angst?

And now it had been confirmed what she knew about him. If she did get out alive, what relationship would they have? What could they have with him behind bars?

Lewis was right. He'd lost her. His own stupid fault, maybe, but she was gone and she wasn't coming back. The woman who left that office complex would be on a mission to destroy him. He'd lose his job, his money, his wife, his legacy.

Yes, Lewis was right. And O'Brien hated him for it.

He addressed Roy, avoiding Lewis altogether. "Quick. And painless."

"You have my word." Roy stood, the first sign that he was eager to get this show on the road. He extended a hand to the mayor, his version of a binding contract. O'Brien looked at the outstretched hand for a moment, licked sweat off his upper lip, then shook.

Roy turned without another word and headed for the door.

Lewis rose to his feet, buttoning his sport coat. "You've made the right decision, sir."

"Shut up and get out of my office, Lewis." The liquor cabinet beckoned O'Brien again.

STILL ON THE 7TH FLOOR

This is my punishment, thought Dale. *It's finally catching up with me and all the vengeance in the universe is falling from the sky on one goddamn day.*

Seemed about right. He'd gotten away with too much for too long. He knew it. How many times had he thought about extricating himself from his deals? Of going straight? But once you were in with someone like Tat—it was near impossible to bring yourself out.

The stupid thing was—and Dale realized this now when his hopes of escaping the high-rise were dwindling to nothing—he never spent any of the money.

The fastest way to get busted for taking bribes and kickbacks was to drive up to the precinct in a new Aston Martin. The surefire way to spark an IA investigation is to take the wife to Aruba for two weeks. No cop has that much money.

He'd done the math not too long ago and figured he'd taken in over two hundred and fifty grand over the years, and he'd spent maybe three grand of it. Most of that was paying for the new gutters on the house, the transmission rebuild in his car, and a new washer dryer for Dahlia's birthday. He saw now how insulting that was to his wife. Buying her a fucking chore machine? How had she stayed with him so long?

* * *

Dale wanted to wrap his hands around the ruined foot, but he also didn't want to touch it. He wanted to scream, but he didn't want to exert his body that much for fear of setting off the exposed nerves in his foot.

He pressed a cheek into the floor, squeezed his eyes shut, and sucked against grinding teeth.

Lauren stood over him, shuffling nervously and waving her hands as if she'd seen a dead mouse in her kitchen.

The foot came cleanly out from under the metal emergency door. All that could be seen of Dale's missing toe beneath the door was a charred bit of rubber from his shoe. His foot jumped like a frayed electrical cord at the end of his leg. The curve of his shoe rounded the slow arc over his smaller toes, then cut off suddenly in a jagged line of red where it should have continued a slow curve down.

Still in his lab coat, Elton lay a few feet away on the floor clutching his left calf where a bullet still burned hot below the muscle. Even still, he sounded like he felt bad for the pain Dale was in. "Jesus Christ, man."

"I had to do it." Lauren still hopped from foot to foot, feeling phantom pains and hot guilt. She tried to get a good look at the wound but found it hard to see Dale's bouncing foot clearly. "I think we should wrap it in something."

"Here." Elton pulled his lab coat off and tore a sleeve. He handed it to Lauren, a ready-made tourniquet.

She bent down and put a hand on Dale's shoulder. "I need to wrap it up, okay? Honestly, it doesn't look that bad."

He knew she was lying, but he couldn't bring himself to look at it yet. He nodded his approval and Lauren went to work. He tried to stifle low, guttural screams as she tied the sleeve over his foot and cinched it tight to slow the blood. It wasn't bleeding as much as she thought it might and when she was close, she could see that part of the wound had been cauterized by the proximity of the gun blast.

She finished and bent down to his ear again. "It looks like

only the one toe. The big one."

With the torture over, Dale flopped onto his back and opened his eyes for the first time. He could feel the heat of the fire in the room next door coming through the metal barricade. He came to terms with the pain, accepting his punishment. He still had jail time to look forward to but that would require getting out of the building, which looked like a dim vision on a foggy horizon.

"We should get moving. More will come soon." Elton was trying to stand.

Lauren, the only one without a bullet wound, looked around the tiny landing where they stood. Blocked from entering the rest of the floor by steel safety doors and with an open elevator shaft behind them, the controls all shot to hell, she didn't see much of a way out.

"And how, exactly?"

Elton nodded to the shaft. "We climb."

Dale knew he wasn't an active member of the negotiations, but he agreed with Elton. They had to keep moving. The fire would go out and more of Tat's militia men would come. Someone would fix the elevator and they'd show up to the strains of soft jazz, but they'd be there. And they couldn't sit around and wait for that to happen. They hadn't come this far only to stall out now. Dahlia was still out there. Lauren still had to get home.

"He's right."

Lauren met his eye from directly above him. "Are you sure you can do it?"

"No. But I'm not staying here."

Elton was already dragging himself to the open elevator shaft. Dale grabbed on to Lauren's pant leg. "Help me up."

She bent down and got him to his one good foot. He leaned on her like a crutch and they all went to look down into the black hole of the shaft. No one spoke for a moment as they followed the cables down until they were eaten by darkness. The walls of the shaft were a crisscross of metal support beams and the mechanisms for the doors were substantial and could make good footholds for a climb. But for two gimps and a woman who had never been rock climbing, even on one of those fake indoor walls? And who had a terrible fear of heights?

This was not a sure bet, but it was the only game in town, so they all anted up.

"I'll go first." Elton swung his legs over the edge and sat with his feet dangling above the blackness. Hs face showed the pain, but he bit through it.

Lauren was unsure about his qualifications as a team leader. "How's your leg?"

"I'm shot, but it's in the meat. Hurts like a leg cramp. I'm not bleeding too much. I'll be fine."

Didn't sound fine to Lauren, but she didn't like the idea of volunteering to go first. Plus, she needed to stay behind to help Dale who would surely not describe his toe pain as a cramp. As she looked at him, he still contorted his face in a closed-eyes grimace.

She speculated. "No one has a flashlight, I guess?"

Elton shook his head. "Gotta just go for it." He reached out and found he couldn't get to the cables from where he sat. He needed another eight inches, maybe. Steadying himself against the side of the doorway, he pushed to his feet. He hopped on one foot when he stood.

Lauren squirmed. "Be careful."

He turned to look at her. "Thanks." He looked at the cables in front of him, then back to her. "And thanks for getting me out. I needed the kick in the ass to do it."

"I wouldn't thank us just yet."

Elton smiled. "Yeah, I guess it's kind of a messed up way to quit your job."

"This is the most messed up day of my life."

The pain was evident in Dale's mocking voice. "Yeah, yeah, everything's real messed up. Can we get going here?"

Elton turned back to the shaft, leaned as far as he could with one hand still on the doorframe, then let go and hopped out the last few inches to the cable. There were three of them grouped together. Steel cords the thickness of a garden hose. The thing he hadn't anticipated was that they were greased up, lubricated to keep the elevator cruising along nicely.

Elton dropped, sliding down a full body length before he wrapped his legs around the bundle of cables and slowed his progress. His calf with the bullet in it rubbed against the cables, the pressure of his tangled legs keeping him from plummeting into the black. He let out a scream.

Lauren rushed to the opening. "You okay?" She left Dale leaning against the wall next to the blown-out call buttons.

It took a few moments for Elton to regain his speaking voice. "I'm all right." The cables rattled up the shaft, the long cords echoing a high-tension note. Fifteen story-high wind chimes in a breeze.

As Lauren gazed into the hole, the blackness seemed deeper now. Before, she could calculate the distance from the seventh floor to the bottom, but now it seemed as if it went to the center of the earth. Dale's voice broke her trance.

"My turn, I guess."

Dale hobbled forward and got his first direct look down the shaft. Elton clung to the group of cables in the center of the void like a child refusing to climb down a tree. That moment when he's realized he got in way over his head here and it was time for Dad to come with the ladder.

"I think I'm going to take the side walls. Looks like there are enough footholds to make it."

Lauren examined the walls, skeptical, but no more so than of Elton's plan. "From what we can see, but what about down there?"

"It's going to be the same in a repeating pattern all the way down. Didn't you study this building?"

"Not the elevator shafts. I'm a reporter, not a building inspector."

As if anticipating the pain to come, Dale shut his eyes and grimaced once more before turning his body and starting his descent along the inner wall of the shaft. He knew there was no way he could support his whole body weight on his damaged foot, so he hung that leg out over the opening and eased himself down on the power of his good leg and his hands gripped onto the doorframe.

Lauren moved in to help him, but he protested. "No. I have to know how much of my own weight I'm holding up. If I need you, I'll let you know." She stayed close by.

In the shaft, Elton began slow slips down. He'd loosen his grip on the cables, slide down a few inches, then tense up again and stop. Black grease coated his cheek as he hugged the cables. His hands already burned from the effort and his leg felt like the bullet had entered his calf anew, but he kept his face turned away from Dale and Lauren. All they could see was his slow progress downward, not the agony on his face.

Dale knew this next part was going to suck. He couldn't tell if he was quite as scared as when he was waiting for Lauren to blast his toe off, but for this he had to have his eyes open and all his senses aware, so he thought it might end up sucking more. One way to find out.

He started feeling along the cinder-block wall of the shaft with his bad foot. Wrapped in a makeshift bandage and missing a toe and a bit, even the slightest touch against anything but air sent a new electric shock of pain shooting from his foot to every corner of his body. He tried to keep his pinky toe turned to the wall so he wasn't hitting the open wound on every hard surface he could.

The first support slid under his foot. He tested the strength through gritted teeth. It would hold. He pressed down with his foot, feeling the narrow steel beam through the bottom of his shoe. It was only about three inches wide. Enough to support his weight, but not without a hand firmly griped on to something else. This would not be easy. Sweat already beaded on his forehead and the intensity of his heartbeat pumped a fresh flow of blood to his ear and his toe.

Dale eased his hands down the inside of the open door. The knee on his support leg bent higher and higher until it was time to let go and allow his lopsided foot to carry the burden.

Above him, Lauren watched, holding her breath. Elton continued to slide down the cables by inches. The journey down to the first floor would take hours unless they figured something else out.

Dale dropped his other leg into the shaft and he heard Lauren let out a slight gasp. His good toes found the beam and he eased off the pressure on his bad foot. The oppressive pain ebbed away to merely tolerable. His hands came off the open doorframe and found any small hold they could. Dale was fully inside the shaft and pulling himself up now seemed more impossible than scaling the rest of the way down.

He thought of Dahlia. What a crazy story this would all make when he got out; the extent to which he went to get back to her. Would she appreciate it? Would he even get to tell her before he was whisked away to a holding cell to await a working over by internal affairs?

In the middle of his questioning thoughts, he heard a scream.

Lauren kept a close eye on Dale, waiting for him to lose his grip and drop away into the dark, but it was Elton who let go. She heard the rattle of cables a split second before his yell. Her eyes darted toward the sound in time to see him vanish from sight straight down.

The strain of holding on had been too much. He loosened his grip to travel another four inches down and his body didn't obey the command to cling on again. The bullet in his leg shut down all muscle response. His hands had enough. The sweat slicked his grip even more against the grease and it became too much to hold on. Elton's scream faded into an echo and then cut off abruptly, the dull impact sound following the scream up the shaft to disappear overhead.

Lauren turned her eyes to Dale who stood clinging to the wall a few feet below her. He looked up at her and a thin light caught his eyes in the darkness. The desperate look seemed to say, *no turning back now.*

CHAPTER 22

There was blood, but she didn't know if it was hers. Dahlia stood straight, her head woozy. She looked down and saw the blood on the front of her pants. The baby. Stinging bands of pain ran across her abdomen from where the seatbelt gripped her to the front seat.

She touched the spot and the blood came away warm. The surface was soaked through. She lifted her shirt and a cut had opened up along the waistband of her pants. Dahlia pulled the front of her pants out and waited for the flow of blood from inside. It never came.

The blood wasn't from inside her body. Not the baby.

Tires eased to a stop on the asphalt, the last few feet a crunching of glass and metal pieces from the engine and bumpers. Dahlia looked up.

T's familiar black car slowed to a halt. How far back had he been following?

Dahlia muttered to herself under her breath. "No."

T stood, watching the driver's seat for movement, wary of the crash. Dahlia buzzed around the edges from the impact, her balance a little off, the pain still making itself known. But time had come to stop running. She lifted Pooch's gun and fired.

T jerked his shoulder with a grunt. She fired again. He bent in the middle and fell against his own car door, slamming it shut, then he slid to the ground. Dahlia walked toward him. Between two vacant buildings she saw a man hunched over an overstuffed shopping cart watching from a safe distance.

She reached the car, engine still running. T sat on the sidewalk, one hand holding him up and the other around a wound below his ribs. A bright spot of red grew across his left shoulder. Dahlia aimed the gun down at him.

"Where's my husband?"

T was in shock, his eyes staring at nothing, wondering how he got there. He didn't answer. Dahlia stuck the gun under his chin and lifted his face to hers.

"Where is my husband?"

Breath didn't come easily, but after a few attempts T squeaked out a word. "Tat."

She knew the name. By reputation, by stories in the papers, by Dale mentioning a case a few years back, then more recently hearing his name in overheard phone calls.

"Take me."

Shock gave way to pain and T curled in on himself. His knees came up to his gut and he rolled over onto his side. Dahlia could see his back and saw no exit wound. The bullet was still inside him, a hot coal touching the tender flesh of organs never meant to see the outside world.

The gun was heavy in Dahlia's hand. Her elbows ached from the impact and even the weight of Pooch's 9mm became too much. She knelt to where T was curled, fetal, on the curb. Her knees protested and her abdomen didn't like being folded in two.

"Take me to see him or I'll leave you here to die."

With her head still blurry, the voice sounded like someone else. She felt drunk, overhearing her own conversation and wishing she could sound tough like that chick. And two shots— two hits. She hadn't been to a gun range in over two years since Dale made her go for training with the gun in her nightstand. She was glad for the training now, and glad she was bad enough not to kill him right away. She needed him to find Dale. Dahlia had no idea where to find this Tat person.

Going there would be a dumb idea. She knew that. But if she was anywhere Dale was, he would handle things. He'd grown distant, his communication skills were shit, they seemed to have different values lately, but one thing she knew: he could be counted on was to protect her. No matter what, he took the job of caring for and protecting his wife very seriously.

In that way she knew he'd have been a good father. Pity the boyfriends if they ended up having a girl. Dale would not be the dad you'd want to have to impress. It made the decision even harder.

But the other side to that coin, if Dale was the one to save her from this man, he also seemed to be the one who brought him to her door. He'd explain it away as a peril of the job. But none of the other cop wives had been abducted. Not that she knew about.

Dahlia tapped the gun on T's forehead. "Let's go."

"I'm shot." He seemed surprised that she didn't already know.

"I see that. You drive, I don't know where I'm going." She reached over and pulled the driver's door open. The car's electronic warning *bong-bong-bonged* at her with the door open and the keys in the ignition. T looked up from the sidewalk. He knew she wouldn't take no for an answer and wouldn't take any more stalling.

He rolled onto his knees and climbed into the car with considerable effort, slumping into the seat and pulling his hand away from his belly. Holding out his bloodstained palm to her, his eyes pleaded for help or mercy.

Dahlia slammed the door and went around to the passenger seat.

"Let's go."

ELEVATOR SHAFT

A stenciled 6 rose out of the darkness in white paint on the back of the elevator doors as they passed. Barely enough light penetrated the shaft to make out anything, but the ghostly number cut through.

Dale let his foot hang in the air for a moment, dreading when he'd have to set it down again, igniting the pain like new. His leg up to his knee had gone numb except for a dull pain that radiated up his thigh and into his hips. The foot dangled, lifeless, like it had been amputated and sewn back on. But when he touched his remaining toes down on one of the support beams bolted into the wall—the steel beams with the three-inch lip keeping him from falling to his death—the foot came alive and sparked with new pain. How so much pain could come from something no longer there bothered Dale, but he'd have the rest of his life to ponder it. That could mean as much as five more minutes.

He and Lauren hadn't spoken since she entered the shaft and started her own slow climb down. Seeing that 6 tempted words out of him.

"Should we try to open it?"

"No. Keep going."

"I don't know if I can."

Lauren clung to an adjacent wall. She'd come even with him, moving faster with her two good feet. Her fingers burned from the tight grip she held on the beams. She wanted to stop, but

159

they had to get down. It was the only way. "The hard part is over. Just keep moving."

Lying had always come easy to Lauren. Ever since she caught her dad lying during the first campaign when he'd slept with that media consultant. Mom had a temper, one she kept in check during campaign mode. She smiled like a dutiful house-wife and supportive candidate's spouse. Never a hair out of place, never rattled. But when she boiled over, she was Vesuvius. Lauren heard about her father's lies from two rooms away.

After that and the other lie that nothing would change once he moved into office, Lauren changed as well. She was escorted to school by two bodyguards. No more going out at night or on weekends. She was to be in by ten and had to take the body-guards with her. Most of her weekends were taken up by photo ops at small business openings, fundraisers, and ribbon cuttings.

She began lying to her parents as a way to get back and seize some control. She told harmless, pointless lies. She was studying with Julie when she was really studying with Stephanie. She loved *Little Women* when she really thought it was a bore. Lies just to prove she could, and to prove what a fool her dad was. It occupied most of her teenage years and became so normal that she forgot what was a lie and what wasn't with her parents. They might call out some incongruity in a story she told and she'd have no recollection of the lie or why she'd told it.

So now, she could lie like a champ. It served her well as a re-porter, and it served her well when she had to tell someone to keep going even when she felt certain they would die in a tall shaft of darkness.

The stenciled 5 was over their heads now. She heard each pained inhale of breath whenever Dale would set his foot down again and have to support his weight for a brief moment while transferring weight to his good foot. Lauren felt deep guilt for shooting his toe off, but she knew they'd still be there now,

Dale pinned under a fire door.

And Elton would be alive. But damn it, none of this was her fault. She rescinded the earlier blame she put on herself. If she took any blame, she'd have to take it all, so she chose to lay it all at Tat's feet for kidnapping her in the first place and for running such a devious criminal empire. Elton's blood could be on his hands. The other men she'd killed may as well have been shot by Tat's own hand. Telling herself that was the only way she could keep going down the shaft. Lying to others came easy—lying to herself was harder.

She felt a fingernail crack and winced against the pain, but she didn't let go.

To break the silence and get her mind off the slow climb, Lauren asked a question that had been on her mind. "Why are you doing this?"

"Because the elevator is broken."

"No, why did you come here in the first place? Seems like a crazy thing to do."

Dale couldn't argue with her. Being here was crazy.

"I guess..." He felt along the edge of a beam with his foot. Winced in pain as he set it down. "I'm looking for some sort of good karma."

"You believe in that stuff?"

"No."

"Then I don't get it."

"Look, I'm not here because I'm the world's greatest cop. I'm here because I'm expendable, and I'm the only one who could get in here without getting shot immediately."

She voiced her realizations. "That's how you got up to Tat's office. You have business with him on the side."

"See? I knew you were a good reporter."

"A good reporter would have known that already."

"Well, either way. You could write an article about me and

it would be the story of one more ordinary crooked cop. One more asshole who couldn't say no to the money. One more jerk who thought he could get away with it. I'm here because if it all went to shit, nobody would cry over me. And it has gone to shit, don't get me wrong, but we're not all the way in it yet."

"Meaning we're not dead."

"Exactly. And plus, I've got some making up to do. I need to try to set things right with the department and the chief." Dale looked off into the darkness. "And my wife."

Lauren could smell the sweat coming off her body. "What, like AA or something? Making amends?"

"Sort of. I've got a lot to make up for. This was a chance to turn things around." Dale thought about his choice to accept the job. He thought about the first time he crossed the line and took the money Tat offered him. His only defense against the shame he felt had been to turn deeper into the take. He hadn't known at first the toll it would take on him, on Dahlia, on his career. "Yeah, a chance. Step one, anyway. First step of a long journey."

"Like that Chinese saying."

"Yeah. I'll have a lot of time to memorize Chinese sayings in prison." Dale had to take a break. He drew three deep breaths, felt the cramping in his fingers. "Mostly I needed to prove to myself that I still know what the right thing to do is. Saving you is the right thing to do. Getting to my wife is the right thing."

"Well, thanks, Dale."

He smiled. It was the first time she used his name. Made him feel like a human again.

Dale saw the stenciled 5. His feet had reached the beam directly on top of the elevator door to the fifth floor and he knew he had to get out of this shaft.

Below them, somewhere, Elton was decomposing as a stark example of the dangers of falling down to the bottom. They had descended another fifteen feet from where he fell, but it wouldn't make any difference. You drown the same in ten feet of water as you do in twenty-five.

He went to set his foot down on the beam below, but he slipped. With an involuntary moan, he grasped the wall and pushed hard with his good foot to stay clung to the narrow out-croppings he used. The foot and his missing toe were giving out. He couldn't put pressure on it anymore.

"I'm getting out."

"What?" Lauren looked at where his voice came from in the darkness. She could see a shadow in the blackness and the white number five.

"I gotta get out."

Dale put a hand on a bar in back of the door. His hand wouldn't reach far enough to wedge his fingers in between the two doors. He pulled toward him, his arm straining as if he were locked in an arm wrestling match with a steel rod.

Dale didn't try to stifle the grunt of effort and the sound car-ried off up the shaft. The door opened slowly. When he had the doors opened, Dale let go and spun his body toward the door. He tried to land on his good foot but it immediately collapsed under him when he hit. He banged a knee and rolled half way over before sprawling out and laying on his back, sucking wind.

Lauren made a slightly more graceful exit from the shaft, then also immediately lay on the ground to catch her breath. They both had to shut their eyes from the glare of overhead lights.

Lauren craned her neck over her shoulder to get a look at the floor. What she saw jogged her memory of the space from her studies. The money floor.

CHAPTER 23

"Fifteen minutes." Chief Schuster ran two fingers over his upper lip, an old habit from when he sported a mustache. The bare skin still felt like a rubber band over his teeth. "No, twenty."

There hadn't been any outside pressure—from the mayor, from the media. He'd just had enough of waiting. If Dale was taking this long, then something had to have gone wrong. A part of him felt an ulcerated pain of guilt digging at his insides for sending a man to such a fixed fight. Dale may have screwed up, and screwed up badly, but he still wore a badge and Schuster's job was to keep the men behind the shield safe, not send them on mini missions impossible.

And Dale was no Tom Cruise. He wasn't even Peter Graves.

"Move in twenty?" Greely, the team leader, was poised to give the command, all he needed was a confirmation from the chief. For the past hour and change, he'd watched the normally decisive man dither and do nothing. He still didn't know exactly what was going on inside the building that they had to wait to deploy. His men were ready.

"Your men should get ready in twenty." A few minutes more, thought Schuster. But he knew the SWAT team was ready to go in a moment's notice. They remained locked and loaded, geared up and eager to take down the city's most notorious gangster.

They even had the department's sole helicopter on standby.

"God dammit, Dale." Schuster rubbed his upper lip again.

164

The crooked cop had robbed Schuster of the pleasure of prose-cuting him as well as a clean, casualty-free extraction of the mayor's daughter.

Now a blood bath was coming. Lauren O'Brien was proba-bly already soaking in her own blood. And Schuster would be soaking in a pool of red ink and bad media coverage when this was all over. How long until the mayor fired him? And how long until it came out about Dale's connections to Tat? A black cloud would cover the whole department unless Dale could somehow pull one out and save the girl. Then they could con-tain, control, and manage the situation.

Schuster watched the tops of the trees, imagining the building beyond. He listened to the team leader call out the command to start the countdown to twenty minutes. He could hear the an-noyance in Greely's voice.

Wasn't his ass on the line, though.

Esmerelda Losopo, Tat's mom, flexed the fingers on her right hand, finally free of the ropes that bound her. Her left hand wouldn't move after she'd crunched her hand small enough to slip through the loose knot. Whoever that guy was who tied her up, he was a goddamn amateur. When she was younger, she would have been able to throw off those boy scout dropout knots in two minutes flat, but time marches on. As it was, she barely had to break anything. Felt like a series of bad sprains more than anything, and half her extremities were numb most of the time anyway these days.

Back home, on Guam, she'd been through the rite of passage that was being kidnapped by local gangs in the slums. Poor people kidnapping poor people's kids, getting twenty or maybe fifty bucks for the trouble. It wasn't a high-stakes game, but the men carried machetes anyway.

At fifteen she was held for nine and a half hours. At nine hours and twenty minutes, she got loose of her bindings and killed the man in the room with her. The one eyeing her with bad intentions in his bloodshot stare. If you were a girl in the slums and you got kidnapped, prepare to get raped. Honestly, Esmerelda was surprised it hadn't happened already.

But she saw the look in the young man's face. Left alone with him, he was getting ideas.

She beat him first with the tiny tin plate they gave her for food. The plate bent easily so she turned it on its side and brought the thin edge down on his throat until she cut a path to his windpipe and left him whistling on the dirt floor of her cell.

She found his machete in the corner and walked out the front door to slash open three more men before walking home in bare feet toting a new, blood-stained machete that she rinsed off and gave to her father, who kept it in the closet and used it frequently for yard work.

Setting her feet into the lush carpet of her bedroom, Esmerelda cursed herself for taking so long to escape. She didn't have a machete to carry out of there, but she held the same murderous feeling in her heart.

When the elevator didn't come, she marched through her apartment to the back stairs. The bureau was already pulled away from the wall, leaving a path for the door, and Esmerelda went out.

5TH FLOOR

A large steel cube sat in the middle of the otherwise open floor. Built nearly to the ceiling with rivets like off a battleship and no windows except for a thin metal flap Dale recognized as similar to the gun ports on armored cars, the cube was built to keep something inside. And to keep everything else out.

A keypad and card swipe blinked red beside a narrow door.

"What the hell?" Dale almost forgot the pain for a moment as he marveled at the impenetrable box.

"It's the cash." Lauren stared at it, imagining what was inside. "This is Tat's bank."

"All his money?"

Lauren nodded.

"Jesus—"

The emptiness of the floor echoed the machine gun fire and the ricochets until they crossed each other in the air and made a white noise of destruction. Dale spotted the thin barrel poking out from the gun port and spraying indiscriminately at the perceived threat.

"Shit!" Dale rolled away from the bullet impacts, bumping his already battered body across the floor.

The person inside had such a small gap to fire through, they couldn't focus on aim. The major deterrent was fear and rounds per second.

The first burst of shooting stopped. It took several seconds for the echo to fade in the cavernous, floor-length room. Dale looked to Lauren who had scurried several feet away to the other side of the room. "What do we do?"

"I don't know."

Dale silently chastised himself for asking her. *He* was the damn cop here. She may have two good feet still, but he had training and experience. Although nobody in the world had experience with his day so far.

The black nose of the gun poked again through the slit. Dale could see a small peephole below and to the left of the gun port. The kind of fish-eye view of the world you get from behind the door of your average apartment.

There was no way to tell how many people were inside or how many guns they had, but getting in wasn't the goal. Not being shot was mission number one. Dale saw the only way he thought of to avoid being sprayed with bullets.

He got ready to run on his nine toes and take command of the situation again. He called to Lauren. "Follow me. You know how to serpentine?"

"You mean run in a crooked line?"

"That's it."

"Where are we going?"

"To the box."

Dale took off like a sprinter with a cramp. He pushed forward and let the momentum drag him along with a heavy limp. He grunted every time his bad foot slapped the floor.

Lauren thought he was nuts. Rush the place where the gunfire was coming from? What kind of plan was that? But she had no ideas of her own so after she watched him lope four ugly staggers forward like he was in a three-legged race with an invisible man, she followed.

Almost immediately as she stood, the machine gun roared to life again. She zigged and Dale zagged as the gun sprayed a rainbow arc of shots too high to be much danger. The design of the cube wasn't suited to marksmanship. With the peephole offset in a parallax view from the slot of the gun port, and the distorted warping of the fish-eye lens, it was no wonder the shooter inside couldn't seem to find them with a decent shot.

As they sidewinded toward the box, the shots became even harder. She had to admit, Dale was right.

She beat him to the thick steel walls of the cube, but he was close behind, dragging his leg, which had given up even working a limp about half way across the room. He pushed his back against the wall below where the door was cut into the steel structure and Lauren could see the agony on his face. Eyes clenched shut, hand holding the knee of his injured leg, not daring to go any closer to the bleeding wound.

The lab coat sleeve she'd wrapped around him had gone from white to deep red. Blood didn't spurt, but it definitely leaked.

Lauren turned her eyes up and noticed she was directly below the gun port. Above her she saw the black metal barrel of the gun poking through like a crow's beak. It panned left to right as the shooter inside frantically looked for his missing targets.

"What now?"

Dale kept his eyes tightly shut. "I don't know. I got us out of the line of fire." He dared to open his eyes. Lauren watched him scan the rest of the floor. She looked too but saw nothing. She leaned over to see behind the cube to the far side. There was a door leading to the back stairwell where they had begun this hellish descent.

She leaned back and pointed to the spot. "The stairs."

Turning around seemed to be too much effort for Dale, but he trusted her and didn't need to see for himself. "Is there a gun port on the other side?"

Lauren kept her back to the steel box and shuffled her feet around to where she could peek onto the opposite wall. She tried not to think of how much money was beyond the five-inch-thick steel behind her back. Knowing Tat, it was a lot. And knowing her dad, some of it was designated for him.

She craned her neck and saw an identical gun port on the opposite side with a direct line of fire to the stairwell door. "Dammit." The black finger of the machine gun barrel peeked out from the slit and searched the back of the room. Lauren crawled back to Dale in front.

"Yeah, there's another one."

"Shit."

Their luck had held out so far, but how much were they willing to risk to make the mad dash with their backs turned to a firing squad?

Lauren looked over Dale's head to the keypad and card swipe. It reminded her of how she needed her ATM card to gain access to the bank vestibule after business hours. Probably the same style unit since there really isn't a retailer for super strong money boxes the size of a studio apartment.

A fuzzy memory, all of an hour old, played across her mind. She smiled and reached into her pocket.

Dale watched her, leery of that smile. What could she possibly have to smile about?

She drew out a thin silver card, like a section taken out of a tin can and pressed flat. Where had he seen that before?

Upstairs, when she cleaned out Tat's pockets before they stuffed him away. He slowly realized, a few beats after she had, what it was for. Access. He turned to look above him. A tiny red light blinked on the card swiper, waiting for just that— access.

What was her plan? Open the damn door and let the gunman out so he can look them in the eye when he kills them?

"What are you doing with that?"

"He's not going to come out, right?" Dale nodded, reluctantly agreeing. "Then the only way to make a hundred percent sure he doesn't shoot us in the back is if we go in and get him."

Breaking down her logic, which, on the surface was very

logical, required brain cells Dale didn't have at his disposal right then. Too much of his mind power was taken over with furious pain and exhaustion. When Lauren moved toward the card reader, Dale wanted to protest, but he reached around his back and drew his gun instead, preferring to be ready to fight the man with the machine gun rather than Lauren.

She hovered the card beside the thin slot. "You ready?"

Dale shook his head. "No. But go ahead."

Like paying for groceries, she slid the card down the slot and the light turned from red to green. There was a click from inside and the door hissed open an inch, looking like the opening to a mausoleum.

Dale rolled out of the way, scooting himself around the corner of the cube. Lauren retreated back to the spot under the gun port with the added protection of now being behind the heavy steel door as it swung open.

Nobody moved. Nothing happened. Dale half expected a flood of armed men like a clown car of death. Instead, he pictured a lone man inside trembling with the same fear he felt, wondering what the protocol was for something like this. This had to be the first time the vault was ever attacked. And now someone used an entry card. Presumably, Tat had the only one. The shiny, silver, one-of-a-kind key to his riches. The numbered keypad the way in for the guards.

"Mister Losopo?"

The voice inside was timid. Dale could imagine the man shitting his pants thinking he'd just been shooting at the boss and maybe some special guests. Well, if the hired gun wanted to think it was Tat, let him think it.

Dale rolled and flopped onto his stomach in the doorway, gun at the ready. He saw the shooter, looking at head height and waiting for Tat to step in. It was enough of a surprise for Dale to shoot first. Three quick bursts and the man jerked with three bullets to his legs, one of them up near his hip bone. He dropped the machine gun, fell to his knees, and seemed to see

Dale on the floor for the first time, as if an alligator had crawled in to his miniature fortress. The strange creature slithering on the floor so out of place in his insulated world.

As the man gave him a confused look, Dale aimed at the man's head.

"Don't make me do it."

Dale couldn't believe the man wasn't screaming. Three bullets in him, probably shattered bone, and he held himself up on his knees by will. The man bent down and put a hand on the machine gun.

"Come on, man. All we want is to get out of here."

The man struggled to get a grip on the gun. Dale scolded him angrily.

"We don't want the money. Just let us walk out and nobody else has to get hurt."

The man got a hand on the grip of the gun. He bent at the waist and put his other hand on the weapon, started to straighten up.

"Please, don't." Dale gripped the butt of his gun, but kept his finger slack on the trigger. Enough killing. He'd had more than he could handle. He felt like he knew what soldiers must feel like. What other choice is there when someone is trying to shoot you?

"Fuckin' cut it out."

The man lifted the machine gun in both hands. Dale fired a single shot into the man's right arm. The machine gun dipped but lifted again in his left hand.

Whatever they pump this guy with, Dale thought, *I want some when I get out of here.*

Dale fired again. The bullet entered his chest on the left side. Finally the man fell face forward and lay still. Dale let the gun go limp in his hand. His chest pushed against the hard floor as he tried to get a deep breath. He squeezed his eyes shut and cursed the man for not listening to instructions. Dale's instructions, anyway. He seemed to have followed Tat's rules to a T.

And what did it get him?

Dale opened his eyes again. What he saw eclipsed all other thoughts from his head.

Lauren came around the door and stopped. Dale was already staring, his body low enough to the ground to be in danger of literally letting his jaw hit the floor. Money. Cash. Stacks of it. Pallets of it. Stacked NBA-player high and row after row so deep that the shooter who'd been stationed in here only had about a ten-foot strip of real estate to move in.

A tiny TV played and a mini fridge buzzed in the corner. Otherwise, the room was devoted to money, and nothing but.

Lauren moved into the room like Alice entering wonderland. She took slow steps, not wanting to break the spell. There was more money in the world. Men traded this amount daily in firms all over Wall Street, often losing an entire cube worth of money in a single transaction, but that was all electronic. This was paper. Faces. Engraving. Real money.

She reached out a hand and it hovered over a stack about waist high on her, a palette not yet filled to capacity. Somehow, she couldn't bring herself to touch it. It had nothing to do with fingerprints or liability, it just didn't seem real and she felt if she touched it, the stacks would all vanish or turn to dust.

Behind her, Dale whistled long and low, almost like a cat call to a sexy girl on the street.

Lauren knew she had to get out. She knew she could stay here and think thoughts and wrestle with pros and cons all night if she let herself. But not even one stack of cash would make its way into her pocket, and she wouldn't allow herself to give any credit to her father for being weak in the face of all this cash. She felt queasy in its presence and no one was standing there offering her any.

"We gotta go."

* * *

The spell was broken. Dear God, it was so much. From his per-spective on the floor, they were great towers of cash, enough to crush him if they fell. How had he done it, this gunman? Every day working his shift in the presence of the answer to all his problems. It must be like working security inside a genie bottle and never being able to ask for a wish.

But she was right. They couldn't stay.

"Yeah."

Dale got to his knees, took a break, and felt Lauren's hand come under his arm to help him up. They both turned their backs on the money and refused to look behind them as they walked out leaving the door wide open.

"Wait." Dale stopped limping and Lauren had to comply or else topple over. "I can't leave everything behind."

Dale broke free and went back inside. Lauren started prepar-ing a lecture on the evils of stealing and how all the money stacked inside the cube was blood money. Besides, they still had to get out and he was sad enough as it was with his half a foot and zombie walk. She didn't think adding the bulk of a few thousand dollars was a good idea.

Dale emerged, but his pockets didn't bulge. He was only marginally heavier, all of it coming from the machine gun slung over his shoulder. He'd slipped a spare clip and his pistol in his belt. Whatever else the building had for him, he was ready. They walked to the stairwell.

CHAPTER 24

The tires bumped over reflective dots in the center lane. T veered the car back in line again, but Dahlia could see his eyes were unfocused. He took it slow, which was fine with her. She didn't need someone who could barely control the car to go speeding and kill them both.

She'd never had a bullet in her gut, and she didn't plan to, but some of the reading she'd been doing compared the pain of childbirth to all sorts of things, one of which was being shot. Apparently a woman in upstate New York took part in a study of childbirth experiences and she had once been shot by a hunting rifle accidentally and she claimed the pain to be strikingly similar. Of course, the people writing books about the subject latched on to that quote and rode it into the ground.

It brought pangs of guilt, but Dahlia couldn't look at T and his blood-soaked shirt front without thinking that she would never know his pain or the pain of childbirth. But she slapped that selfish thought out of her head. His agony wasn't a time for her to reflect on the sad turns of her own life.

"How much farther?"

He didn't answer and his one-handed driving style was making her nervous. Dahlia didn't like to look at him knowing she shot him. Actually discharging a gun into another human being wasn't something she ever considered through her Dale-mandated firearms classes. Even though the paper targets all had human forms, even though the instructors all emphasized the gravity of the tool in her hand. She'd gone to class to appease her husband, and she vowed never to fire a weapon again. Then today happened.

"Maybe I should drive and you can give me directions." She realized now she had nothing to fear from him and no reason to keep the gun trained on him. He wasn't going anywhere and was about as likely to make a leap for her while she drove as he was to break out in a tap dance.

"Why don't you pull over?"

Though he didn't answer, T steered the car for the curb so she knew he'd understood. He bumped roughly against the curb and the car bounced and the tires squeaked. It came to a lurching stop after that. T made a weak attempt to put it in park, but his arm wasn't up to the task.

Dahlia leaned over and moved the lever into P and unbuckled herself. "Slide over and I'll drive."

She got out and walked around the hood of the car and opened the driver's door. T had slumped over on the seat, but not moved into the passenger bucket as she'd asked. She nudged him with the gun, not as a threat but because she didn't want to touch his bloody shirt with her hand.

He didn't move. She poked again, still nothing. *Great,* she thought. *Passed out.*

She looked at his body slopped over the center console and didn't think she could move him as dead weight. She decided it would be easier to pull and went back around to the passenger side and leaned in. She lifted his hands, floppy as dead fish, and tried pulling him over to her side. His hip hung up on the arm rest/storage console and she gave up.

Dahlia thought of grabbing a leg in hopes that might raise his hip so she could slip him over the obstacle. She reached down and wrapped both hands around his thigh. His jeans were soaked in blood and he squished when she grabbed hold. Immediately she recoiled and drew her hands back. She stopped herself a second before she instinctually wiped her hands on her shirt.

Her palms were painted red.

Nothing to do about it now. She went in for another grab. She got his leg up and his knee over the console. One-fifth of his body down, the heavy bits still to go. She moved his other leg up and set his knees side by side on the console. His torso had shifted around so he sat against the door, his head lolling to the side.

Dahlia went back around to the driver's side and pushed. She tried to get low on his back and push up, not just forward. His hips started to move but the more they traveled forward, the more his head and shoulders fell back until she had to put one hand on the back of his neck and one hand in the small of his back, then shove forward with a shoulder like a linebacker in practice with a dummy.

His body flopped up and over and folded into the passenger seat looking like a pile of dirty laundry.

Sucking wind from the exertion, Dahlia leaned against the car door. Both arms were bloodstained almost up to her elbows. The shoulder where she rammed him home had a smear on it and she forgot herself and pushed a strand of hair out of her face, getting blood on her cheek and temple.

Lord save her if she got pulled over by a cop anywhere on the rest of her drive.

Now, about the drive...she couldn't exactly take directions while he was sleeping it off. She needed smelling salts or a bucket of cold water to splash him with. With neither of these at her disposal, she thought of pain. A jolt could bring him back around. It was cruel, but after all, this was the guy who started it by breaking into her house uninvited that morning. He killed Mrs. Joosten and shot at those other people, not to mention breaking that boy's nose and slashing the other one on the arm.

He deserved what he got, she told herself.

Poking a finger in his bullet wound ought to do the trick. But rooting around in an open gash wasn't exactly something she wanted to do. Like poking him before, she decided to use the end of the gun.

Dahlia sat down in the driver seat and cringed. The sticky blood he'd been stewing in as it dripped from his gut was warm on the seat and she could feel her pants soaking through. No other place to sit while driving the car, though, so she shut the unpleasant feeling out of her mind.

The seat squished as she leaned over and pushed the barrel of the gun into the hole in T's shirt. He didn't flinch. The pain hadn't roused him. She pushed harder. Nothing.

She pulled the gun back, a half inch of the barrel stained with blood. She'd pushed hard enough, deep enough, but nothing could bring him back to consciousness. Then Dahlia had a thought.

She reached over and put two fingers on his neck, below his jawbone, and felt for a pulse. Nothing pushed back at her fingertips. His skin did not jump under her touch. He was clammy and growing cold. Dead.

Shit, thought Dahlia. *What do I do now?*

CHAPTER 25

The sounds could have been them coming back. The crazy one-time employee and that bitch who shot a hole in his hand. Tat stayed quiet as he listened to someone moving in his home.

He tried to picture the inside of the closet and think if anything in his vicinity could be used as a weapon. All he could feel in the pitch black was the coats around him. An idea passed, but he silently cursed himself for his *Mommie Dearest*-level rule of no wire hangers. Something about them spoke of people who couldn't afford better. He hadn't even seen the movie, but if he did, he'd have been on Joan Crawford's side on that issue.

Whoever was outside didn't speak and it sounded like only one set of footsteps. What if Dale had called in the troops? Was the first of a SWAT tactical team soft-shoeing around his home? And what did that mean for the rest of the compound?

Tat worked hard to create his world and mold it to his own design. He wanted a place he'd never have to leave. A place that held everything he could possibly need. Headquarters, bunker, dormitory. He loved James Bond films and always wanted a supervillain lair. He knew it was silly—massive encampments carved out of active volcanoes or uncharted islands housing moon-melting death rays, but he admired the ambition of the bad guys. When chance came to have his own, he took it.

Something about the industrial wasteland look of the unfinished complex appealed to him. He knew cartel leaders in Central America who still lived in hovels, practically, out of fear of being detected. Tat thought they were fools. He admired the brash drug lords who built thirty-thousand-square-foot villas in the jungles of Mexico, a hundred miles from the nearest town.

He got the property for a song. He'd been saving his money, hoarding it was more like, for years. A cash payment put through by one of his shell corporations set up by one of his team of crack accountants was accepted without counter offer. For every new floor and new idea Tat came up with, he hired a new contractor. No one person knew the extent to which he'd altered and designed this building from the inside out.

He'd built a stronghold but somehow the parasites always got in, and now one of them was walking around outside his closet.

Tat felt with the back of his skull to an empty hanger and considered if he would be able to lift it down. A wooden coat hanger that he couldn't bend into a sharp eye-poker, but which still had a large hook good for gouging out eyes, catching in cheeks, tearing at jugular veins. Everything in the world is a weapon if you use it like one. His first attempt at lifting his arm caused a riot of pain shooting from his shoulder.

The slow shuffling footsteps got closer. The thin rope of light at the bottom of the door dimmed in one corner, then dark breaks in the line of light walked from one end to the other as feet outside passed by. Tat shifted his body to follow the shadows. A coat, loosened by his shifting back, fell and the rustle of sound made the feet outside come to a halt.

Tat tried to adjust himself and get his body in a position to leap if the door opened. He tried again to reach for the hanger and got his arm as high as his hip before the pain of dislocation stopped it there.

The feet crept back to the closet and stopped, two black interruptions in the line of light. He heard the doorknob turn.

Light spilled in and blinded Tat as his eyes struggled to adjust. The moment of disorientation threw off any attack he may have made. As his eyes adjusted to compensate for the new burst of light he saw his own mother, Esmerelda, standing before him.

"Momma?"

She saw the dark maroon blood stains on her boy. "Oh, baby boy, what have they done to you?"

"Momma, how did you...?"

"Never you mind that now. You got intruders. You got trouble."

Don't I know it, thought Tat. *But I got something else. A second chance.*

CHAPTER 26

Two visits from his wife in one day wasn't normal for Mayor O'Brien, but this wasn't a normal day.

Lori swept in to the office before his secretary had finished announcing her on the intercom. O'Brien could tell she was tense and thought to offer her a drink, but he knew he'd pour himself another and he couldn't afford to get any softer around the edges than he already was.

"Is there any news?"

"Nothing yet."

She paced. "Can't you call someone? You're the damn mayor after all."

"If I want them to let me do my job, I need to let them do theirs. The police chief is handling it, Lori. I know it's hard."

He had no idea how he was keeping it together. To talk of Lauren's rescue as if he hadn't stacked the deck against it. Even if this lone ranger they sent in managed to get her out, a long shot at best, O'Brien had just sent a man out to make sure his daughter never got more than a few steps out of that building.

Lori stopped pacing. "I'm sorry, Michael. About earlier." As she spoke, she straightened her spine, letting him know this wasn't a knee-crawling act of contrition, but a mature adult coming to another to apologize and leave the door open for his apology in return.

"I'm sorry too. It's been..." He exhaled, exhausted. "A hell of a day."

Lori went to her husband, wrapped her arms around him in a show of intimacy they hadn't shared in a long time. "Oh, Michael. Our little girl. Our baby girl."

She began crying and O'Brien wondered if she'd hadn't had a few drinks of her own since she saw him last. Lori had been known to take two or three martinis with lunch when she met with rotary clubs or auxiliary groups of one stripe or another. Doing her first lady duties and trying to enjoy herself while doing them.

The unexpected moment of vulnerability confused O'Brien at first. He hugged her back but didn't know what to do with the sobbing woman in his arms. He'd spent the past fifteen years of their marriage wondering what it was she wanted to hear from him and usually getting it wrong. And when he got it wrong, brother, look out. This was a delicate situation beyond most he'd been through with her. Sometimes all it took to set her against him was choosing the wrong place to go for dinner. This was their daughter, their only child.

As he pondered what to say, he gripped harder to her. She responded in kind and soon they were clinging to each other for strength and being held up by the other the way a real married couple does. But for him, it was the realization of what he'd done.

Removed from Lewis' stark revelations about the consequences to his career, O'Brien saw again the girl behind the threat to his office. Lauren, who at age five had presented her father with a homemade construction paper crown knighting him the World's Greatest Dad. Lauren, who came to him for scraped knees, lost teeth, and bad dreams. And his words, his embrace, healed the pain and scared away the demons. His daughter who trusted him at one point. Such unconditional devotion in her eyes as she trusted that he would be there at the end of the school day, he would be there to walk her down the aisle someday, he would be there to listen when her heart got broken.

ALL THE WAY DOWN

And now a man named Roy was on his way to shoot her.

Lori's sobs slowed and she settled in to a calm embrace with her husband. He had no idea what she could be thinking. Perhaps her mind was fully occupied by Lauren and the fears and unknowns of her situation. Or perhaps she was as baffled by their sudden reconnection in the face of tragedy as he was. But O'Brien knew exactly how he felt. A sureness that wasn't in the room when Lewis and Roy were here. He knew wholeheartedly. He'd changed his mind.

4TH FLOOR

The money called to them from one floor above. There had been so damn much it was like it had its own gravitational pull. But Dale and Lauren dutifully ignored the siren's call. Dale added another item to the list of things Chief Schuster had better damn well appreciate when this is all over.

Dale reached the landing for the fourth floor first. They moved cautiously, but with intent. The first floor, lobby, and exit were so tantalizingly close now.

"We need to stop here."

Dale froze in his tracks, unable to believe what he heard from Lauren. It had to be someone else, right? He turned to her and she looked at him expectantly and with a little apology behind her eyes.

"Did you say stop?"

"Yeah." Lauren shrugged. "This is Tyler's floor. The offices. Accounting and all that stuff. I need to see him."

"For your story."

Lauren wouldn't meet Dale's eyes. "Yes."

"You're still worried about the damn story? You don't have enough?"

"I'm missing the smoking gun on my dad. I know Tyler will have access to the right file or account or something to show a direct link between Tat and the mayor's office."

Dale took a longing look down the stairs. Four short flights and they were out. He didn't have time to argue with her. The sound of the door opening filled the stairwell. They were going whether Dale liked it or not. He and Lauren stepped slowly into the fourth floor. He saw offices, desks, floor lamps, potted palms. All the trappings of a completely average office suite. Business-attired workers hummed around with the mid-morning laziness of typical office drones. It all looked like an artist's rendering of exactly what this building had been designed for. Dale looked back at Lauren.

She spoke low, the two of them huddled against the doorway relatively out of sight. "Tat's running a business after all."

"Yeah, but...this is so normal."

"These are the front businesses. This is all legit."

"Well, talk to Tyler and let's get the hell out of here."

"Okay, I just have to find him."

"You don't know where his office is even?"

"We've only been seeing each other a few weeks."

Dale rolled his eyes. *Seeing each other* was code for *using him*, and Dale knew it. "Does this guy even know why you're here?"

She ignored him. "He'll help me."

At first no one noticed the bloody and armed strangers in their midst. The windows on either side of the narrow floor let in light in a way nothing above them had. Each office was a mirror image of the one across the hall. It seemed a bright, cheerful place to work. Office walls were glass, creating an open work environment. The fixtures and furniture were new and modern, the lighting was all energy efficient. The plants all meticulously groomed and watered.

A young woman at a desk tapped on her keyboard, eyes focused on her monitor.

While Lauren scanned the floor for her "boyfriend," Dale thought he could at least use this strange scenario to his advantage. "Can I use your phone?"

The secretary looked up and her mouth gaped. The front of Dale's shirt was a splotched mess of dried blood and his ear looked chewed by a raccoon. She couldn't see his foot yet, but she could see the machine gun slung over his shoulder.

One by one the other workers began to notice the intruders. Work slowed, then stopped. Fingers lifted off keyboards, rendering them silent, phones were hung up.

"Sure." The woman slid her chair back on the plastic pad that covered the carpet under her and let the wheels of her chair roll. "Go ahead."

Lauren watched the faces of the fourth-floor workers as Dale dialed the phone. She saw fear, something she never thought she'd inspire in people. She didn't even realize the gun was still in her hand until she saw one young secretary whisper behind a cupped hand to another and point. She thought at first the woman must be pointing at Dale's ruined foot since he was the scary one in their midst, but she followed the woman's finger and it led to her.

Dirty, bloody, and the only one besides Dale who was armed, Lauren hated to think what she looked like.

"It's okay, we won't hurt you." She felt compelled to say something reassuring. "I'm looking for Tyler." When she was met with blank stares, she suddenly realized she didn't know his last name so she couldn't even ask a more pointed question in case maybe someone only knew him as Mr. Smith, or whatever the hell he was called. Creeping guilt invaded her normally cool demeanor. "Anyone know where he sits?"

Dale hung up the phone. No answer. Still. He remembered Tat's instructions, "Bring her here." Dahlia could already be in the building. They would take her to the top floor, but find Tat wasn't there. None of the possibilities he could think of were good. Still, the only thing he could do was to get out and go look for her. Get out and hope for the best.

A thought lit like a match head in his thoughts. "Oh, Jesus." *Why hadn't he thought of it?*

Dale dialed again. A woman answered. "Chief Schuster's office."

"Danni, get me the chief."

"He's on assignment, may I take a message?"

"Danni, it's Dale. Put me through."

There was a pause. Dale heard it as an unspoken statement. *I thought you'd be dead.* Then, "Hold, please."

Schuster checked his watch. Any minute now, Greely would be on his ass again for a decision. He'd have to send the boys in, guns blazing. Well, shit, better to be seen as too tough on crime than too soft.

The phone buzzed on Schuster's belt. He jerked a little bit at first, startled by the vibrations, then clawed at the clip to release the phone. "Hello?"

Danni put him through.

"I have the girl, we're almost out."

"Good God, Dale, where the hell have you been?"

All eyes in the tactical van turned to him, awaiting word.

Dale didn't even know where to begin. It was all so ridiculous when he thought of it. "It's been...a challenge, sir."

"But he gave her up? You've got Lauren?"

"I have her. I wouldn't say he gave her up." Dale wanted to make a deal then and there, to plea bargain for a reduced sentence, but he knew it was stupid. "It's been a hell of time, Chief."

Schuster exhaled for what felt like the first time in an hour. "But you're almost out. Good. Damn good."

"Let's hope so."

"Are you bringing Tat out with her?"

"No, sir. Just the two of us. You want Tat, you'll have to come in and get him, but I wouldn't recommend it."

Schuster kept his back to the men awaiting orders. "Where are you now?"

"Fourth floor."

"I'm sending out the welcoming committee."

"We'll be damn glad to see them, sir."

They hung up. Schuster turned with a look of pride in his face, of having made the right call. "Prep your men, Captain."

The team leader nodded. "They're ready to go."

"When they come out that door, I want them escorted and brought right to me."

"Yes, sir."

"Aw, shit." Why hadn't Dale thought of it before? He redialed Schuster, got him on the line again.

"Chief, my wife. You've got to send someone out to the house to check on her. Tat said he was going to grab her, bring her back here to prove some point to me. I haven't been able to get in touch with her."

"Settle down, Burnett. I'll send a patrol car. I'm sure she's fine."

"Thanks. Can you make sure they stay there? Leave a few guys to act as sentry."

"Will do. Now get that girl out of there."

Dale tried sounding official, respectful. Try it on for size, see if he still knew how. "Yes, sir." Dale hung up. Lauren was gone, off wandering the floor in search of her contact. He spoke to the secretary, "The elevator work?"

The girl at the desk hadn't stopped staring at Dale when he was on the phone. His words didn't seem to penetrate the shock at the man in front of her.

"I asked if the elevator is working on this floor."

She snapped to attention, afraid she might have angered him

with her daydream.

"I think so. I don't know, I haven't used it since this morning."

Dale looked to the far end of the floor. "That way?"

She nodded. Dale thanked her and went to follow Lauren as the workers silently watched him. Higher ups in their glass-walled offices sat still at their desks, secretaries rotated silently in their chairs as he passed by.

"Lauren? What are you doing here?"

She had almost walked right past his office. She knew her head was scrambled from the day she was having, but she chastised herself again for not knowing a whole hell of a lot about this guy.

"Tyler, thank goodness." She went to hug him, but he pulled back.

"They said he had you upstairs."

"He did." She noticed him looking at her soiled and blood-spattered clothes. Outside the glass wall, Dale arrived looking even worse. Tyler gave him a look, then came back to Lauren. "I got away and now I need your help."

"You got away from Tat?" Tyler couldn't seem to wrap his head around that one.

"Yes. And I need files. Accounts. Something to link my father and Tat's organization. Something direct. Something that could be used in court."

Confusion on Tyler's face turned to shock and disappointment.

"You're trying to bring him down?"

She wasn't sure which him he referred to, but it didn't matter. The answer was yes on both fronts. She eyed his laptop.

"Can you let me borrow that for a few days?"

"Lauren, did you use me to get inside here? Is that all this was?"

She didn't have time for this broken heart shit. "No. No way. But now I need your help."

* * *

Dale chimed in from the hallway. "And the clock is ticking, pal."

All around him the workers started gathering in small cliques, whispering behind their hands. They moved slowly and reached into drawers. Something felt off about it and Dale became even more anxious to hit the elevators and get out.

Lauren didn't seem to be making much progress with Tyler. He sat down at his desk and made a slow reach for his own drawer. Dale instinctively tightened grip on his gun.

Lauren tried to soften her voice, play the girlfriend role—a role she had to admit she'd been playacting since the first.

"Look, you're not like the rest of the people who work here. You can help me. I bet you don't even know everything that goes on here. You want this brought down just as much as I do. You're not like one of the soldiers on the higher floors."

Tyler gave her a level stare. "We're all soldiers here."

Lauren wasn't sure what that meant but didn't like the look in his eyes.

"I know what goes on, Lauren. I help make it run. And yes, your dad helps us, too. Do you know how much money is at stake here?" He pointed to his laptop. "Do you want to see the numbers? Is that what you want?"

"I just want to see justice done." Her words came out weak.

"We have our own justice here."

Tyler lifted his hand out of the drawer. A mean-looking pistol sprouted from his fist. Behind her, Lauren heard Dale lift his machine gun.

"Stop!" Both men froze.

Lauren turned to Dale to make sure he complied. That's when she saw the other office workers mimicking Tyler, drawing weapons out of hiding places in their desks. He was right—they were all soldiers here. The floor came alive with the sounds of safeties being clicked off and bullets being racked into their chambers like a chorus of crickets on a summer night.

Dale turned and raised the machine gun. Five gun barrels aimed back at him. He looked beyond the glass office walls. Managers held even bigger guns on them. Dale spun back around to face front and discovered the other side of the floor had taken up arms as well.

Twenty-two people in all. Twenty-two guns. Guess they did know who they were working for all along.

We're not making it to the elevator, Dale thought. He couldn't muster the same animosity for a bunch of office workers in their sensible suits and polished shoes as he could for a bunch of thugs with too many push-ups and not enough brain cells. Then again, they were holding guns on him.

Dale eyeballed the secretarial pool from his stance in this standoff. Twenty-somethings, all of them. Fit, attractive. A world away from the whores up on the eighth floor, but he didn't know yet if they were as loyal.

He didn't want a slaughter. He didn't want a bloodbath among the young men and women. That didn't play into his plan for contrition, his turn for good. Even though if SWAT ended up coming in, none of these people were safe.

"We don't want to hurt anyone." His words were met with blank stares. It was like they'd encountered a floor of automatons. "All we want is to leave with no trouble."

Nobody lowered their guns.

Lauren had her pistol raised at Tyler, tears now brimming in her eyes.

"Don't do this."

"This was you." The hurt in his eyes turned to steel. "You brought this here."

She couldn't deny it. She also couldn't deny that she had started going out with Tyler for his access. But there were feelings there. Enough to overcome a gun pointed at her? Maybe not. He'd shown his loyalties, but did she have the guts to take what she needed by force?

"Tat's done. It's over already and he's going down. You've got nothing to fight for."

"Bullshit."

"See that guy?" She pointed to Dale. "He's a cop. There's more cops outside. It's done."

"We own the cops. Want to see a record of payments?"

"He's on that record. Even your lackeys are turning. It's over!"

She could see on Tyler's face that the only reason she was still alive was some sort of feeling he held for her. Muscles in his hand twitched, his finger tightening on the trigger and then backing off. She thought she saw the beginnings of tears in his eyes. They'd all been trained for this moment, but now that it was here, they were still only accountants. But they were paid well and money can buy loyalty. Plus, there was what would happen if they didn't follow orders. Money and death—the ultimate motivators.

Muscles in Tyler's arm flexed again. A long, slow reaction that started at his shoulder and moved down his arm. Synapses firing in slow motion, his brain fighting with itself to do it and not do it at the same time.

Lauren had learned a thing or two about survival in the past hour. Rule number one: don't hesitate. Swallowing a lump in her throat, Lauren fired. She hit Tyler in the chest. He fell back with a look of betrayal frozen on his face. She didn't have time to mourn as the entire floor erupted in gunfire. Dale saw it coming and was ready. He dropped to a knee, aimed low, raking the barrel of the gun across the feet of desks and the glass walls only a few inches off the floor. The sudden burst of machine gun fire scattered the office workers like cockroaches with a light on. The sound of pounding bullets became swallowed by shattering glass as floor to ceiling sheets like the walls of giant fish tanks exploded under the relentless firing.

"Let's go," he called out to Lauren. He saw her step quickly over to Tyler's desk amid a hailstorm of falling glass and snatch his laptop off the desk.

Dale moved forward as he fired and Lauren was right behind him, getting off a few of her own suppressing shots with the laptop tucked under arm. Several shots came back their way, but they were fired by people in retreat and didn't come close.

The barrel of the gun spit bullets at an alarming rate as Dale kept his finger pinned to the trigger. He hoisted his bad foot as he shuffle-stepped as fast as he could across the carpet. He aimed for the elevator at the far end of the floor, but knew it was a long shot.

Lauren swung her body around as she retreated with Dale. She remembered something her mom used to tell her about a woman's place in the world. It seemed like an excuse for how she felt her own daughter must see her—as a spoiled rich wife attending gallery openings and well-orchestrated charity events meant to give the appearance of social do-gooding while keeping the patrons hermetically sealed away from the true blight of the issue they were raising money for.

Lauren remembered her words as she back pedaled behind Dale, swinging her gun side to side hoping not to have to use it. Her mom told her a woman's work often goes unseen. After all, remember Lauren, Ginger Rogers matched every step Fred Astaire did, only she did it backwards and in high heels.

To her right, a woman stood from behind a desk. She popped up like a creature in a haunted house and fired a shot at Lauren almost point blank. The bullet passed Lauren so close her hair puffed out like a hummingbird had flown by. Lauren spun without thinking and fired a return shot. The secretary stiffened, her face went slack and Lauren saw the burst of red in her chest. The woman slumped and fell back into hiding behind the desk, but Lauren knew she wouldn't be coming out again.

God dammit. Killing did not get any easier the more she did it. Lauren felt that the building and the people she killed would be with her forever, provided forever was more than the next sweep around of the second hand. She'd taken lives, something never in her life plan. The faces would haunt her, even if they were devoid of detail. Blank skin over nondescript human-shaped forms who would crawl around in her brain and wait for a moment when she didn't remember. A tiny respite when her actions had faded away. They would be there quickly to crawl through her brain and loose the memory again from slumber.

She would never forget, and yet, what choice did she have? Someone shoots at you, someone evil, you shoot back. Its primate logic played out with all-too-human tools.

Dale saw the kitchen and angled for it. His clip ran out, the gun clicking a rapid empty sound as his finger still clamped down on the trigger. He thumbed the release, let the empty clip drop, and reached into his belt for the new one.

Four rapid shots shattered glass next to Dale. He turned to see one of the manager types inside an office, but one with no walls, only shards of falling tempered glass. The manager held a black pistol at arm's length and fired two more shots. Dale felt the air move as they went past. He banged the heel of his hand on the new clip and rammed it home, turned the gun on the manager, and let him see the barrel and the sight trained on his chest.

The manager dove for the floor, sliding among the bed of glass to hide. Dale turned the gun away and kept moving for the kitchen.

White floor tile ran the length of the narrow room. A fridge, double sinks, coffee maker, microwave, juicer, and a wide array of snacks and fresh fruit awaited him. At the end of the counters stood the silver doors of a freight elevator.

Dale turned and upended a desk nearby, slinging the gun over his shoulder as he toppled the black rectangle. Lauren reached him and he pushed her inside the kitchen as he slid the desk to cover the doorway. Bullets clipped the wall and exploded a thermostat. A ficus tree in a wicker basket took a bullet and slumped forward on a broken trunk.

"Press the button." Dale pointed to the elevator. Lauren followed his command, cradling the laptop like a football in her arm. Dale stood at the overturned desk and felt like Rambo as he laid down a wide arc of suppressing fire. This time he shot high, taking out an exit sign, the last of two glass walls on this end of the floor, and several ceiling tiles. Workers dove for cover and burrowed in place until the shooting stopped. Soldiers, maybe, but quick to retreat, luckily.

"Come on." Dale turned to see Lauren waving him in to the open elevator. She stood with her hip against the door to keep it open. She looked like a Navy Seal. If this ordeal hadn't reignited a love for his wife, he'd have fallen for her there with a gun in her hand and a command in her voice.

He turned and ran. When his firing stopped, several bullets followed him into the kitchen. As he hopped on one foot, then pushed forward with the other, shots took out a trio of bananas, a selection of teas and several boxes of cereal.

Dale reached the elevator and spun to face out as Lauren slid inside and reached for the button. There was only one, marked with a K.

Dale hoped the next stop came with friendlier natives.

CHAPTER 27

O'Brien rarely came to the staffers' floor, by design. Make them come to you. Slumming it in their cramped offices was a sign of weakness. They weren't that important for him to come down two flights of stairs. All eyes were on him as people watched him march with laser focus to Lewis' office.

Lewis' secretary, a bright-eyed girl named Dianne, started to say something but noticed quickly that Mayor O'Brien wasn't going to stop and ask permission to enter Lewis' office.

She called to his back. "Go right in, sir."

O'Brien entered his chief of staff's office for the first time in over a year. It looked like his own office in three-quarters scale. Lewis had plans to move up a few floors, it was easy to see.

"Call it off."

Lewis rushed off the phone without a goodbye, slamming the receiver down like a husband caught talking to a girlfriend. "Sir? What brings you down here?"

"Call it off, I said." O'Brien reached the edge of Lewis' desk and loomed over.

"That's..." Lewis checked the door. Still open from O'Brien's flamboyant entrance. Lewis stood and walked to close it. "I can't do that."

"You did it, you can undo it."

Lewis shut the door. "No, sir. *You* did it."

O'Brien puffed up his chest, not wanting any of Lewis' tricks. "You know what I mean."

"I do, Mr. Mayor. And I know Roy won't change any plans on my phone call. It has to be you."

"So give me his number."

Lewis stood in the center of the room, two men as equals. The mayor was in *his* space now and he owned it the way a spider hangs proudly in the center of a newly spun web. Lewis didn't answer.

O'Brien took a step forward. "Give me his number so I can call it off."

"Changed your mind, did you?"

O'Brien swallowed. He didn't seem to like the tone in Lewis' voice. "Yes, I did."

"Guilty conscience?"

A stiff finger came out from O'Brien's clenched fist, waved in emphasis at his subordinate. "Just give me the goddamn num—"

"No."

The finger hung between them, impotent in Lewis' face. O'Brien lifted his chest as he breathed heavy. Lewis stood perfectly still. O'Brien dropped his hand, lifted it again, then let it fall to his side.

Lewis became calmer the more frantic the mayor became. "It was the right call, sir."

"You don't understand—"

"Apparently you don't understand, *Mister* Mayor." Lewis raised his tone in volume and in hardness. His feet stayed set in place and he wished for another few inches so he could stand taller than the mayor, a space he always felt he should occupy. "She'll ruin us."

There it was, thought O'Brien. *Us*, not me. This wasn't about preserving the current office, it was about protecting his chance to sit behind the desk upstairs. A derailment of this administration meant Lewis would never work in politics again, not after the revelations came out. Lewis' own kickbacks, while only a fraction of the mayor's, would come to light and not only would those relationships be ruined, meaning losing out on millions of revenue from his future term in office, but he would be drummed out of town by an angry constituency and most likely spend some token time in prison while O'Brien lived out his exile under house arrest in his four-thousand-square-foot lake home.

O'Brien dropped his voice low. "It's my daughter."

"She's a liability."

"She's a person, God damn you."

Lewis took a step forward. "She's a threat."

O'Brien could feel his cheeks flushing and his ears grow hot with blood pumping through from the angry beats of his heart. If this young bastard in front of him didn't make this stop, he might as well be pulling the trigger.

He saw the punch land on Lewis' chin before he even knew he'd thrown it. Lewis staggered back, caught completely unaware by the mayor's fist. Once he'd started, O'Brien felt like he was back in the Navy, taking swings on the deck of the USS Stennis.

He chased Lewis as he fell away and swung hard with a left, catching only Lewis' shoulder. It had been years since he'd thrown a punch and already his knuckles ached. O'Brien wasn't sure he'd ever hit anyone bare knuckled.

Lewis jerked up and raised his hands in defense. He ended up looking like a boxer from the twenties ready to engage in fisticuffs over the virtue of a lady. He rolled his fists around like he was kneading salt water taffy. O'Brien launched a jab in between the youngster's hands and hit him in the sternum.

A pained wheeze escaped Lewis' lungs. O'Brien knew the feeling and knew it hurt. He moved in and shoved Lewis to the floor, trying to spare his knuckles any more abuse.

"Give me Roy's number, you son of a bitch."

Lewis gained half a lungful of breath. "I guess I'm fired, huh?"

"You're damn right."

"Well, then..." Lewis scissored his legs while doing a spin on his back. O'Brien's legs went out from under him and he crashed to the floor. Lewis pounced on his boss' back. Right away O'Brien could tell Lewis had done some high school wrestling. That Greco-Roman grappling crap always rubbed O'Brien the wrong way. If you're going to fight someone, stand up and fight them. Don't give them a hug and wait for someone to count to three.

O'Brien rolled and slid out from Lewis' grasp. The sleeve of his jacket tore as he went. He shifted his wingtips under him and got into a crouch. O'Brien waited for Lewis to do the same. When Lewis had his feet set, O'Brien lunged forward and tackled him. They banged into a leather chair and it rocketed into a set of bookshelves lining the wall. A cascade of leather-bound editions fell to the floor.

O'Brien stood quickly and landed another punch to Lewis' jaw before the kid had time to stand up.

Behind them, Dianne opened the door. "Is everything all right in here?"

She blanched and put a hand over her mouth. She stood, one hand on the doorknob, and watched as Mayor O'Brien punched Lewis in the stomach.

"Oh my God." Dianne looked back to her desk as if she might break for the phone, but she stayed in the doorway.

O'Brien leaned in to Lewis, who slumped against the bookcase, both men out of breath. "Are you going to help me call this off?"

Lewis ran a tongue across cracked and bloody lips. "Fuck you."

The mayor turned to Dianne. "He's fired. Get security up here to take him out. And call my car for me, tell them to meet me downstairs in three minutes." He picked up a book that had fallen off the shelf, a volume of city ordinances that looked as if it had never been opened. "Got that?"

Dianne nodded. "Yes, sir."

O'Brien cracked Lewis across the cheek with the hard spine of the book.

CHAPTER 28

The bodies hadn't been moved.

"No need for you to see this, Momma." Tat turned his mother away from the sight of the men sprawled on the floor of their dorms, dead only an hour now and already stiff as the wood floors they lay on. "Take her back to her room."

One of Tat's six men stepped out of the small crowd to escort Esmerelda downstairs.

"What are you gonna do about it?" Tat's mother stood firm, jerking her arm away from the man trying to help her out.

"I'll take care of it, Momma."

"How?"

Tat was annoyed, but never rose to the level of anger with his mother. "So that it never happens again."

"That's right." Esmerelda crossed her arms and nodded once for emphasis.

"Now will you trust me to take care of this and go back to your apartment?"

"I suppose so." She uncrossed her arms and set a hand on her son's shoulder. "You take care of yourself now."

"I will, Momma." Some leaders would never let their militia men see a tender side like Tat held for his mother, but he wasn't shy about it. He kissed her forehead and she walked out on the arm of a six-foot Samoan boy.

When she had gone, Tat looked back down at the wreckage in front of him. Bodies on both sides of the hallway. Loyal men.

ALL THE WAY DOWN

* * *

The men had come once Esmerelda went upstairs to get them. As Tat suspected, they were huddled and waiting for orders, but terrified to breech the sanctity of Tat's residential floor. With Esmerelda's blessing, the men came to the rescue.

First order of business was to reset Tat's arms. One man split off and untied Tat's girlfriend from her shirtless binding in the living room. Tat ordered her taken away as he lay on the floor waiting for one of the heftier men to stand over him, lift his arm, twist it slightly, then pull up sharply until it slid back into joint with a pop.

The heavy blocks of ink on Tat's arms twisted under the big man's grip as the second arm was reset. Tat grunted like an animal but stood right away and got down to business despite the ache in his shoulders. His mom nodded slowly, approving her son's tolerance to pain. They both knew if he'd started crying she would have been quick to tell him to be quiet or else go put on a dress.

Now, patched up to tolerable and staring at a floor full of bodies, Tat was eager to get down to the business of vengeance.

"The mayor wants a war, we'll give him a war." He clenched his unwounded hand into a fist. "The police want a war, we'll give them a war." Tat turned to his small assemblage of men, his last troops. He held his fist out in front of him, then lifted his injured hand, curled his fingers down into a fist over the crude wrapping of the hole in his hand. The pain twisted his features and a fresh flow of blood oozed out from his clenched fist. The other men fed off flowing endorphins watching their leader endure such pain in the name of vengeance.

"Anyone who wants a war, we'll give it to them."

CHAPTER 29

The empty warehouse threw a shadow onto the car. Somewhere in an alley beyond, a bottle broke. Dahlia stood looking at the state of her abandonment and was no closer to coming up with a solution. With T dead she had no way of getting to wherever he was taking her—presumably where Dale would be and she could get both answers and protection.

Alone and with the clock running, Dahlia again thought of her appointment. No way to make it now. Not with so much else to do. That was on the off chance the baby was still alive inside her after the crazy day she'd been having.

The resolve—or was it resignation?—she possessed that morning had vanished. In the face of all evidence telling her she shouldn't bring a child into the world because of more factors than she could count, she reached for the notion that maybe this was a sign.

Dahlia wasn't usually one of those everything-happens-for-a-reason type people, but her day was enough to convert anyone. When she saw the car pulling slowly to a stop behind her, the initial thought was that a kind Samaritan had stopped to help a woman in need. Now how the hell was she going to explain the dead body?

A man got out from the driver's side with a phone pressed to his ear. Olive skinned and muscled, he wore a tight black T-shirt and buzz cut hair. He moved slowly and eyed her skeptically, she thought. Then Dahlia remembered the gun in her hand. She tucked it behind her, but before she could call out to her rescuer to explain, a chirping sounded from inside the car and at first, she thought maybe a bird had been trapped.

She looked inside and a cell phone vibrated its way out of T's pocket, the chirp gaining volume when it cleared the cloth dampers on the sound. She looked from the phone to the man in the new car, then to the two other men getting out of the passenger side. Both clones of the first and, now that she looked at them, all three were subtle versions of T.

Everything clicked into place. These weren't saviors—they were more kidnappers. T must have been on the phone with backup when he rolled up on her with the crashed car and Pooch dead in the front seat. Then what? They must have tracked him with his cell phone signal. They can do that, right? Leave it to Dahlia to get mixed up with high-tech gangsters. Most likely it was something any kid with an iPad could do in ten seconds, but to Dahlia, checking her email sometimes made her feel as satisfied as a Russian hacker who brings down the US military mainframe.

The calm pause she'd been experiencing by the side of the road shattered into panic and frantic, empty-fisted hunts for a plan. The man hung up the phone and put it in his pocket. He reached behind him and Dahlia knew he was going for a gun.

"Stop right there." To her shock, he did. The other two men stood on guard. All three seemed to respect the gun in her hand, even though she still had it pointed at the ground. Synapses fired in her brain and somehow made the connection that they were going to take her hostage, and to counteract that, she needed a hostage. In the absence of any other plan, she aimed the gun into the car.

"I'll shoot him."

She watched as the three men strained to get a good look inside the car where T slumped dead in the passenger seat.

"Yo, T, you all right, man?"

Dahlia cut off any potential answer. "He won't be if you don't back off." Now she was committed. She had to up the ante.

Dahlia had read about those women who lift a burning car off their child with some untapped reserve of strength only the threat of death gives you, but she never knew what it felt like until right then. Surging with a cocktail of adrenalin and fear blasting through her bloodstream, a mixture that would render heroin and cocaine obsolete if you could crystalize it and sell it on the streets, she reached in and put and arm under T and hauled him up next to her. She did her best to make him look as alive as possible, but she knew it was a losing battle.

"I already knocked the shit out of him. Don't make me finish the job. Guns on the ground."

The three men looked skeptically at her puppet show. Dahlia knew she was losing the crowd.

"Fine. I warned you."

She did it before she could think too hard about it. She did it with the same mindset her grandmother had talked about having when she walked her through the steps of beheading a chicken for dinner. She did it to save her own life.

Dahlia put the gun to T's temple and fired. She let go as she shot and he fell like the dead weight he was. A spray of blood and bone coated the car, but Dahlia was too busy clutching at her ear from the incredibly loud noise of the blast.

The three men all jumped at the shot and stared in wonder as their comrade fell to the street with half a head. Who was this crazy bitch?

Dahlia shook off the ringing in her ears and tried to ignore that warm sticky stuff on her cheek. She raised the gun to them. "Drop them."

One of the passengers was first to comply. He set his gun down and kept his hands up and gave her what Dahlia could only describe as a don't-shoot-my-head-off look. She took two steps forward and the other two men set down their guns.

A looping refrain of *this is working, this is working, this is working* played in her head as she walked over to the car. She went to the driver, stopped five feet away from him to protect against any anxious grabs for her gun, and gave the orders.

"Take me to your boss. That's where he was supposed to take me. The man wants to see me? So let's see him."

She tried not to get too frustrated that all this effort had been spent trying to avoid going to see this mystery man and now she was hijacking a car to get there, but the hope that Dale would be there made it a risk worth taking. She couldn't trust anyone else, and the thought surprised her as much as anything all day long.

The driver got back behind the wheel. She aimed the gun at the other two men still standing in the street and she got in the back behind the driver like she was taking a casual cab to the airport.

Once in, she made sure he knew the gun was pointed at the base of his skull. *Good God*, she thought, *What the fear of dying will make you do.*

"Get going."

"Lady—"

"I said, get going."

"I'm just telling you for your own good, you can't roll up to Tat's place with a gun waving around. We won't get a hundred feet from there."

"Then we'll get two hundred feet and you'll call him. You like making phone calls, right?"

He sighed. "It's your funeral."

"Y'know, this morning I'd have thought so too. But I'm starting to think I've got nine lives. I may have used up five or six of them, but as long as I have more to go, I'm going to find out what the hell this is all about and what it has to do with my husband."

He dropped the car in gear and they drove off, leaving two stranded thugs with T's corpse. When they were beyond the sight of the two men left behind, and with the driver's back to her, Dahlia frantically wiped at her face to remove the wet, slightly viscous mess on her cheek. She pawed with her sleeve pulled down over her palm to clear away blood that was not hers. Her breath came out in huffed panting and somehow, she held back tears.

3RD FLOOR

The ride down was short. One floor. The elevator bumped to a stop and Dale pushed himself against the back wall, giving enough space to raise the machine gun in front of him. Lauren clung to the side wall, using the eighteen inches of protection the sides of the elevator offered.

On the ride down she had time to explain the floor they were entering was the kitchen. A central hub for the entire complex catering three meals a day to the entire staff. Since they were so far out of town, and since coming and going from the secure location was a chore and a potential breech of security, Tat provided all meals complimentary. He even imported a chef from Guam to cook special dishes for his mother to make her feel at home.

But after the gunfight upstairs, Dale didn't even trust a room full of cooks and dishwashers.

No bell dinged as the doors opened. Dale was ready for a fight. What he got was a nose full of garlic and the humid air of a long galley kitchen filled with bubbling pots and sizzling pans.

Four men in white chef's jackets stared back at him. The elevator, a service-only lift to bring meals up to the office staff, was tucked in the far corner of the floor. Crates of vegetables and bags of linens waiting to go out the laundry nearly blocked the elevator door.

The men stared blankly. One heavyset man held a squash in his hand he was midway through peeling.

Dale called out to the men. "This elevator go all the way to the ground floor?"

Three of them shook their heads. Only the heavyset one answered. Must be the head chef. "Only up and down between here and four. Deliveries only."

The doors began their automated close and Dale stepped forward, poking the gun in between the closing doors. They sprang open again and he stepped into the large kitchen area. Lauren followed.

"We thought we heard shooting." The heavyset man seemed to be their spokesperson. Two more heads poked around a corner farther into the kitchen.

"We're not looking for any trouble." Dale seemed to have appointed himself spokesperson for his side of the conversation.

"Then you shouldn't have come here."

In each man's hand a knife appeared. Except for the heavyset man. He held a cleaver.

Dale sighed and let his shoulders slump. "We don't want to hurt anyone. We just want to leave."

Lauren checked her grip on the gun in her hand, tightened her arm around the laptop. "He's right. We don't want to hurt you."

The group looked to the heavyset man and he turned his head first left, then right. Behind Dale and Lauren, the elevator doors closed, sealing off any escape; though back up to the fourth floor would hardly be a safe zone.

The heavyset man screamed something in a language Dale didn't understand and the fight was on. Six men in matching outfits came at them with knives meant for cutting meat, separating flesh from bone, cleaving ribs apart.

Dale dodged to the left, lining himself up with a long row of stovetops and ovens. Large pots boiled water ready to accept lobsters or corn cobs. Pans sautéed sauces, onions, and garlic. Two men were headed down the line toward him. Dale didn't want to shoot. He didn't want any more blood spilled by men who were just a part of the machine of Tat's business.

He took aim at a large pot of boiling water. He fired a quick burst and the pot exploded off the stove, toppling over and sending scalding hot water and a dozen small, grenade-sized potatoes spilling out to land like hot little land mines in the path of the approaching chef assassins.

The front man veered off course to avoid the waterfall of boiling water. The man behind him stepped on a potato and sipped on the soft flesh, landing hard on his ass in a pool of still bubbling water. The front man was distracted enough that Dale could step forward and plant the butt of his machine gun on the man's chin. His head spun, his neck rocketing around, and he was out cold before he hit the floor. *Sorry about that, buddy. Better than being dead though*, Dale thought.

Lauren faced down two chefs of her own, including the heavyset man and his cleaver. He charged and by instinct, she tried to block him using the only shield she had—the laptop. Holding it out in front of her, she felt the cleaver sink in and saw the sharp angle of the cleaver's tip break through the casing. The chef yanked his arm back for another swing and took the computer with him, jerking it out of Lauren's hands. She watched it go—all her evidence, the whole reason she was there. The lives lost because of it, Tyler and the others.

A searing rage rose inside of her. She noticed she stood next to a wire mesh supply rack. Four shelves of tools for cooking a meal for a whole building. Ignoring her gun, she reached over and picked up a small saucepan. She flung it at the heavyset man. He deflected it away with a swipe of his cleaver, now free from the destroyed laptop. It rang high pitched, like two swords coming together.

Lauren picked up another one, flung it, and saw it fly across the room as it got swatted away. She succeeded in slowing the progress of the men coming toward her, but eventually they would be close enough to swipe at her with those sharp objects.

She didn't want to shoot them. Didn't want to kill anyone else after the torment she felt with Tyler. She searched the shelf for other potential weapons. She put a hand on a carrot peeler but lifted it off when she saw a small set of paring knives. Tiny knives in varying shapes with different color handles. They were miniatures compared to the eight- and ten-inch carving knives the chefs wielded, but they were better than nothing—and better than more saucepans.

She lifted one out of the small case. She thought of throwing darts with her nanny when she was younger. How much harder than that could it be?

Lauren held the knife like a dart from her youth and let it fly at the heavyset man. The tiny weapon landed soundlessly in the meat of his upper thigh. He screamed as the sting of a hundred wasps all bore into his leg at once. The heavyset man went down in front of his troops. They were blocked in the narrow aisle, but they also saw their captain down, and the only place more loyal to their commander than the army was the line in a kitchen. Two men were quickly at his side.

Dale limped past the stoves, heat from the blue gas flames of the burners warming one side of his body. He heard a cry of pain from the other side of the room, but it was male so he knew Lauren was still with him.

Another chef turned into his aisle. The man brandished a ten-inch butcher's knife, freshly used and still dripping with meat juices. The chefs seemed undeterred by the machine gun in Dale's hands. He charged and raised the knife over his head ready to slash down and cut Dale in two.

Dale's finger brushed the trigger. It would be so easy to blow this guy away. Might even scare the others into giving up their knives. But with each body in his wake, his chances of leniency shrunk. Whether they wanted to believe him or not, Dale really was trying not to hurt anyone. Perhaps it was the cages of the sad-eyed whores, but he'd gone off killing if he could possibly avoid it. It was looking less likely he could and still ensure his and Lauren's survival.

He had time to spin the gun in his hands and punch the butt into the chef's gut. He gasped and blew out air. His arm, high up next to his right ear, froze in place and his finger slackened. The knife fell. Dale braced for the pain, but it never came; even after he heard the dull *thunk* of the knife tip burying itself in the rubber mat on the floor.

Dale looked down and saw the knife poised, tip down, in the space left vacant by his missing big toe. Had it been there still, he'd have lost it to a clean sever. Either way, it was still gone, and this time it saved him, rather than caused, a great deal of pain.

Lauren put the gun in her waistband and held four short knives in her hands now. One with a red handle was poised between her fingers like she was aiming for a bull's eye in the local pub.

One of the chefs hovering over the heavyset man stood and focused a deep anger toward Lauren. She didn't wait for an invitation, she flung the knife away from her. It landed in the tennis-ball-sized muscle of his triceps. He shrieked and went down.

Lauren almost smiled to herself. She had no idea she had a talent for knife throwing. She vowed that when she got out of this, she'd buy another dart board and start playing again.

She grabbed up two more knives in her hand and dashed forward. The one man still standing broke and ran away from her. She flung a knife at him while in stride and it nicked the back of the man's neck, then fell harmlessly away. Lauren vaulted herself over the heavyset man and moved on past the prep stations and warming lamps.

Only one man remained in Dale's way. The chef stood, recovering from the body blow, and filled the pathway to freedom on the other side. Dale drew back the butt of his gun to pound the man in the gut again in hopes he'd go down for good. The chef lifted a foot as if to block the gun, but instead brought it down on the handle of a pan sizzling on the stove. His foot levered the hot pan up and an arc of boiling hot oil and browning garlic flew through the air.

Dale barely had time to pull his body back. He turned his shoulders and watched the hot oil curve through the air and land with a splash on the man who'd slipped on the potato. The man shrieked in pain as Dale felt his back grow hot and realized he'd put himself up against one of the stoves licking the air with blue flames. Dale pulled away, but the heat didn't go down. His back got hotter.

He spun in half circles, trying to see his own back. He saw enough—a glow of orange and a rush of air and flickering flame whenever he spun his body. Dale was on fire.

Kindergarten lessons played in his head. Stop, drop, and roll. Dale hit the floor. He spun his body in a barrel roll and went up and over the man agonizing in pain after the hot oil spill. Dale rolled until he came to the feet of the man who flung the pan at him. Dale kept rolling and took the man's knees out from under him. He fell in front of Dale, making a speed bump for him to get over.

Dale rolled up and over the man as he reached out for Dale but readjusted his arms to swat at the licking flames that moved from Dale's back to the front of his shirt. Dale reached the other end of his roadblock and fell still, a burnt cotton smell coming off his back and the heat of an intense sunburn on his skin. The fire was out though and Dale stood.

He turned to see the three men in his wake. None of them stood to follow. They'd done their duty, enough was enough. Let the guys who get paid for security handle it from here. Dale turned to the far end of the kitchen, to the exit.

Lauren was waiting there for him. "Come on, hurry it up."

Dale limped quickly along to her, a trail of smoke in his wake.

CHAPTER 30

The official car of the mayor's office was American made, of course. O'Brien pushed the engine up to sixty. He knew the way to Tat's compound, though he'd only set foot inside once. He was summoned as a candidate and was told the election could be his if he played ball with Tat. When he asked how Tat could deliver on such a promise, he was told, "I think it's better if you don't know."

It was a philosophy that served him well for six years in office.

He never went to collect money from the drug lords and mafia types he accepted payments from. He barely knew names. He always found out so-and-so or what's-his-name was dead months after it happened. Better that way. It kept the graft at a distance, made it unreal.

He'd never met Roy before, truly had no idea what other jobs he'd done on O'Brien's behalf. But now, putting a face to the crimes, peeking behind the curtain made it all too real. And now that his daughter stood in the crosshairs…it became too much.

The not knowing was the worst. There was a chance Lauren was already free and in Chief Schuster's custody and protection. No one had called to inform him, but there would be a debriefing with Lauren and the cop who went in to get her. And no way Schuster would let anyone else make the call. That guy loved all the credit he could get, deserved or not.

Or, O'Brien thought, he could have waffled just one minute too long. Could have been indecisive for the split second it took for Roy to fire a shot. She could be coming out of the building right then, and he'd be too late because he couldn't make up his mind on such a stupid decision. You don't order your own daughter killed. He saw it now the way any sane, rational person would. Temporary insanity, that's what it was. The only explanation.

He urged the car up to sixty-five.

CHAPTER 31

The fourth floor was abuzz. Several of the managers wanted to follow the two intruders down the service elevator into the kitchen. The cooler heads of the secretaries prevailed.

"He had a machine gun."

"They'll handle them down there."

"We followed protocol. Now we sit tight."

Everyone agreed they never thought they'd have to use the guns provided to them. Some even confessed they forgot where the firearms were stashed in their offices. But everyone agreed they were glad to have had them. A small group gathered around Tyler's office, shaking their heads and wondering what his connection to the woman had been.

The chatter stopped on one end of the floor and quickly spread like a fog oozing through the office to silence everything. Mr. Losopo was on the fourth floor.

The office workers stopped and stared as Tat walked point with six security guards fanned out in a V behind him. Everyone looked at his hand, which hung uncovered at his side, a messy hole in the center of it. He looked like a general who'd been through war, and the men following him were poised to march back into battle.

"He's been here?" Tat asked the question to the room, not to anyone in particular.

Several people nodded. One woman spoke. "There was a girl, too."

"Still with him, huh? Anyone hurt?"

Several people turned their heads to Tyler's office. Tat nodded, seemed to think a casualty rate that low was acceptable. Tat surveyed the ceiling damage. "Lousy shot, huh?"

"I don't think he was trying to shoot us." The secretary behind the desk where Dale used the phone cast her eyes down, regretting speaking out.

Tat looked at her. "No?"

"I think it was just supposed to scare us."

Tat looked around at the shattered glass and bullet casings on the floor. "And were you scared?"

"We all fought back. Just like it says in the book."

"Good, good." Tat didn't smile. He couldn't, didn't think he was capable for the near future. "They went down?"

The secretary nodded.

Tat waved his guards to follow him. "Then we go down."

STILL ON THE 3RD FLOOR

The elevator made no sound when it opened. Tat and his six men saw the carnage. Men in white chef's jackets writhed on the floor, two had knives stuck in them. One held both hands over his face, crying and saying, "I'm burned. I'm burned."

At least the trail was easy to follow with these two.

Tat looked up first and saw Dale and Lauren at the far end of the floor.

"Burnett! You bring her back to me."

The six henchmen all came to attention, guns leapt to the ends of outstretched arms. They could barely hear from the far end of the space, but it sounded like Dale cursed. "Fuck me."

A bunch of chefs and office drones they could handle—barely—but Tat's right-hand men? Not a chance.

"Go down. Now."

Dale shoved Lauren toward the elevator doors, the open shaft beyond them. She slapped both palms against them in a stance like she was about to be frisked. "Down?"

"It's the only way. C'mon, help me open this."

Dale began prying at the doors, Lauren slid her fingers between the two brushed aluminum doors and together they pried them open. The black pit of the elevator shaft welcomed them back.

Lauren looked at Dale, his foot, the smoke curling from his

back. "Can you do this?"

"It's this or die, and we've come too far." He put a hand on her back. "You go first."

"Why, so you can fall on me?"

"No, so I can—"

The first shots ripped into the walls beside them. Dale spun and raised the machine gun. He squeezed the trigger and a quick burst of shells sprayed in the direction of the kitchen. Bullets pinged off metal racks and counters. The men racing toward them dove for cover, buying a few seconds more.

"So I can do that. Now, go."

Lauren knew there was no time for the slow climb from before. She also knew that Elton couldn't keep his grip on the cables. The only thing giving her the courage to jump was that it wasn't as far of a fall now. As the bullets began flying again, Lauren leaped and grabbed the cables in both fists. She gripped a bundle of three thick cables, wet with grease. She slid down immediately and had to pinch hard with her legs to slow her fall. She hoped that would be the only echo of Elton's attempt at the cables.

She looked up and saw Dale backing into the shaft. He fired a fast burst of cover fire, then turned and hesitated a second. Lauren slid down a few feet, giving him room enough to jump. She braced herself for him to slide down and land on her head. She made a quick glance down, hoping to see bottom, but saw only darkness.

"Do it, Dale. Go."

Using his good foot to push off, he jumped. The machine gun was slung over his shoulder and he reached with both hands. While he was in the air, bullets cracked around the elevator doors, ricocheting off the metal and sending echoes up the shaft into the black.

Dale bear hugged the cluster of cables and hung on. He didn't slip onto Lauren's head.

"Okay, good, let's go before they get here."

Lauren started a semi-controlled slide down the cables. She'd slip four or five feet, have to pinch her whole body tight to stop herself, then repeat. Slowly the light around her disappeared and she slid into darkness.

Dale loosened his grip, then tightened back up a second later. He bobbed down in eight-inch increments. Not enough to be gone by the time they got to the open doors.

"I can't see you. I don't want to land on you."

Lauren called from the darkness below. "You're fine. Just keep coming down. If they shoot you, you'll fall for sure."

Motivation enough. Dale started sliding down a few feet at a time, then gripping the cables to stop. His clothes were getting slick with grease, his hands could barely grab hold. He knew exactly how Elton had died. He tried to hang on with one hand and wipe the palm of his other down the ungreased side of his pants, but it only helped for a moment.

Dale heard footsteps, then Tat's voice. "You can't get away from me, you fucks. You shot me. You stole my property." Tat's face appeared, leaning beyond the precipice of the third floor. "You hit my mother."

A fierce-looking gun appeared in his hand and aimed at Dale who was ten feet down, but still lit up by the light spilling into the shaft. He had one option and he wasn't sure it was a good one.

Dale unslung the machine gun from his shoulder and slid his hand over the grip. Already his other hand slipped on the cables, inches at first. He began firing as his slide down picked up pace. Falling away into darkness Dale emptied the clip at the open door. One man slumped and fell, his head and arm hanging over the edge. The rest of them, and Tat, pulled back for cover. Dale's shots pounded into the doorframe, the ceiling outside the door, the walls of the shaft. He was spraying bullets as he slid backward in a controlled fall.

He hadn't realized it, but he was screaming while he fell. A war cry he'd never heard before from some place primal inside him. He fell away from the light spilling in to the shaft and all details of his body were swallowed by darkness. Only the orange flashes of his gun lit the walls of the shaft.

The scream ended when he ran out of bullets, which he did at the same time he landed on Lauren's head.

CHAPTER 32

"Last chance, lady. You sure you want to do this?"

Dahlia wasn't sure at all. All she knew was that for some reason, she needed to see Dale. She needed the protection of her husband. She'd taken it for granted, him being a cop. She hadn't realized how much she depended on it.

It wasn't the guns, or the extra patrols the local uniformed guys did around their street at night. It was Dale. He was a protector. He enjoyed it. And she felt safe. So safe she started to ignore it.

When he fell silent, went on his weird jags of not communicating, she decided two could play at that game. She mimicked him, unconsciously. They'd forgotten all the things that brought them together, and now she wanted it back.

Dahlia set a hand on her stomach. She knew she'd need to reschedule the appointment, and still felt fairly sure it was the choice she was going to stick with. But it was the other reason she needed to see Dale. To know for sure.

She'd made the choice without him. Her body, her choice. She didn't feel like the argument, either. But she never looked him in the eye and thought the thought. *You're going to end this baby. His baby. Our baby.*

She needed to see him and then she'd know. And maybe then he could explain all this craziness.

Her knees were propped up on the seat in front of her. The driver surely felt them dig into his back. Dahlia kept her head hunched down into her shoulders like a moody teenager getting a ride from Mom to the mall, only with a gun.

"Yeah." She sat up straight in the seat. "I'm sure I want to do this."

CHAPTER 33

The city slid past and into the rearview. O'Brien crossed out of city limits and into a fringe land as lawless as the Wild West, because he allowed it to be so. Whoever made up the expression "crime doesn't pay" surely meant it to apply to the criminals. They obviously had no idea how well crime paid for the officials who kept it in business.

He checked the dashboard clock again. Same time as his last glance. The digital numbers hadn't even clicked over yet, so frequent were his compulsive time checks. Seconds counted in the life of his daughter.

O'Brien composed the first draft of a resignation speech in his head. He'd have to keep this one for himself, the speechwriters could stay out of it. Made him realize how shitty he was at writing speeches.

Maybe he'd do it through the media. Line up some exclusive interview with a TV anchor and let them film the train wreck. But no, that would undercut Lauren's story. And if anything good could come out of this, at least he could give his daughter a leg up in the journalism world. She was pretty enough for cable news, opinionated enough for sure.

A dip in the road sank the shocks almost to the pavement as he rocketed along. No radio, no distractions. A time check. One minute had passed. O'Brien hoped it wasn't one minute too long.

A whoop of sirens sounded behind him. He checked the rearview and saw a police car with lights on. He checked the speedometer. Seventy-two. He hadn't looked, but no way this road was more than a forty-five speed limit. He slowed.

The car idled on the shoulder, the engine panting deeply after such a workout. The damn cop was taking his sweet time getting to the window. When he did, O'Brien already had it rolled down and turned his face to the officer, offering himself up as his own ID.

"License and—" The officer stopped. He took at the sight of the city's mayor behind the wheel, let it process, then dropped his tough guy behind the badge stance. "Sir?"

"Yes. I'm sorry Officer..." The man's badge read Burkes. "Burkes. I'm in a bit of a hurry."

"Yes, sir. You were speeding."

"I know and I'm sorry. Official business though."

Burkes shifted on his feet. "You were going really fast though, sir." He sniffed the air by habit as he leaned in to rest an elbow on the window frame. He got a whiff of what he didn't want. Alcohol. The stress pushed sweat out of O'Brien and it carried the stink of his slow but steady visits to the in-office bar that morning.

"We can discuss this with Chief Schuster together, but tomorrow. I really need to get somewhere now."

"Where are you headed to, sir?"

O'Brien balked. He couldn't explain. Didn't feel he needed to, and God dammit this was taking too long. "Look, Burkes, I don't want to pull rank or anything—"

"Have you been drinking today, sir?"

Son of a bitch. This guy...

"Son, you really don't want to do this."

The thing O'Brien didn't know about Officer Burkes, the thing he wanted least of all in the cop who pulled him over, was that Burkes was a third-generation cop. A rule follower. A by-the-books man.

Burkes pulled on the door handle and the door opened. "I need you to step out of the vehicle, Mr. Mayor."

O'Brien sighed and put his face in his cupped hands. "You don't understand."

"I need to administer a field sobriety test, sir. If you pass it, I'll let the speeding go. Please step out."

O'Brien unbuckled his seat belt. He felt Lauren slipping away. He put a foot out onto the gravel of the soft shoulder. He saw Roy aiming a rifle at his daughter, the crosshairs fixed between her eyes. He stood up and watched Burkes square off against him the way he would with any drunk who came down his stretch of road. He watched Lauren fall, her lovely face a smear of red and her hair floating behind her in blonde and blood streaks.

He whispered, "My daughter."

"What's that, sir?"

How could this kid understand? And if he explained, wouldn't the cop be obligated to run him in for a host of other offenses? A drunk driving rap would be a footnote at the bottom of the report.

"Sir, please stand with your feet together and your arms outstretched like this. I'm gonna need you to touch your nose with the tip of your index finger like so."

Burkes demonstrated what he wanted. He went from his Jesus on the cross pose to touching his nose first with one finger and then got half way to touching his nose with the other when O'Brien hit him.

O'Brien nearly fell over on top of the cop as he tipped forward after his haymaker shot to Burkes' chin. He missed most of the punch but landed enough so the cop fell backward. O'Brien straightened and looked at his fist like he'd only just found it there at the end of his arm. Had he really punched a cop?

He had, and there was no coming back from that now. O'Brien dove to the ground and on top of Burkes. He wrestled the gun off his belt and tossed it behind them into the ditch on the side of the road. He went next for the handcuffs. Burkes gathered his senses enough to slap a hand over his pepper spray, where he thought the mayor was headed.

This had to be beyond anything the officer had planned on for the day—the mayor assaulting him on the side of the road, whiskeyed up and itching for a fight like a weekend bar patron.

Seeing Burkes back in fighting form, O'Brien punched him again. With the advantage of hovering directly over his target, O'Brien landed a much better shot and Burkes went foggy. O'Brien slipped the cuffs from the leather holder on the cop's belt and clamped them onto his hands.

O'Brien rolled off when it was done and looked back at the man. Burkes was back from the stun of the last punch and looked at his hands, then angrily shot a look to O'Brien.

"What the hell are you doing?"

"I told you. I need to get some place right away."

Taking Burkes' own cue, O'Brien reached over and grabbed the pepper spray and blasted Burkes in the face. The cop screamed and threw his cuffed hands to his face. O'Brien stood and pulled Burkes by the scruff of his jacket along the gravel toward the police car. O'Brien reached into the driver's door and unlocked the back. He dragged the angry and cursing Burkes to the door and tried to haul him inside. Like an angry drunk or a kid high on meth, Burkes refused to get inside his own vehicle.

O'Brien stepped over Burkes, straddling him over his shoulders as he stood at the door and grabbed hold with both hands. He pulled sharply out and clipped Burkes in the head with the heavy door. Burkes tilted and went down to the gravel.

O'Brien slid into the backseat and pulled Burkes inside before backing out the other door. He shut the cop in and made sure to lock the doors again.

He went around to the front of the cop car and bent over to suck in air for a moment. What a stupid thing to do, but what else is new? And if it helped Lauren at all, it was worth it. All apologies to Officer Burkes.

As he straightened, O'Brien noticed a small red light. The

roof lights were off and Burkes was still in a ball on the back seat. O'Brien had to look closer at the black square in the window of the police car, but he knew what it was. He'd signed the bill to make it a requirement.

A dash-mounted video camera. His assault had been captured on video for all to see on the nightly news, or in the courts when the time came. His shoulders slumped in defeat.

O'Brien turned to the camera and decided to turn it into a confessional.

"Look, I'm sorry for what went on here just now. If anyone is seeing this, then you know the truth of it. I'm going to try to save my daughter's life and I hope I'm not too late. If I am, I don't blame Officer Burkes. He was doing his job. I blame myself for not doing mine. I'm a fuck up. Everything you've read about me is true. But I deserve to pay for it, not my daughter."

He turned and the camera watched him climb back into his official city Town Car and spit gravel as he peeled away.

BASEMENT

Death couldn't be any blacker. The bottom of the elevator shaft, the basement level, sucked all light from the world and swallowed it into the bottom of the pit as if it were the center of the earth.

Dale felt around, his body aching and his foot on fire with pain. He wanted a drink of water. He needed to know if Lauren was alive. "Lauren? Are you all right?"

A low groan off to his left. "You fell on me."

Good. Not dead. "Sorry. Is anything broken?"

A pause while she evaluated the stabs of pain and dull aches throughout her body. "I don't think so." Didn't sound like she felt good, though.

From above, echoing through the shaft, came Tat's voice. "I'm coming for you, motherfuckers."

A tiny light sparked overhead and fell. The lighter tumbled in the darkness, illuminating the sides of the shaft as it spun. The flame whipped in the wind of the descent but never went out. An endorsement to the brand.

The lighter landed next to Dale and the bottom of the pit was lit with a dull glow. Bullets followed the flame down into the shaft. Dale rolled and squished his body against the wall as shots exploded where Tat's boys could now see them in the firelight.

Lauren shrugged off where she had landed and finally noticed what broke her fall and probably saved her life. Elton's body was sprawled like a half-deflated airbag across the gear-driving mechanism of the elevator.

Bullets punched the ground, spun off the giant spool for collecting the cable. Dale reached out a hand and put it over the lighter. His hand burned as his palm covered the flame, then he closed his fist around it and shut the lid, plunging the bottom of the pit into blackness again.

Above him, Dale saw shadows move away from the open door where Tat and his men had been. He knew that meant they were on their way down the stairs.

"We gotta move." He got to his knees, the machine gun he had slung over his shoulder lay on the blank bottom of the pit now, cracked and useless. Empty of ammunition anyway.

Another grunt from Lauren said she knew, but she wasn't happy about the need to move quickly. In the brief firelight, Dale noticed he was against the door and he pawed at the backside of the opening in a blind man's search for a finger hold. "Over here. Help me get this door open."

Dale wedged his fingers in between the two doors and tried to pry. The exertion in his muscles screamed rage at his entire body. The fall hadn't been too bad. He'd gotten almost even with the first floor before he lost his grip on the cables, and even then, his legs never came loose from being wrapped around. And Lauren held on like a bull rider, trying her damndest to slow them both down with Dale sitting on her head.

Landing on Elton helped, too. His girth cushioned the impact.

Lauren climbed over Elton's crushed body and shoved off, shivering as if a tarantula had crawled over her bare skin. She joined Dale at the doors and got her fingers in the slot. She pulled left and he pulled right and the first sliver of light broke through.

Dale urged them on. "Keep going." They tugged again and the gap widened. Dale knew every quarter inch they opened the door was another step downward Tat and his boys took. They would meet them there in the basement and this thing would finally be over, but not the way Dale wanted.

He and Lauren both let out grunts of pain as they pulled the elevator doors open and got their first glimpse of the basement. Dale put a hand on her shoulder. "Go, go, go."

Lauren squeezed through, widening the gap a little more with her body as she slid through sideways. Dale followed, pushing the doors open with his hips and arms when he was half way through.

The basement was a storage facility, that much became obvious. Rows of crates and stacks of boxes made a maze of thin footpaths between the inventory. As Dale tried to examine the maze for a solution that would get them out of there, Lauren noticed something else.

"Uh, Dale." She pointed to the side of a stack of boxes and the stenciled letters there. "Look at this."

Mario was two steps behind Tat, keeping pace. A dedicated servant to Tat for six years now, he felt he'd earned the right to speak up.

"We're gonna take them on down there?"

"Yeah." Tat sounded annoyed already.

"I mean, with all those—"

"Yeah, with all those." Tat hit the landing for the first floor; he turned and continued on down the stairs toward the basement, a tank with no brakes. "Anyone else got a problem with that?"

Several of them did, but no one said a thing.

"Then hurry the fuck up and it won't be a problem. They're probably too dumb to figure out what they're in the middle of anyway."

Dale and Lauren stood in the middle of a stockpile of weapons enough to start a small war.

Crates of AR-15 machine guns. Boxes of hand grenades. Rifles, pistols, ammunition by the crate. Three long wooden boxes with rocket-propelled grenade launchers and the RPG ammo to go with it.

"What the hell was he planning?"

Dale looked around at the boxes blocking his every move to get out of the basement. "I don't know, but he's serious about it."

Lauren stopped. "It's this."

"What is?"

"This is what he'd been planning for. An invasion. A breech of his compound."

"Don't you think this is a little overkill for just you and me?"

"Obviously he didn't think it would be just one guy and a girl reporter he kidnapped."

Dale took a quick inventory of only the boxes around him and felt scared shitless at the explosive power of the contents. "Looks like he thought it would be the entire US Marine Corps." Sales was more likely, Dale thought. Why settle for dime bags of drugs when you can take in a few grand a pop for a crate of machine guns sold to a South American cartel?

"Look." Lauren drew his eyes to a box in front of her. The lid was off and neat rows of two dozen Desert Eagle .44 magnums showed themselves. Full clips were nestled next to them in form-cut foam holders.

Unarmed since the fall, Dale picked up a gun and two clips, loaded one, and put the other in his pocket. "You should get one, too."

"I'm good." Lauren reached around her back for her gun. She paused, patted the small of her back where it should have been, then sheepishly brought her arm back around to her front and dipped into the box to get her own Magnum.

A loud bang, duller than gunfire, sounded across the basement. A door being kicked in. Tat had arrived.

Dale heard the sounds of men spreading out, though he could see nothing past the rows and angles of the crates stacked head high all around them.

"Tat, I know it's you." Dale held his new gun according to

police academy regulations for entering a fire fight. "It would be really dumb for you to start shooting right now, considering where we are."

Dale waited for the bullets to fly anyway. He got silence.

"Tat? There is some serious shit in these boxes. Stuff you don't want to hit with a bullet."

"So what do you suggest?" He sounded pissed, but Dale expected that.

Dale looked at Lauren who shrugged. "Don't suppose letting us go is on the list of options?"

"Let me ask you this, Burnett, did you punch my mother in the face?"

Dale nodded, not bothering to answer the rhetorical question. A free pass was not an option. They'd gotten their wish— they made it down to the bottom. Only, this was a little farther than they expected.

Nowhere else to go. This was the final standoff. This would determine if Dale would get a chance to face his fate in court and learn how much this rescue mission had cleared his name. And Lauren would get to confront her dad and go win her prizes and take her new job at CNN.

Dale noticed a box marked Land Mines. Land mines? Tat was just fucking with them now.

CHAPTER 34

"Vehicle approaching, sir."

Schuster turned and looked back inside the tactical team van. "Where?"

An officer at a video monitor pointed to his screen where a car was turning onto the road leading into the compound. Bad timing. The SWAT team had been deployed and currently lay in wait in a half dozen strategic points near, but not in direct view, of the building. They were armed and waiting for instructions. They had orders to shoot to kill if anyone but Dale and Lauren exited the building.

Schuster hadn't thought of someone driving in.

"Who is it?"

"Unconfirmed, sir."

They didn't look to be speeding. Only the driver was visible.

"Pick them up. Don't let them get close. We can't screw this up now."

Dahlia sat forward in the back seat. "You can get me to see him? Your boss, I mean."

The driver shook his head, sounded dubious. "I can ask. I doubt you're gonna get very far with that gun in my back, though."

"I don't want to hurt anyone."

"Shoulda thought of that before you shot that dude in the head."

Dahlia wondered for a second what the hell the guy was talking about, then remembered in a muzzle flash the inhuman act she'd done. "He was already dead. I just needed you guys to think I was serious."

"Yeah, well, mission accomplished."

The car rounded a corner and Dahlia pitched forward as he hit the brakes. Four men stood in the road, cops by the look of it. Dark navy jumpsuits over Kevlar vests. Tactical helmets. Each held a gun out and a hand demanding that they stop.

"What are you doing?"

The driver lifted his hands off the wheel. "When four dudes with guns tell you to stop, you stop."

Dahlia's heart rate tripled. Were these more men out to kill her? Her last run in with the police hadn't gone well. Maybe they were here to finish the job. "Drive through them. Or go around."

"Look, lady—"

Panic got the better of her. "I'll shoot you."

"And you'll drive from the back seat?"

The four men started approaching. Dahlia hopped on the seat, unsure what her next move should be. The only thing she knew for sure was that she wanted to live long enough to see the baby born. If the day's weird events hadn't already killed the child in her womb, she had no intention of rescheduling her appointment. The decision came to her like a bright light in her mind. She wanted this baby. Dale would want it too.

Dahlia stepped out of the car, gun in hand. "All I want is to see my husband."

The four men stopped, raised their guns, and stood their ground. One of them radioed back for instructions.

"A woman, sir."

"A woman?" Schuster squinted at the tiny image on the monitor. One of the team's shoulder-mounted cameras showed a woman now out of the car and brandishing a gun at the team. She hadn't identified herself or indicated if she had anything to do with Tat, but she was armed and that was a threat. "What does she want?"

"She asked to see her husband, sir."

"How the fuck is that my problem?"

The team leader lowered his weapon, shifted to hostage tactics. "Ma'am, set the gun down and tell me who your husband is."

"No. You'll shoot me."

"Not if you put the gun down. Let's see if we can help you. Who is your husband and why do you think he's here?"

Dahlia pointed her gun beyond the curve of the road to the compound. "Dale Burnett. He's in there, I think."

Schuster put a hand to his forehead. "Son of a bitch. Bring her in here. Tell them not to shoot."

"Ma'am, if you come with me we'll see what we can do. But put the gun down first."

One of the men split off and went to the driver's door to get the man out from behind the wheel. He knew when he was beat so he complied without problem.

Dahlia kept her gun on the men now taking baby steps forward.

"You're going to take me somewhere and dump my body."

"No, ma'am. Why would we do that?"

"Do you have any idea the amount of bullshit I've been through today? Do you?"

The team advanced slowly, almost invisible to Dahlia. "Let's get you safe then. In our custody and out of danger, but Mrs. Burnett, you need to drop that gun."

"The last cop I went to said I'd be safe. The guy who gave me a ride said I'd be safe. My neighbor, Mrs. Joosten said I'd be safe. Why should I believe you?"

"I have no reason to lie to you."

"Then tell me why they wanted to kidnap me."

"I don't know that, ma'am."

Dahlia felt hot tears brimming her eyelids. No one had answers. Dale had been keeping secrets, now everyone else was too. She was tired of it. If these men were here to kill her, she wasn't going down without a fight.

"I can't trust you."

"I'm going to need you to, ma'am."

She watched their boots shuffle synchronized steps over the road, moving as one body toward her. The only way she was still alive was by her own wits. Her unwillingness to lie down and let other people dictate her fate. She wasn't going to give that up in the last stages.

Dahlia lifted the gun and fired.

With practiced efficiency, the four men in the team fired back.

CHAPTER 35

Mayor O'Brien let the car idle as he listened to the phone ring. He'd placed a call to Lewis. Like so many times before, he was the only person to turn to. When his wife wouldn't do because she needed to be kept in the dark, when other members of his staff wouldn't do because they weren't ruthless enough, Lewis was the one to call.

He listened to the third ring, then the fourth, and thought he may have used up his last chance with Lewis.

The phone line clicked. There was a pause. The air crackled between them until finally, "Yes?"

"Lewis. Please. I need to know where to find him. It might already be too late."

O'Brien could hear the muffled breathing of Lewis struggling through his blood-clogged nose. His career was over, too tied to the mayor's to do anything but burn from the residual heat when O'Brien went public and let his daughter ruin everything they'd built. They'd be lucky to have the state protect them by putting them in prison out of fear of what Tat and his men would do to them once the operation was exposed. And then, when they were behind bars, they had to pray for a white-collar facility or fall victim to one of Tat's many minions lurking with shivs and strangulation wires in every max-security cell in the state.

O'Brien listened to Lewis snort a clot of blood up his sinuses, then spit it out into a trash can. "Where are you now?"

O'Brien let go a sigh and felt his body melt into the seat. He described where he was and Lewis told him how to find Roy, but he knew it might be too late.

BASEMENT

Dale had never played shuffleboard, but he thought he might be good at it. He pushed another land mine across the cement floor of the basement and it skidded to a halt within inches of where he wanted it. The thought did cross his mind that he was boxing himself in a corner, but better to be protected while they figured out a plan than to sit around and wait for Tat and his boys to come and get them.

It had become too much to remember. Lauren wished she brought her voice recorder, a nifty little tool Arneson gave her when he hired her. She still had so much to learn about reporting. This was looking more like a book than an article, though. If she survived, that is.

Damn, that would have been the way to go. She should have been making notes all along so if they didn't make it, Arneson could run her diary of the final moments. Shit, no one would believe it.

Now Dale was tossing land mines across the floor like hockey pucks.

There hadn't been much time to think about her parents. She wondered if they were sitting by the phone waiting to hear their daughter's fate. Were they holding a press conference? Were they even aware she was missing?

Fighting so hard to survive just so she could go destroy her family as she knew it was a weird feeling. She held a match in her hand and could see the fuse; it was up to her to light it and run. She didn't know if Mom would be angrier at Dad or at her for exposing him. She'd feel lied to by her husband (nothing new) and betrayed by her daughter (not exactly breaking news there either). Whatever the outcome, Lauren would find out soon enough.

Then there was Dale. This weird guy who seemed to be on some mission of contrition and soul salvation. He was here for her, sort of. More like she'd been a passenger on his own journey down river. He was taking the trip away from, rather than into, his own heart of darkness. She admired that. As much as she could understand it. He was still a crooked cop, still part of the machine she was going to bring down with her reporting. And it still could all fall apart around them in a fiery blaze of land mines and hand grenades.

Yeah, they'd made it to the basement all right. In more ways than one.

Tat's hand had grown stiff, like a part of his body had already gone rigor mortis. He tried to ignore it while he commanded his troops.

"No shooting, okay? We don't want the whole place to go up. Unless you have a clean shot. If you can take him or her out, do it. Head shots. No question. I want dead, not wounded. And as much as I'd like to say leave them for me, I know I'm not a hundred percent. Just kill them. I'll get the next ones."

A large man to his left, Junior, looked down a row of tall boxes. Guns on the right, ammo on the left. "Don't the cops know he's here?"

"If he was here with the cops, where are the rest of them?" Junior shrugged. Tat went on. "He's trying to be the guy from *Die Hard*. He's an idiot."

The six men surrounding Tat all nodded. "Now lock and load."

* * *

Dale peered around a stack of boxes, looking for a way out. He wondered if there was more money in this room—in the value of arms to the highest bidder—than in the safe room a few floors up. And he wondered who Tat dealt to. A front for a front for a front could lead back to ISIS or something. Dale wouldn't be surprised, and he doubted Tat would feel any guilt.

These are the men he got in bed with, he accepted money from. Sweet fucking Jesus, where had it all gone so wrong?

He beckoned Lauren close to him. When she came, he whispered in her ear: "I think if we stick to the walls and go along the outside we can make it to the stairs. I see some gaps where we can keep a row of boxes between us and any view. I'm gonna guess he's going to come more down the center of things."

"Guess based on what?"

"Based on making myself feel better about a plan. You got a better one?"

Lauren shook her head.

"Okay, so let's start out—"

The explosion rocked the cinder-block room. Dale's chest rattled with the concussion and he prepared for a barrage of shrapnel to tear through his body, but none came. He checked on Lauren and aside from looking very freaked out, she seemed fine. He peered around his stack of boxes again.

Midway through the room was a small cloud of black smoke rising to the ceiling. After a delay, a man's screams started. "Fuck, my legs!"

A land mine. It must have been one of the first ones he laid out, before they started making their retreat deeper into the bowels of the basement. Still, too close for comfort. They needed to move.

Dale put a hand on Lauren's arm. "We've come too far. We're getting out of here, okay?"

"Okay." She gave him a look that was equal parts fear and

trust. Dale led and Lauren followed.

He started by putting his back to the wall and moving as far as he could until he came to a stack of boxes. He gave a quick look around the edge, then motioned for Lauren to follow. They bent low, not allowing their heads to bob above the line of cover they found behind the row of boxes. Ahead, the maze veered right and dipped away into unknown corners. Each turn could be an ambush, a pit of vipers or one of the land mines Dale himself had tossed. He tried to remember where he put them all, but the jumble of crates and narrow passages made it impossible. He tried his best to keep one eye on the floor and one eye ahead where he knew Tat and his men waited.

The screams faded as help arrived for the wounded man. His cries went muffled as a hand obviously went over his mouth. Dale kept moving forward, Lauren at his heels.

He was trying to stick close to the wall, to follow the line of the building to loop them around to an eventual staircase. He knew it was a good possibility Tat had ordered a man to stay there and watch the potential escape route. Dale told himself this was the same as it was upstairs. If a man aims to do you harm, you must shoot first. His old partner his first years on the beat lived by the adage: when in doubt, take him out.

Lauren had never been claustrophobic but being underground gave her an uneasy feeling. Something about being up high made escape seem much more tangible. Down in the basement she felt that much closer to being in a grave.

Dale was moving fast up ahead, snaking along the disheveled rows of crates. Arms dealing was a part of Tat's business she'd been unaware of. She wondered if some of his South American suppliers got paid in guns and grenades. Not that he didn't have enough cash on hand. She saw that for herself, and as impressive as this stockpile of arms was, it didn't compare to the stacks of cash upstairs. Why the hell hadn't she brought a camera?

Oh, yeah. Because Tat and his men stripped her of everything she came in with.

A bullet splintered a crate next to Lauren's head. She threw her hands up and ducked lower, not bothering to look for land mines as she dove for the floor.

Dale was beside her in an instant. The single shot had pierced an unmarked box. Dale searched for the shooter but saw nothing.

"You get her?" The goons were communicating in shouts from their different hiding places.

"Not sure."

Dale wanted to yell out, to let them know they'd missed, but he didn't want to give away their position. He bent down and put a hand under Lauren's arm. "Let's move."

Tugging her along, Dale resumed his wall-hugging escape route. He rounded one jutting stack of boxes and turned again to the left to rejoin the wall and found himself facing one of Tat's men.

The man raised an arm, caught off guard by the sudden visitors. He leveled his gun at Lauren's face. She froze momentarily, caught in the proverbial life flashing before her eyes.

Dale flung his arm up, catching the barrel of the gun with his forearm and bumping the pistol toward the ceiling as it went off. The flash of heat from the gun singed his arm hair, but the bullet sailed north of Lauren's skull by inches.

Dale was in close. He could smell the gunpowder and the sweat on the man in front of him. He could grapple the man down to the floor, disarm him, hope for the best. But now was not the time for hope.

His arm stayed bent as the gun came up. Dale couldn't straighten his shooting arm with the man so close. He shoved upward, pushing the barrel into the soft flesh under the man's jaw. Without thinking—he fired.

The Desert Eagle was a powerful gun. The man's head jerked

back and the crates behind him were painted red. The man went limp instantly and he fell away, the top of his head down to where his skull met spinal cord was gone, evaporated in a rain of red splatter.

As if roused from a nightmare, Lauren jerked the trigger on her own pistol and shot the man as he fell. A token gesture to her own near death.

The sudden exchange of gunfire alerted the rest of Tat's crew to their location and Dale heard footsteps coming. Dale took up Lauren's arm again and started a retreat, backing down the aisle in the direction they came.

The dead man's body hit hard against a tall stack of boxes and the tower tilted forward. Already Dale and Lauren's backs were to it, but the five-high stack of crates tipped and fell. A set of thundering footsteps rounded a corner in time to see the boxes fall. He wasn't in time to see the black letters stamped on the side: Grenades. Nor was he in time to see the land mine Dale had skidded across the floor earlier laying in the path of the falling boxes.

When the crates landed, the land mine went off. The explosion shook the building and took out both legs of the man fast approaching. Before he could stop his legs from moving, he was amputated below the knee. The electronic message of pain had barely made it to his brain when the first box exploded. A dozen hand grenades went off all at once.

Dale had put two stacks of boxes between them and the carnage behind. They felt the concussion like the ground had risen up to pound them on the back. Both Dale and Lauren stumbled forward but kept moving.

Several residual explosions popped like aftershocks of an earthquake. The sole eyewitness to the explosions had been reduced to a puddle of liquid and shards of bone.

Concrete dust shook loose from the walls and ceiling. The room was packed too tightly to echo. The sound of falling debris and settling shrapnel went on for longer than Dale imagined.

"Who's still with me?" Tat's voice called out from ahead of them, in the direction they were heading. He was near the back of the room where Dale and Lauren started from. Dale reversed course again and marched toward the explosion. He figured they wouldn't look for them in that mess.

Three distant voices called back to Tat. "Here." "Over here." "I'm okay."

Dale turned to Lauren and checked on her. "You okay?"

Her eyes were wide. "We're not going to make it."

"Yes, we are."

"How?"

"I don't even know how we made it this far. But if the world wanted us dead, it sure as shit had enough opportunities. We may be cats on our ninth life, but as long as we're still moving, we have a chance."

She gave a slight smile. A what-the-hell, it-can't-get-any-worse smile.

Dale turned the corner around the stack of boxes and found the scene of the explosion. A charred black hole was hollowed out in the concrete floor. There was no evidence at all that two bodies were in the wreckage. A wood slat on one crate burned a tiny matchstick-sized flame.

The wall beside Dale seemed different. It took Dale a moment to realize what he was seeing. At first it looked like a black scar on the cinder blocks, but as he looked closer, he saw it was a hole. And beyond the hole, not just earth.

Dale stepped closer. The blast had opened up the side of the basement wall and exposed an open space big enough to stand up in. Dale craned his neck into the gap. It was some sort of sewer line. A wide pipe put down there years ago to feed the needs of the vast industrial park to come. A pipe that never got used.

He turned to Lauren, a smile on his face. He didn't know where it would lead, but they no longer needed the stairs to get out.

CHAPTER 36

"What the hell was that?" Schuster stopped walking when he heard the explosions in the distance.

"Unclear, sir."

"Sounded like a goddamn bomb."

The officer at his side peeled away and got on his walkie to try to figure out what had happened. Schuster stepped over to where Dahlia lay on the ground. He leaned over her, checking her pale face.

"Dahlia?"

Her eyes fluttered. The pain had sent her under the cover of a welcome blackness for a little while, but now she was back. Both her legs burned from the bullets in each thigh. The SWAT team responded to her shots with defensive fire of their own. Her aim was lousy, theirs was dead on. A bullet to each leg put her down and the team quickly disarmed her and radioed in to the tactical van. That's when Schuster came running.

"Christ, you had me scared."

Dahlia didn't answer, only grimaced in pain.

"Dale had me checking up on you. How in the hell did you make it out here?" Schuster waved the question away. "Forget it, there's time for that. Let's get you fixed up. Dale's almost out."

He hoped, anyway. And what the hell was that explosion?

CHAPTER 37

Two years in the ROTC hadn't made O'Brien a master of stealth. He spotted the dark outline of Ray in the trees right where Lewis said he would be but getting to him was difficult. Pine needles crackled underfoot and in the quiet of the woods, O'Brien's Armani suit made all kinds of noises heard never heard from it before.

With thirty paces still to go, Roy turned and aimed the rifle barrel at him. When Roy saw who it was, he relaxed. It was the first time O'Brien had seen an ounce of stress on the man.

O'Brien was allowed to approach.

"The hell you doing here?" Roy turned his attention back to the building down at the bottom of the ridge at least five hundred yards away. The scope on Roy's rifle reminded O'Brien of a pirate's spyglass.

"I'm calling it off. It's over."

O'Brien nearly broke down in tears. If Roy was here that meant Lauren hadn't come out yet. The job wasn't done. He'd made it in time.

"It's not over. The job ain't done."

"There is no more job. I'm calling it off."

"All due respect, Mayor. I don't take my orders from you."

O'Brien couldn't believe it. Why wasn't this man listening? "Well, who then? Lewis?"

Roy sighted down the scope. O'Brien's voice pitched higher, in a frenzy. "I spoke to him. We called it off. Call him. Talk to him." O'Brien fished in his pocket for his cell phone.

"He would have called me."

"There isn't time for this. It's my contract, my job. I'm calling it off."

"No can do."

O'Brien moved next to him. "It's my daughter."

Roy kept his eye to the scope. "To me, she's just another target."

O'Brien dove. He landed on Roy's back and put a bare hand around the barrel of the rifle. Roy rolled, fast, and flung the mayor off him, but that hand stayed attached. The gun jerked in Roy's hand and his finger slid over the trigger. A shot blasted nearly straight up. The barrel burned with the sudden heat of the shot and O'Brien's hand sizzled against the metal. He opened his fingers and let the gun go.

Roy gripped the rifle and whipped the stock around to catch O'Brien in the jaw with a crack. The mayor fell back against the thick carpet of pine needles and inhaled the smell, one of his favorites until today.

Standing, Roy put the scope to his eye again. This time he saw a door open.

CHAPTER 38

"We got movement."

Schuster pushed his way past a SWAT member to get a look at the video monitors. "Is it them?"

Tiny shapes emerged from the glass doors of the building. One, then a second, then a third. Large men. Tattoos ran down the arms of the man in front. He held a stiff arm and a wounded hand out in front of him.

"It's Tat, sir. Looks like two of his own with him."

Schuster pounded the console desk in front of him. Despite himself, he'd been rooting for Dale to make it, and not only because he didn't want to deal with the phone call from the mayor if this plan failed.

"Is she there? Do they have the girl?"

Two technicians scanned four different angles on the monitors. "Negative, sir."

"Fuck." He turned to the open back door of the tactical van. The pine trees blocked his view of the compound like they'd done all day. With his back to the monitors he balled a fist and steeled himself to give the command.

"Take them out."

In the distance, firecracker pops sounded. On the monitors the three figures shook and flailed their arms in a dance to the beat of the SWAT team's guns.

* * *

Roy turned at the sound of gunshots. O'Brien cried out an anguished scream and tore the rifle from Roy's grip. Each blast from the SWAT automatics, an angry beehive buzz of shooting, could be his daughter dying.

O'Brien turned the gun and hit Roy across the temple with a swing he'd perfected by countless hours on the golf course. With Roy out, O'Brien put the scope up to his eye. It took him some time to find what he was looking for through the powerful magnifying glass. When he steadied his view, he saw three men face down on the sidewalk in front of the building. He recognized Tat from his tattoos. The others could be any of the generic henchmen always surrounding Tat. No Lauren.

He lowered the rifle, certain that she was inside—dead already.

The polished black boots of the SWAT team came out of hiding and hustled to where the three bodies lay. Barking out commands and heads sweeping the area for other potential targets, the overdue adrenaline rush of the troops spurred them on to a near sprint.

Behind their attention, what would be a block away down a driveway leading to a building that was never completed beyond a rectangular concrete pad, a manhole cover lifted from underneath.

Wary of the gunfire he'd heard moments ago, Dale peeked out through a one-inch gap. Seeing no danger he pushed the rest of the way up and let the manhole cover clank to the road beside the hole. He climbed out, then reached back for Lauren.

Dale smiled. "Told you I'd get you out."

Lauren smiled back at him, then wrapped him in a hug. Dale hopped on one leg, his injured foot awash in a new pain now that his body began to relax. The agony his brain had been staving off for survival's sake broke loose from the dam and flooded his pain receptors.

Dale crumbled to his knees, laughing the whole way down.

CHAPTER 39

Dale waited outside Chief Schuster's office, the same empty coffee table in front of him. His week in the hospital had barely been enough time for the story to unfold in the press, with Lauren's reports leading the way.

He'd made it this far along as an "unnamed inside confidant" within the department. Lauren was protecting her exclusive source, and protecting Dale from the certain attacks of the press once his hero story was revealed to be the work of a dirty cop. Nothing the press likes more than to tear down a hero of their own making.

Out there, at the compound, Lauren had called out to the SWAT team to come help her with Dale. The team advanced on them with guns out until Schuster could be heard over their earpieces screaming at them not to shoot and to bring them in.

Dale was laid out on a stretcher next to his wife. They cried and held hands, each with an IV in a vein of their wrist.

Dale tried to explain. "Dahlia, I'm going to get in trouble when this is over. I've done some bad things."

"Me too."

"No. Some real bad things. You're going to hear a lot of things about me you won't want to. I won't deny anything. I won't lie to you anymore. I want you to know, though, that's not me anymore."

Dahlia told him that she understood. If he'd confessed to her eight hours earlier, she wouldn't have. But now, all she wanted was a new start.

"I'm pregnant."

He squeezed her hand tighter and they cried together.

Mayor O'Brien had almost been shot when he came out of the woods dragging a man's body behind him. It took the officers onsite a long time to recognize who stood in front of them. O'Brien had dropped Roy's body on the ground, the man rolled and groaned, blood soaking the side of his head and his shirt. O'Brien threw the gun down on top of him. "Arrest this man." He held out his hands, ready for handcuffs. "And then arrest me."

Before the cuffs went on, Lauren broke free from the man applying alcohol swabs to her cuts. She ran to her father and hugged him.

He spoke quietly into her ear. "I know what you need to do. I won't stop you. Everything you think of me, all the reasons you hate me. They must all be true."

Lauren hugged him tighter.

"Chief Schuster will see you now." The girl behind the desk knew who Dale was. She knew her version of the story about what happened out there that day. Her version was lacking eighty percent of the facts, but even that much was enough to make her watch him go by like a combination serial killer and rock star.

Dale propped himself on his crutches and opened the door, then put his crutch back under his armpit and entered the office. "Sir?"

"Ah, Dale. Come in."

Schuster was flanked by Bardsley, the grey-haired man from Dale's first meeting. The man from the mayor's office—Lewis, Dale recalled—was missing.

"Have a seat." Schuster waved Dale onto the couch. Dale

hobbled over, still getting used to the new way of walking, and sat down inelegantly. Schuster got up and sat on the edge of his desk, like a concerned college professor.

"We were just going over the inventory." He gestured to a pile of papers on his desk. He rambled off facts, ticking them off on his fingers. "Forty-one men and women in office suits with guns, a kitchen staff with their share of scrapes and other wounds, almost three dozen girls who looked like refugees."

Dale nodded, remembering. While he was on the stretcher, he saw the SWAT team leading clusters of Tat's employees out the front entrance. Floor by floor they came out, hands raised in surrender or cuffed behind their backs. The girls all clumped together and chattered like hens. Last out the door was Tat's girlfriend and Esmerelda, his mom. She fought against the two beefy SWAT members who each had a hold of an arm. She swore like a sailor at them, detailing all the ways her son would rain down revenge upon them—until she saw the white sheet draped over the body, a heavily tattooed arm peeking out the side. She began to wail to the heavens and beg Jesus for an explanation.

She was hustled into a waiting squad car while larger transport vehicles drove away the others to their own fates. Dale watched as the tower became vacant once again.

"So." Schuster folded his hands together. "How you feeling?"

"Getting by."

"How's Dahlia?"

"Fine. Another week of bed rest to be safe."

"Good. That's good." He gave a look over his shoulder to the grey-haired man. "Dale, I'm sure you've noticed your name has been kept out of the papers."

"Yes, sir."

"This is by design."

Dale sank back a little deeper into the couch. "I understand sir. While you build your case. I'm healthy enough for interviews with I.A.—"

"It's not that."

Dale cocked his head at an angle. Schuster and the grey-haired man shared another look. Last time they called him in here with an agenda, things didn't work out so well. Or maybe they worked out better than he expected.

"Dale, that rescue of yours was mighty impressive."

Impressive? thought Dale. *It was pathetic.*

"Being able to send in a single man, a man like you, proved to be quite an asset. It saved that girl's life for sure."

Dale wasn't so sure at all, but he let Schuster talk.

"I'm thinking." He waved a hand between him and his second in command. "We've been thinking…a man with your skills could come in handy."

The grey-haired man finally spoke. "A man with your connections."

"Could be very valuable when the need arises."

Dale sat up straighter. "What are you saying, sir?"

Schuster exhaled sharply, as if he didn't like what he was about to say, but it needed saying. "You're not going to prison, Detective. You're going to work off your debt to the department by being more useful to us out on the streets than you would behind bars."

"More rescue missions?"

Schuster leaned forward, emphasizing his seriousness. "Whatever we want you to do, Detective. Understand?"

Barely wasn't a good answer, Dale knew. He lied a little. "Yes."

"Good. Then we have a deal."

Schuster extended his hand. Dale didn't know exactly what he was signing on for. If it meant more days like the one at Tat's compound, he might rather take his chances in prison. But with Dahlia at home carrying their child and a chance, a real chance, at a new start—he couldn't say no.

Dale leaned forward on the couch and shook Chief Schuster's hand. "Deal." He couldn't help thinking the chief was squeezing extra hard.

ALL THE WAY DOWN

* * *

Out in the hallway, Dale tried to process what had just happened. He wasn't going away, but his job just got a hell of a lot harder. He stood and stared, leaning heavily on his crutches, a phantom pain where his toe used to be.

Dale shook his head, breaking out of his stupor. He reached for the elevator button and stopped. He turned his head to the stairwell, then back to the elevator, his finger an inch away from the button.

Dale smiled.

ACKNOWLEDGMENTS

I want to thank Bobby McCue for that day in The Mystery Bookstore when he first put a copy of Duane Swierczynski, Victor Gischler, Steve Brewer and Allan Guthrie in my hands. And to John Rector for reading this early and giving some great thoughts. The first and only time anyone has ever read anything of mine early. That's how much I trust him.

Thanks to everyone who had something nice to say about the book and who let me exploit their good name for my own use. Thanks to Lauren O'Brien for allowing me to use her good name in an entirely different but equally exploitative way.

Thanks to the Down & Out team for the unwavering support. Always and forever thanks to my family who puts up with my writing addiction.

Photo by Mark Krajnak

ERIC BEETNER has been described as "the James Brown of crime fiction—the hardest working man in noir." (Crime Fiction Lover) and "The 21st Century's answer to Jim Thompson" (LitReactor). He has written more than 20 novels including *Rumrunners, Leadfoot, The Devil Doesn't Want Me, The Year I Died 7 Times* and *Criminal Economics*. His award-winning short stories have appeared in over three dozen anthologies. He co-hosts the podcast Writer Types and the Noir at the Bar reading series in Los Angeles where he lives and works as a television editor.

EricBeetner.com

BOOKS

On the following pages are a few
more great titles from the
Down & Out Books publishing family.

For a complete list of books and to
sign up for our newsletter,
go to DownAndOutBooks.com.

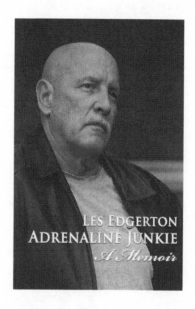

Adrenaline Junkie: A Memoir
Les Edgerton

Down & Out Books
November 2018
978-1-948235-41-9

Adrenaline Junkie is more than a renowned, multi-award-winning author entertaining with his life history. Les Edgerton understands that backstory matters. It influences the present. So he journeyed through his past seeking answers for why he was the way he was. Seeking answers for his thrill-seeking, devil-may-care, often self-destructive, behaviors. Seeking a sense of personal peace.

So settle back. Meet a real-life, twenty-first-century Renaissance man. A real-life adrenaline junkie.

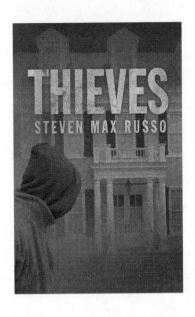

Thieves
Steven Max Russo

Down & Out Books
November 2018
978-1-948235-40-2

Dark, deadly and disturbing, *Thieves* will both horrify and delight you.

In his stunning debut thriller, Steven Max Russo teams a young cleaning girl with a psychopathic killer in a simple robbery that quickly escalates into a terrifying ordeal. Stuck in a deadly partnership, trapped by both circumstance and greed, a young girl is forced to play cat and mouse against her deadly partner in crime.

Gravy Train
Tess Makovesky

All Due Respect, an imprint of
Down & Out Books
November 2018
978-1-64396-006-7

When barmaid Sandra wins eighty grand on a betting scam she thinks she's got it made. But she's reckoned without an assortment of losers and criminals, including a mugger, a car thief and even her own step-uncle George.

As they hurtle towards a frantic showdown by the local canal, will Sandra see her ill-gotten gains again? Or will her precious gravy train come shuddering to a halt?

The Carrier
Preston Lang

Shotgun Honey, an imprint of
Down & Out Books
July 2018
978-1-948235-02-0

It's a bad idea for a drug courier to pick up a woman in a roadside bar. Cyril learns this lesson when the sultry-voiced girl he brings back to his motel room holds him up at gunpoint.

But he hasn't made his pickup yet, and the two form an uneasy alliance in a dangerous game to grab the loot.